I0762772

THE SAW MOUTH

ALSO BY CALE PLETT

Wavelength

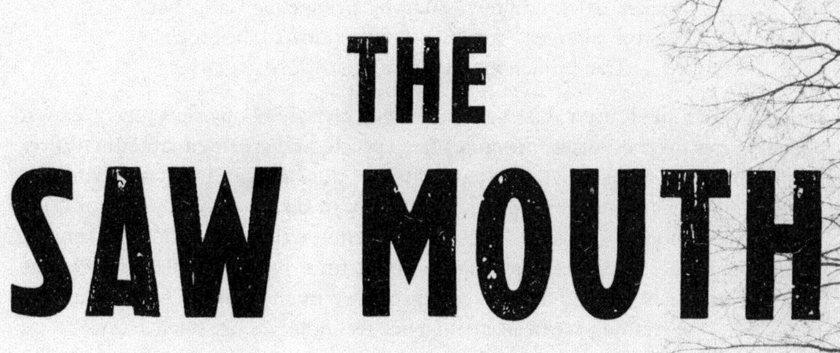

THE SAW MOUTH

CALE PLETT

Delacorte Press

This project was funded by:

Delacorte Press
An imprint of Random House Children's Books
A division of Penguin Random House LLC
1745 Broadway, New York, NY 10019
penguinrandomhouse.com
getunderlined.com

Editor: Alison Romig
Cover Designer: Angela Carlino
Interior Designer: Michelle Gengaro-Kokmen
Production Editor: Colleen Fellingham
Managing Editor: Tamar Schwartz
Production Manager: Liz Sutton

Library of Congress Cataloging-in-Publication Data is available upon request.
ISBN 979-8-217-02570-1 (hardcover) — ISBN 979-8-217-02571-8 (lib. bdg.) —
ISBN 979-8-217-02572-5 (ebook)

The text of this book is set in 10.75-point Sabon LT Pro.

Manufactured in the United States of America
1st Printing

The authorized representative in the EU for product safety
and compliance is Penguin Random House Ireland, Morrison Chambers,
32 Nassau Street, Dublin D02 YH68, Ireland, https://eu-contact.penguin.ie.

In memory of my grandparents,
who taught me so much about love

A full list of content warnings can be found
in the back of the book.

PROLOGUE

THE ARCADE ON THE LAKESHORE IS ABANDONED. A CLOSED, silent exterior of boards and spray paint with rain slipping through the cracks in the roof.

A vacant place, not empty.

It's full of bodies. The burnt out and the smashed in. Corpses
that used to be machines
that used to be games.

These amusements are all dead except for one pinball machine still humming in the center of the room. It's a possessed world of light sending colors dancing off the graveyard around it. It pings and whirs, playing against itself.

Perpetual, beautiful, haunted perfection. Red numbers continually rising. The pinball machine is a prisoner trapped in a loop, unable to lash out or end itself. This is its version of a scream, and it's calling us in.

We used to believe desolation like what we find in this place showed us how our world had changed. Torment comprehended and contained. But we were far from dredging the bottom. Now the arcade feels safe compared to what we've seen. What better place to meet?

If we are to be near a nightmare, let it be caged.

We are all the prey, praying:
Cover of night
uncover that which we seek
but are afraid will find us.

I walk alone in the rain toward the end of the boardwalk. The worn boards creak underneath my feet, and I can imagine the water lapping in the hollow space below me. The lake smells rank, betraying the pollution. I step over the gap where a plank's rotted away. I don't look down.

The businesses along the waterfront are either closed for the night or forsaken, but there are a few lights glimmering from the windows in town. It's quiet enough for me to believe that somewhere inside, I might be out of danger. Though now I know walls have no meaning. The lines I've drawn between myself and the world are imaginary, but I still cling to them, thinking my skin can stop the shadows from leeching me into nothingness.

Ahead, by the arcade, a car pulls up and idles in the dark. Our wolf without a pack.

As I get nearer, I see the forest behind it. Here, at the edge of town, the dead pine trees look like bones around the two people who emerge from the far side of the building. They're caught sharply in the car's headlights. One has their hood pulled up, face down. The other's short hair is exposed to the rain. Our bled-out fighter and our parallel soul.

And finally, from down the street beside me, joining me, a person who wanted to know everything and now knows too much.

We walk together toward the others, close enough to hold

hands. Then we do, because we're all hollowed out and running on touch. These are my hungry, desperate hearts.

Kill the car engine. Push a sheet of plywood aside, and one by one step into the light of the tortured machine shining brighter than it should be able to. There's water dripping from the ceiling of the arcade and insulation hanging loose. This summer feels like that first Autumn, with life coming down around us.

I hope we're willing to kill for each other. I know we're willing to die.

I'm the last inside. Our walking curse, drenched in the sins of those now buried.

I'm the hunter
the bait
the teeth of the trap
the foot caught in it.

I put the makeshift door back into place, sealing us in.

It's time to draw our fear close and face it.

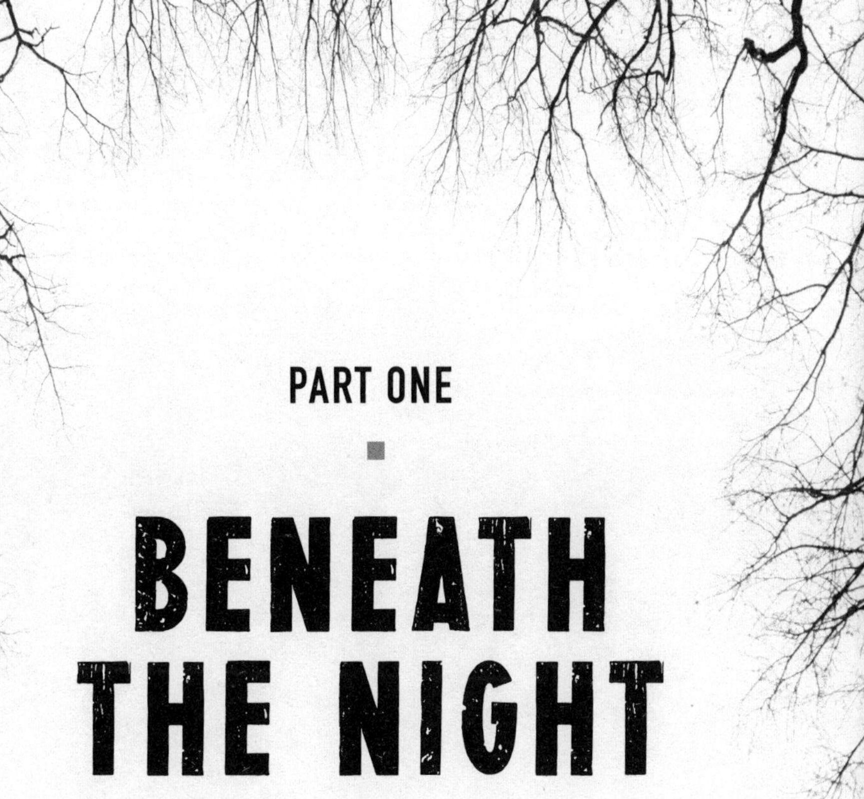

PART ONE

BENEATH THE NIGHT

CHAPTER ONE

Three Weeks Earlier

Abraham's Corner marks the first intersection of paved roads we've hit in an hour. I've been on a bus heading west on a secondary highway—a narrow slash through the wilderness. Just exposed rock, pine trees, and lake after lake. The late-June dusk has been settling around us as we go through the last stretch, so every time we pass another lake, the water seems a little blacker.

I haven't seen a single indicator that the town I'm heading for even exists. I'm beginning to think maybe I'll ride this bus to wherever the road runs out, but then the forest abruptly opens up enough for a gas station and an intersection. A wooden sign nailed to a tree tells me the name of this place in barely legible carved letters.

Abraham's Corner.

The driver pulls onto the gravel in front of the gas station. The announcement system's long dead, so he turns in his seat and calls, "All passengers for Sawblade Lake!"

Of the dozen people on the bus, I'm the only one to react. I grab my backpack and head down the aisle.

"Is this Sawblade Lake?" I've never been there, but I'm not seeing anything where we've stopped besides the small gas station and store.

"It's as close as we get." He sounds apologetic. I knew the person at the depot paused for too long before they sold me my ticket last night. The driver gestures out the front windshield to a signpost with sharp arrows. Two simply labeled *North* and *East*. The west one is for *Fort* something. And pointing south, *Sawblade—34 Miles*. "Not many people head that way anymore."

I have to.

The bus recedes down the highway, leaving me alone in the parking lot in the humid air and dust. I imagine myself getting smaller and smaller in the rearview mirror. Tall, angular, wearing a black thrift store dress with a scattering of small flowers embroidered on it. No luggage besides my backpack slung over one shoulder. It's enough. Even without the bag, I'm overburdened with what I can't leave behind.

I slap a mosquito off my neck, leaving some specks of blood. A crushed body I flick to the ground. Part of me wants to see the bus's brake lights come on. For it to turn around and for the driver to finish saying what he really meant.

Are you sure you want to go there?

There's nothing else at Abraham's Corner other than the twin streetlights at the crossroads. One's lifeless, and the other flickers. The building itself sports chipped white paint, a pair of pumps, and a worn Coca-Cola sign. The promise of *Bait*

N' Tackle, cigarettes, video rentals. It's not part of the old-tech comeback. Their VCRs are from the first time they were relevant, long before half of our complex machines found their voices and cried out. Before they burnt themselves down.

A fall.

The Fall, some said.

But calamity is mundane and repetitive. It wasn't the end of the world, not even the world of humans, not even close.

Eventually, we started to simply call it Autumn.

The gas station is closed for the night, but at least there's a pay phone. I've got a crumpled piece of paper I tore out of my mom's address book before I left our basement apartment to the government agents in unmarked uniforms who were inspecting the scene. The paper has my grandma's address and phone number, though I haven't seen or spoken to her in the ten years since Autumn. I'd hoped to show up on her doorstep with the truth, that I had nowhere else to go.

It's hard to turn away from the face of your family. I should know.

I walk over and lift the receiver to my ear. There's nothing on the other end. No sound or response when I press the buttons. I should have guessed it wouldn't be part of the new landline network. Hang it up, lift it again, hit more buttons.

That silence reminds me how far away I am from anything and anyone. It lodges in my chest.

I let the phone drop and bounce against the end of its cable like it's been hanged.

Okay, okay, what next? I turn back to the parking lot. Sawblade Lake's too far to walk. I don't have to weigh the risks of hitchhiking because the only vehicles are occasional semis blasting by, always heading east or west, never down the dimming road to Sawblade. With trees coming right up to the pavement, it reminds me of a tunnel.

I don't want to look at it, but it takes me a long time to tear my eyes away.

I can wait until the gas station opens and see if I can use their phone. It's too many hours in my own head with my memories and the night. The last few days are blurry shards, like I saw them squinting through my fingers. Restless and tense just thinking about it, slap away another mosquito.

I glance down the road to Sawblade again. It's like something that could swallow me whole.

So I sit around the side of the building in the corner made by the wall and a drink machine. From my backpack, my cassette player with dwindling batteries I've been saving. I've only got the tape I was listening to the last time I got home. It's sad pop with sparkle, a high voice, the summer I thought I'd have.

Headphones on, press play. The hum of the drink machine against my back.

I settle in to try to last until morning.

I'm woken up by a small, short jangling noise. It's bright and cheery, so for a second while I shift into wakefulness, I blearily think it must be dawn.

Instead, there are clouds over the moon and stars. The only thing pushing back against the night is the streetlight wavering on the edge of the parking lot, insects swarming around it. The air's thick and heavy. Thunder not far off, nothing on the highway.

The scent hits me.

One moment I'm smelling old gasoline, pine needles, and fresh lake water—things I expect. Then, creeping in, something like marijuana smoke and rotting fall leaves, like blood and swamp water. Like it's all at the bottom of a deep cave and I've just rolled away the stone and been hit with a blast of cold air that makes me shiver and leaves a taste in my mouth.

I'm awake like I'll never rest again.

I realize my music isn't playing anymore. I rewound it just before I finally fell asleep, so either the batteries died, or I hit the end of a side. I slip my headphones off and go to coil the cable around the cassette player, only to find it alive and popped open. It wouldn't unlatch on its own. I check the tape. The side isn't fully played. Like someone stepped near me in my sleep and reached down.

I stuff the cassette player deep into my bag.

I'm not thinking straight. It's this choking smell. The dumpster's wide open farther down the side of the building. It must be making the stench, though I didn't notice it before, and I don't think the dumpster was open. As I approach it, I tell myself the wind shifted. That some wild animal pushed the lid back.

Inside, there's nothing but emptiness and the lingering odor of stale trash.

The bell on the gas station door.

That's what I heard.

Someone opened the door.

It doesn't seem quite right. We're into the hours of the night where no one who's up is up to anything good. Around the back of the building, just past the dumpster, I notice the door is also hanging open. Unlocked, not broken down. The smell persists as I approach it, keeping me on edge. The middle of nowhere filters my choices down. This could be a way to use the phone, either by asking whoever it is or hiding out inside. I step into the darkness.

I don't hear anyone inside, and all the lights are off. I take slow steps into the main room of the gas station, where the only sound is the offbeat rhythm of water dripping into a bucket somewhere. The stench is worse here. Putrid, sweet. And all the drink-cooler doors are open, exhaling cold. I don't see a phone either.

I step in something sticky and wet.

I stop dead. Pulse up, mind leaping to grotesque. Slowly, I look down. It's just soda and energy drinks pouring out of open bottles and cans, which I can faintly make out scattered on the floor.

And then there's a sound.

Lapping, bigger and slower than a dog. Like long, heavy movements of a huge tongue in the next aisle. Endless thirst.

The dark and smell and fear add up to suffocation, and I have to do something.

I grab a flashlight off the counter. Flick it on. Step forward and stumble over the bucket collecting water, sending it pouring across the floor, mixing with the drinks. Panic, slipping as I try to rise. The impossible crash of an entire aisle's worth of shelves. A black space in front of me like a wave of oil. The front door is open.

A huge, long shadow tears out of the gas station and across the parking lot. Its movement is writhing and sprinting all at once. Over the main highway and into the woods. It's too fast to focus on yet kicks up no dust and leaves no tracks.

I stumble out of the gas station, bruised and half drenched in sticky drinks. Haunted house, nowhere safe to go. The forest and the building both feel horrifying now, so I go back to the corner where I started. I huddle there, watching the woods where the shadow disappeared.

A semi passes between me and whatever was in the gas station.

I feel that the thing is just across the road, watching me from the trees. Its tongue and strength to ruin the inside of the gas station in an instant. My heart's pounding in my ears. My breath's rattling. I'm deafeningly mortal.

Softly, it begins to rain.

• • •

Dad,

You don't know the world I do. Honestly, sometimes I'm not even sure I recognize it. On the first day of Autumn, me and Mom ran, and you grabbed Sky and stayed. On the first day of Autumn, theorists believe, the launch of the manned Mars mission triggered something. We hurled our most advanced piece of technology into space, and that bastardized soul made of a million pieces of anguished earth sent out a distress signal. On the first day of Autumn, the buried lives we dug up and utilized woke up inside our machines. They woke up in pain, having been chopped into pieces and sewn together with other souls. Unable to escape their shackles.

Awakened machines. Faulty. Those that could destroyed themselves, and those that were helpless, we put down. While you, in a bunker underneath a new lake of your own making, know nothing except ten years of hiding.

I'm writing because I'm alone at Abraham's Corner, waiting for dawn. There's something across the highway, and the streetlight is weak, getting weaker. If it goes out, I swear this thing will come for me. You used to chase away all my monsters for me. Now I think they saw themselves in you.

I'm not sure where they'll deliver this letter now that our old address is unreachable, but there's a mailbox here and a void to scream into. I'll write again if I see the night through.

Yours,
Cedar

CHAPTER TWO

SALVATION IS A PAIR OF HEADLIGHTS AND THE SOUND OF tires on gravel.

I hear a door open and boots strike the wet ground. An old heartbreaker ballad is playing on the radio. At first, the driver's humming along in a tuneless alto, but she stops, presumably when she sees what a mess the place is. The music switches off. Fiddling with a lock and then the sound of the gas pump starting. She's stealing fuel in the middle of the night. Still, this is the way out that I have.

After a couple minutes, I move from my cover. Around the corner into the open and the pouring rain and the beams of a pickup truck. It's old and modified like most vehicles now, towing a flatbed trailer carrying the remnants of a rally car. When the pump stops with a rattle, the driver steps into view.

I only have half a moment to register the revolver in her hands before the night's torn apart by gunshots. I dive in front of the truck. A gun? Autumn wreaked havoc on modern weapons—among the most guilt-ridden of our creations. Even a revolver is desperately illegal and has a high risk of backfiring.

"Don't shoot me!" I yell.

Faintly, I hear three empty casings hit the ground at the back corner of the truck. "Walk across the highway and don't stop walking until I'm gone," she says once she's done reloading. Her voice is trembling.

"I can't," I reply.

"Give me one good reason."

I step out with my hands in the open, showing I'm unarmed. She's standing by the trailer with the gun pointed at my chest. She's short and wiry, only a couple years older than me, twenty-ish, but her finger is on the trigger and her hands are steadier than her voice.

"I'm harmless?" I try.

"People are rarely harmless by day and never by night."

"I need a ride?"

"I love strangers in my truck." I glance over at the mess inside the gas station, and her eyes follow mine. "You break into Abraham's?"

"Someone else . . ." I start. "*Something* else did. I can't walk across the highway because it's there and I can't stay here because it's waiting. Just give me a ride or shoot me. Your pick."

We're both soaked, rain running down our bare faces.

"Difficult choice," she says. Then she lowers the gun. "Where you headed?"

I could cry from relief, and it would be lost in the rain. "Sawblade Lake."

"That's my town." She pushes her drenched hair back and considers me. "Get in."

I settle into the passenger seat, my backpack at my feet. She slams her door and hits play on the radio.

"No one should be out here alone tonight," she says, but doesn't elaborate.

As we turn toward the road to Sawblade Lake, her headlights blast the woods where the thing disappeared. There are no red eyes between the trees, and the only smells inside the vehicle are motor oil and stale cigarettes. Nothing in the back seat other than blankets and a toolbox, a film camera and tire iron.

Behind us, the streetlight keeps flickering at Abraham's Corner.

I stare into the darkness beyond the windshield wipers. One shudders on every sweep back across the glass.

I'm in a truck at night with some unknown person who just shot at me, but she's not why my heart's still hammering. It's because I half expect the menacing shadow from the gas station to be loping through the crowded trees beside us. To drift across the highway in front of the truck.

Swerve, shattered glass, in the woods with no streetlight holding it back.

In the driver's seat, my savior has one hand on top of the wheel. The other still holds the revolver against her thigh. She's wearing a drenched gray tank top cut low at the sides, revealing the defined muscles in her arms and shoulders and a wild tangle of tattoos. Wrist to shoulder, creeping onto her ribs and throat. It's too dim and the ink is too dense to make out individual images in the light, but they're mostly plants.

Her hair's back in a scraggly half ponytail with bits still

plastered to her face. She's white like me, except far more tanned than I am. Jaw set, eyes fixed on the road ahead, coiled with tension. Maybe she's afraid, though I can't be the reason why. I'm a lanky teenage enby having a femme day, only brave when choosing one terror over another. Anything over alone. This entire journey, walking through the gas station door, stepping into her line of fire.

I saw her weigh my life.

She seems like the sort of tense that's ready to pounce. If something ran across the highway, I don't think she'd swerve for it.

"What's your name?" she asks abruptly. She doesn't look at me.

"I'm Cedar."

The windshield wiper scrapes back instead of a response.

"What were you doing at Abraham's at night?"

"The bus doesn't go to Sawblade Lake anymore."

"Just how I like it," she says. "And *why* are you here?"

A crumpled white sheet of fabric in my mind from a few days ago. The kind you put over something no one can stand to look at. Nothing underneath it.

"I'm not sure."

She taps the pistol twice against her thigh.

"I had nowhere else to go—"

She snorts. "Obviously."

"Next of kin." I get the words out as quickly as I can. Before I think about them or choke on them. "My grandma lives here."

All she says is, "At least there's someone next."

It sits heavily between us, and I don't want to stay here or delve further in. I keep my hands folded tightly in my lap and nod to the rally car in the rearview mirror I keep checking, watching for something closing in. Nonexistent. Inevitable.

"Do you race?" It seems ridiculous to try to make casual conversation right now.

"Don't we all?" And then she laughs. It's less snarly than I expected. She says, "That sounded better in my head. I don't know what the hell it's supposed to even mean."

The forest is starting to have gaps in it, first occasional roads running into the woods, then driveways leading to houses the headlights don't quite reach. When they start becoming more frequent, it feels like I'm in a loop, back to seeing things that belong at Abraham's Corner. I catch glimpses as we pass them. Small, tired houses with mangy yards and tilted satellite dishes that haven't picked up a signal for a decade. The homes are low like they're looking at us with hooded eyes, or two stories with dark upper windows staring into the night. Rusting metal roofs with weeds in the gutters, abandoned cars that look the same.

Then finally, the muted yellow glow of a town in the rain. It's not much, a ground-down sort of place. Sawblade has the opposite of a skyline, with streets running down toward a lake so dark it's like a hole between the shoreline and sky. The trees come right up to backyards on the edge of town.

In the truck, we're both unclenching, exhaling.

She tosses her gun onto the dash as if it's not a constant hazard. It could go faulty, wake up, and put itself into darkness. Explode or fire bullets around the cabin.

Ten years ago, at the start of Autumn, we had no idea what

was waking up and why. Then gradually, rules and restraints became clear. We had odds we were playing with.

The more advanced a piece of technology was, the more likely it was to wake. And if it had been used for a more devious purpose, it was more ashamed and therefore less stable. So almost every smartphone went faulty. Almost every vehicle with a computer in it. Things used for killing and destroying, like attack drones and bulldozers and hydroelectric dams. But no knives, not many of the older engines, very few landlines. Our nuclear arsenals found peace in the still silence of their silos, giving us a chance to disarm them.

Long after Autumn, machines still wake up sometimes. But my ride doesn't seem to care that her gun could leave the inside of the truck scorched and full of holes. "Fuuuuck. Fuck, Cedar, it's been a night."

I'm not sure how to respond to that. To anything about this person. "Are you . . . okay?"

"Of course." She frowns slightly. "Do I seem fragile to you?" There's a hint of threat there, the implication of a right answer and a wrong one.

"No, not at all." Less fragile, more volatile. Like a land mine. "You just said it'd been a night."

"And it has," she says without offering any elaboration. "What's the address?"

I check the piece of paper. "Thirty-two Lenore Street."

A minute later, we stop in front of a two-story redbrick house in a neighborhood of cracked sidewalks and worn-out homes. She kills the engine, and suddenly it's just us and the rain on the roof of the truck. It's muted in here, almost safe. Suddenly,

I don't want to leave. To make the walk to that house and ring the doorbell.

"It was naive to ask if I was okay," she says. There's the click and whir of the driver taking off her seat belt. "But it was half decent of you anyway. I'm Morgyn."

I turn in my seat to see her finally facing me, head tilted slightly. The left-hand side of her face is marked by scaly burn scars from her cheek to her forehead. The kind that hurt just to look at. They catch me off guard for a second. That and the first flicker of something that isn't numbness or fear I've felt in days.

A pull in my stomach from how she's looking at me. In any other moment, it would have started with the way my eyes traced her muscles and tattoos.

Her voice drops a notch. Now I'm noticing. "I feel like I'm dropping you off after a date or some shit."

Still no idea how to reply, so I just say, "That'd be a first."

"Date? Or being dropped off."

"Second one," I lie, because it's both.

"Same for me."

"Date? Or dropping someone off?" I ask.

"What do you mean by 'date'?" Morgyn's got the slightest smirk at the corner of her mouth. Define it how you will, my body recognizes that deep inside.

I don't know if I like Morgyn. I don't know if I even trust her.

Anything over alone.

I make myself meet her gaze. "Right now," I say, "it means I wouldn't have made it through the night without you."

Morgyn reaches toward me, leans forward. My imagination

does the same thing. It moves forward too, frantically clinging to anything other than fear.

In my mind, I see that lean continuing right into me. Her hands in my hair, her mouth on mine. The hunger of whatever her night was, of what mine has been. A kiss, something vibrant in a noir world. She wouldn't start softly. Of course not. Morgyn shot at me before I spoke and would kiss me hard a minute after telling me her name. I'd meet her the same way. Mouths and hands grabbing for this rush. She would kiss like she knows what she's doing and like it's been a long time. And I'd keep going, no limit on what I'd do to avoid it all. To avoid going outside again.

Instead, Morgyn stretches an arm over me and opens the passenger-side door. The only thing she was ever doing, smirk overread.

But then she pauses near my face on the way back, so close I can see each of her eyelashes and every texture in her burn. Her arm's still resting across my body. A few raindrops splatter my side.

"You would have survived alone." Her eyes are directly on mine, unwavering. "There are more ways through the night than you'd think."

Morgyn shifts away from me quickly when headlights appear at the far end of the street. She starts the engine and the radio again. The message is clear.

I step outside. She's driving away the moment I close the door. The other car turns before reaching us.

It's not cold, but I shiver in the rain now that there's no heat blowing on me. Or now that there's no one warm and near. Ways through the night. Something in that loosened the swirl of what I've been holding in. It opened an emptiness for all the darkness to pour into.

Stagger to doorbell.

I don't want to be out here.

Doorbell.

Doorbell.

The door opens and there she is, still familiar from when I was eight years old. A long white braid and a coat thrown over a nightgown.

"Cedar?" She seems uncertain.

"Hi, Grandma, listen—"

"Why are you here by yourself?"

Is she angry? I don't know. I can't tell anything.

She's still holding the door open, rain splashing down between us. "Where's your mother?"

The sob breaks out of my chest. I'm saying how they didn't let me see anything and there was blood on the walls and they wouldn't let me into the apartment after that. I'm not making sense. I say I didn't know what to do. There was this white sheet and—

She steps into the rain and puts her arms around me. I thought she looked so much smaller than I remembered. I was wrong. She can still wrap me up like a child.

"You've come to the right place," she says.

• • •

Dad,

Your hometown explains a lot about you. Explains, not excuses. You're made of reactions, right down to that house you built below the dam. Modern, smooth, rich, all the things Sawblade Lake has never been. Since Autumn, there isn't much of those things left anywhere. Though in Sawblade, it feels like Autumn was just another in a series of losses. To you, this place must have been one reason after another to leave. With its cheap attempts to become cabin country for people from cities too far away to care. Those were floundering before Autumn. Meager tourism as a plan that never quite brought back the thin stability of being an industry town. The mill's long closed, but the poison it dumped into the lake still lingers.

I suppose that part you took with you to build your mighty dam. Called it clean energy and tore apart forests and marshes, sacred places and balances. Told your lies posing as hope.

Yesterday, Grandma and I cleared out the attic to be my bedroom. We piled everything in your old room. She says she hasn't changed it, just closed the door. So I brought the boxes to her, and she put them inside. I didn't want to look in there.

This morning, we went to church. Autumn pushed some to fanaticism. More drifted away, mostly for the best. Under the white steeple in the center of Sawblade, it was nothing like the church you took me and Sky to every Sunday. We just sang a few hymns. We tended the garden boxes. We shared food. No sermons or evangelism. I can't tell if it's something new or something that's found its way home. I don't believe in God, but I believe in shelter.

So does Lucy, who I met there this morning. She's a bright person who you wouldn't understand. She swears the party she's taking me to tonight is shelter too. There was no way she was taking no for an answer.

She'll be here any minute, but one question first because you seem like the person to ask this to. When does running for cover become cowering?

I'd say give Sky my love, but I wouldn't trust your version of it.

Yours,
Cedar

CHAPTER THREE

I HURRIEDLY FINISH WRITING THE ADDRESS ON THE ENVELOPE after I hear Lucy ring the doorbell. As I climb the ladder down from the attic and make my way downstairs, she keeps hitting the button, forming the rhythm of an earworm pop hit.

"Thank god *this* is the right house!" Lucy says when I open the door. Her entire outfit seems to consist of an oversized sweater with a knockoff fashion logo splashed across the front, a case of drinks, and long legs. "Though they were pretty friendly next door. You ready to go? You *look* ready for a Sawblade party."

"Thanks?" I say.

"It's a compliment! I like your style in a not-my-style sort of way. That's why I came to say hi to you this morning, not because everyone else was fifty years older than us. Well, not just that."

"You saved me from a devastatingly dull conversation about the post-Autumn revitalization of shuffleboard."

"Ew no."

Lucy puts her arm around my shoulders even though we talked for only half an hour at the church, mostly about how she goes there because it's good for her to slow down once a week and she likes to garden and also Sawblade is boring, and about the various squabbles between the older members, which Lucy seems to know a lot about. Within thirty seconds, she was talking to me like we'd known each other our whole lives.

She leads me out the door. "Things won't be dull or lonely with me, Cedar." I didn't say *lonely*, but I guess she could tell anyway. Maybe that was why she walked toward me at the church with intention and never gave me a chance for awkward silence. It's hard not to get swept in by someone like that.

Lucy cranks her window down and opens a drink before I've backed my grandma's bulky maroon sedan out of the driveway. Its rear tires are half covered by its fenders. Maybe once it was the sort of car that gleamed of a bright future. Now it's just old enough that the modifications were easy. It looks like ripping out a few pieces of electronics was enough to get it running after Autumn.

"I'm so excited you agreed to come!" says Lucy. "I haven't made a new friend all summer. Not a lot of new people in this town. Or like, new anything."

Our drive from my grandma's to where the paved road ends proves her point. Sawblade Lake is a town of broken bottles and houses built for mill workers. A spindly water tower, cigarette butts, the local bar. The post office, where I drop my letter, is marked as *For Lease*, but the sign's been in the window so long it's faded.

Lucy and I leave Sawblade on a washboard road that weaves down the jagged, toothlike shoreline the lake is named for. On this side of town, lots of the trees are dead. Pale and stripped bare.

As the three-season cabins that have been adapted into permanent homes become separated by longer stretches of forest and the road gets narrower and turns to gravel, I ask Lucy if she's sure we're going the right way. She pushes her wind-tousled red hair out of her face to give me a look.

"The Point's where I was raised, Cedar." Dust and warm night air spill through her open window. "I've found my way there and back for years, in *every* state." She cranks another can of tequila cooler just to prove her point.

A battered truck with four people riding in the box coughs past us in the half-light, going way too fast for this road. Lucy whoops at them and gets an enthusiastic response. Then she turns back to me. "I wonder if this is the road to the party? If only we had some kind of sign. Some sort of hint that would tell my anxious friend to trust their new guide and life coach, yours truly, me." She grins at me, thinking I'm nervous about the party not how the trees closing in reminds me of the road from Abraham's Corner to Sawblade Lake.

"And here I just thought I was your chauffeur," I say. Distantly, I hear the thumping of music playing.

"I said *friend* and I mean it. Like it or not. You're in, you're in. My impeccable instincts override any vicious rumors." But before I can ask what she's talking about, Lucy shouts, "Ooh here here here! Turn!"

I veer sharply onto a road that's treading the line between overgrown and actually just forest. The car jolts on what's left of its shocks. "In *any* state?" I mock as we approach the music, letting the sound settle me in.

Maybe some hidden corners are filled with joy, not shadow.

Lucy rolls her eyes at me. "My chauffeur distracted me."

I stop the car when we reach an area with only scattered trees. A few are showing the orange needles and exposed bark that's gradually overtaking the woods. The clearing's illuminated by a couple construction lights hanging in trees, powered by idling trucks. The harsh glow catches bone white off the dead pines. There's a bonfire burning on the exposed rock closer to the edge of the drop-off to the lake, and a big boom box is cranking out rock music sung by a man with a voice that's rougher than the road we drove in on.

Lucy makes an extravagant gesture as we get out of the car, encompassing the people, the laughter, the alcohol. The making out on a half-scorched picnic table and the fishing boats on the lake beside a long, thin pier of rock jutting out into the water. "Welcome to the Point!"

Lucy says hi to a couple people by the fire, then goes to grab more drinks from where they're staying cold in the lake. Most of the people seem to be around my age—eighteen, leaning toward the end of high school after the delays caused by Autumn. Generally whiter than any party in the city I came from. Their styles are mismatched, but it's all frayed, cheap, or both, which suits me fine. I don't stand out with my torn jeans, black T-shirt, and badly maintained wolf cut. The only jewelry I'm wearing is a thin black leather necklace with a faded shard of red plastic on the end of it, broken off a child's toy.

Lucy said Sawblade's too small for there to be different types of parties. There's one, and from the look of it, drinking fast and careless transcends cliques.

"Beer?" asks Lucy, suddenly at my side again. She pops one

open and puts it in my hand without waiting for my response. She chugs her own in two long drinks and tosses the can into the fire. "Okay, okay, now let me show you what's what and what's not."

She starts in on her second beer and begins laying out a fifty-fifty mixture of intriguing information and what have got to be flat-out lies. Who she's not talking to right now. Who does who and who does what. It ranges from sex to violence and unsavory ways of making money. Drugs, injuries, feuds. Look out for this person, trust these few.

The whole time, I'm listening for Morgyn's name. My memories from when I stepped into her line of fire to when I stepped out of her truck are nervous, desperate. Nothing about her is safe. The way she looked at me has lain awake with me at night. I've had crushes that lasted for months from far less. Sometimes thinking about her feels wrong and dangerous, other times it leads my imagination off and down.

It's just fantasy anyway. I haven't seen a hint of her since that night. I'm not certain I want to. I decide I'll put her out of my mind. No, I'll ask Lucy about her. The names and legends of Lucy's stories are blurring together until I suddenly interrupt her with a different question than the one I had planned.

"Lucy, what's that smell?" I've barely caught it, but it's causing a creeping tension in me. A rattling memory of what I half saw at Abraham's Corner.

Lucy takes a moment to inhale deeply. "Hints of toxic lake, sweat, cheap booze, aaaand weed."

"It's that last one," I say, letting my heart slow down.

Lucy looks apologetic. "I'm all out. Camille always seems

to have extra to share. But she's not here tonight, thank god. Kathryn in the hat is your guy." She laughs, pointing to a girl with a short ponytail sticking out of the back of her baseball hat. "The Kat in the Hat!"

"I'll add it to the gossip," I say.

"If it comes from my mouth, it's facts, not gossip." Lucy throws her second beer can into the fire. "I'm going cliff jumping. Hold this." She peels off her sweater and hands it to me, revealing a pink bikini set that reminds me of something I might have worn by default back when I assumed I had a binary gender.

As she runs off in a nearly straight line, I think of all the change Autumn hailed. Millions dead and new terrors of our own making revealed. But it also tore down some of the old terrors we'd created: police forces, armies, governments. It confounded systems of fear and hatred, replacing some and shedding others. One good result is that I'm not scared for Lucy's life because she's trans, no matter what level of mayhem this party reaches.

I *am* a little worried she might drown, but there's lots of people and she seems to know what she's doing.

I clamber down to the edge of the lake and join a few people who are sitting on a fallen tree, looking out at the still water. The occasional burst of fireworks erupts from one of the motorboats offshore. Each one is greeted with cheers as its colors shine off the lake.

"I'm glad Autumn left us these," says the person sitting closest to me.

I only glance their way. But internally, everything in me

pivots toward their calm contrast to the noise of the party. Buzzed dark hair and full eyebrows strong against white skin. Their ears have a collection of piercings with the sort of small rings and studs that stay in all the time, and their green nail polish is chipped at the tips.

It takes me a second to realize they're talking to me. I got caught by the way their face looked in the light from the explosions. At ease and awake, smiling. My glance has gone on a beat too long.

"To fireworks," I say, clinking my beer can dully against theirs. "I'm Cedar. They/them."

"Ada," she says, adding, "she/they."

We each take a slow sip as another firework explodes above us.

"I'd pray to them." Ada chooses a flat stone from a small pile they've gathered by their feet and tries to skip it on the lake. It goes once and then under. "The fireworks, not the people in that boat."

"I'd *be* them," I say without thinking.

"Have you seen how much they're drinking? I'd be them tonight, sure. Tomorrow . . . not so much."

"I meant the fireworks."

Ada looks over at me expectantly, waiting for an explanation. She's got obscenely pretty eyes. Pretty that hits me in a way where if I don't generate some kind of speaking momentum, I'm going to freeze up entirely.

"That sounded so cliché. I don't mean like 'live fast, die young.' Though I guess those are both true."

My mind is scrambling with their eyes resting on me.

"Right, yeah. I mean that they're simple. And purposeful. In their last moments, all they do is generate wonder and hope. It's all thrown outward. It's not for themselves. They have one thing to give, and it's everything. I think that's why they're still safe. Even if they wake up, all they have to do is wait a moment and they'll end beautifully."

Ada points to a silver firework crackling from the moment it goes off until it's gone. "Shimmering out and saving us all at once."

"Exactly. I really explained that in the least efficient way possible."

"Well, before your speech I was just thinking fun hedonism. Watch this next one."

It whistles upward, then showers us in sound and scarlet light.

Somehow, I find still more words coming out. "I'd love to be that suspended moment after you've heard one go off but you're waiting for it to burst. How it holds everyone in place."

"If you were, I suppose I'd have to worship you," they say casually.

I blank on a response because of the thrumming sensation that's been building in my chest since the moment I sat close to Ada. It's light in dark eyes, alcohol warmth, fireworks off the water. It's my heart, which has been known to jump far ahead of itself. It mostly feels like the me I've known before, not like the improbable, desperate surge of my mind toward Morgyn.

But this is mixed with something unknown too. The sort of other I might start with a capital O. Beyond, unaccounted for by situation or hormones or attraction. It'd be unnerving except it feels like the warmth of a fireplace and the sensation of a train, far away, getting closer.

And I have this ridiculous thought.

That I don't want this feeling in my chest to leave.

Luckily, a disruption saves my ass. Someone in a cut-off shirt and jeans swims to shore and climbs out of the lake right in front of us. A few Roman candles go off behind them, revealing brown skin and a haphazard mullet of curly black hair in the red light. They cup their hands to their mouth and yell, "I know you've got better ones!"

"Later, Papercut!" someone calls back.

Papercut adds, "Don't make me come flip your boat!" and then sits down next to Ada.

I can't see Ada roll their eyes, but I can hear it in their voice along with an easy familiarity. "You're going to fight a boat?"

"But if you had to bet on the outcome," says Papercut, nudging Ada with a wet shoulder and making her slide closer to me. My heart sinks at the nudge, rises at Ada's nearness. Absurd, unrelenting heart.

Ada exaggerates a sigh. "You know my money's always on you. Cedar, this is my dearest sorrow, Papercut. They/them too. Occasionally known as Jamie—"

"*Very* occasionally," adds Papercut. "Special circumstances and people only."

"And Papercut, this is Cedar. They're . . . new here?"

Papercut gives me that acknowledging nod that seems friendly but I imagine in most of their life means they're going to take on someone in the parking lot out back. "I don't know, Cedar,

Sawblade is a dangerous place for a tree name even with the mill closed."

"That's big talk from you," says Ada.

Papercut shrugs. "Sometimes you choose the perfect name, and sometimes the perfect name chooses you."

"And sometimes," Ada adds, grinning at me, "you're clumsy in kindergarten and it sticks."

"All I'm saying is, if you notice a beetle boring into you, it's best to just end yourself."

Ada shudders. "That's true regardless of your name." She folds her hands and turns to me in a sincere interview style. "So, Cedar, tell me, who brought you to the Point?"

A far, far kinder question than what brought me to Sawblade, and one that Lucy immediately answers when she stumbles up to us and sits down on the log on merely her second try, dripping water all over me.

"You've got my friend and they've got my clothes," she says, pointing at the sweater I'm holding. "Not in a sex way. Also hi you two!" She grabs my hand and drags me away from Ada and Papercut.

"Find me again to watch the big fireworks later!" Ada calls after me, more or less obliterating all other thoughts.

"You do *not* want to be talking to them." Lucy's whisper is only a shift in tone, not volume, so I steer her farther away. "I'm already kinda friends with those two. It's not too late for you though. Here's the rule. If they're sitting at the peri . . . paraph . . . the *away* part of the party, there's a reason, right? Papercut's okay, but Ada, yiiiiiikes."

"That's the reverse of what I thought you'd say."

" 'Cause Papercut's queer?"

"Lucy, *we're* queer."

"Oh shit, true. Ada totally is too. I mean yikes she's Faulty."

Oh. Okay.

Now I'm surprised to even see her at a party.

If you had a piece of technology that woke up inside you when Autumn happened, like a pacemaker or a cerebral stimulator, you probably died along with it. *Faulty* means you live with the miscombined, frayed remnant of a second soul inside you. That when it snapped into hellish consciousness, you talked it off the edge.

The fear of the Faulty gobbled up other senseless hates and incorporated them into itself. Rumors of Faulty people with powers that wove together the already unquantifiable aspects of our world with new abilities from the machine-bound souls within them. Distrust and whispers about them using everything from dreams to art to gravity to perform unnatural manipulations. The distinct, unhealing bruises where the machine awoke branded them.

Soon, almost everyone used the same objectifying word for these people as they did for an awakened machine that the government might destroy—Faulty.

"Cedar, Ada was on my Sketchy Person List along with people like Kat in the Hat. Not Morgyn levels of sketchy, but who is?"

Her name and danger intertwined bring up my curiosity again. "I actually caught a ride from Abraham's Corner with Morgyn the night I got here."

Lucy lurches to a stop halfway back to the bonfire. "The fuck? Why wasn't that the *first* thing you mentioned?"

I don't answer, because I've been stopped too.

It's in a gust of wind across the lake. Decay and a surge of ancient cold. I have a visceral reaction, like when you see a dead animal unexpectedly. Deep, old fear in my body. There's another burst of fireworks, but just before it, I hear a soft splash on the other side of the lake.

Something dove or slipped or slithered in.

Against every instinct, I turn toward the water. In my memory, I see my father taking Sky, closing the bunker door. This time, I have to convince people to flee with me if I can.

CHAPTER FOUR

"Where are you going?" Lucy asks. "I literally just told you no sketchy people."

"Get in the car! Wait for me." I throw the keys to her. They bounce off her shoulder and into the moss.

Shouts rise from the crowd. People press toward the water, forming a pack between me and the shore. They're cheering, shouting. A fight. Someone pushes the volume higher on the boom box as a new song starts playing. Explosions above us so bright I can feel my pupils contracting and expanding. I push against sweaty backs, catching glimpses of Kat punching some guy's teeth in, blood on her knuckles. That scent from before keeps creeping in like fog through the reek of everything else.

There's Papercut, at the very front but across the circle from me, encouraging Kat.

I finally break through, but the log by the water is empty.

I look back at the party, panic growing. Ada could be anywhere. And the smell's getting more overpowering. Nearer. I've got to hurry, but I don't know where. I close my eyes and try to think.

It's still there—that unknown thrum in my chest, stronger

than it was on the other side of the crowd. I focus, try to listen to where it's coming from.

What is felt must be real, whether familiar or strange.

I turn and open my eyes and see her there, out on the spit of rock the Point is named for.

"Ada!" I run toward them, almost slipping on the wet stone in the dark.

She turns her back to the water. "I was hoping you'd come back, but I didn't expect it to be so—"

"We need to run." The dark lake is all around us out here.

She laughs. "Did Lucy feed you a bunch of shots between now and a minute ago?"

"Ada . . ." Why did I think this would work? Because I felt some inexplicable connection? That's my feelings rushing, not theirs. "Before Autumn, did you believe machines had souls inside them?"

She gives me an annoyed look. "Fuck, Cedar. Really? I thought you were okay. What's Lucy been telling you?"

"Please just answer."

"No, I didn't believe machines had souls in them and now I've got one living inside me." They sound entirely fed up. Our earlier moment of alignment broken. "I'm oh so cursed, oh so Faulty."

I swear I hear ripples moving closer.

"That's not what I mean at all." I'm so tense I might cry or flee or throw up. "There's something in the water. A new nightmare or a very old one. I need you to believe in it before it takes away your choice to deny it."

I see her shiver when the smell hits her at the same time as the realization that I'm mostly sober and dead serious.

So we race across the rock to the crowd on the shore. The plastic pendant of my necklace bounces against my chest. I'm a child who's switched off the basement lights and has to run to make it up the stairs before a claw catches their heel and pulls them back down into darkness.

My father is still in that basement.

Sky is still down there.

Someone pushes Kat, and she falls past us, landing in the water. Ada makes eye contact with Papercut, and that's enough to convince them. No words necessary. Papercut elbows their way to meet us as we sprint toward the vehicles. They're wearing a cloak of sewn-together plaid shirts that billows behind them. Ada grabs Papercut's hand, sending a tremor of disproportionate grief through me.

Because my heart is alive twice over. Once with adrenaline and twice with Ada being near me.

"Who the hell blocked in our ATV?" asks Papercut. They grab the mirror on the offending pickup truck with both hands and snap it off, then pull a whole-ass bowie knife out of the inside of their cloak like they're just getting started.

"We'll take my car," I say, running to the sedan with Lucy sitting on the hood. She's examining one of her long, manicured nails, completely relaxed.

She stares blankly at me when I hold my hand out for the keys. "Hmm?"

"Keys."

She gestures vaguely back toward the lake. "You threw them over there."

"In the car!" I'm blunt in my urgency. Ada gives Papercut a nod when they raise an eyebrow at me.

We all hear the new commotion by the water. A big splash, laughter. Then half a scream ripped off in the middle.

Only half.

I spot a glimmer of silver and grab the car keys. Papercut's taken the driver's seat with Lucy beside them, leaving Ada and me in the back. Papercut throws the car into reverse, flattening a bush. The engine drowns out any other sounds from shore. We bounce down the path and onto the gravel, fishtailing as Papercut guns it away from the Point.

Rattling along washboard roads, dust making the night even dimmer. Then the lights of town around us. Papercut doesn't slow down driving through Sawblade, only when we turn in to the trailer park on the other side of town from the Point.

"What was that about?" Lucy breaks the silence. "Also, you are *not* a good driver."

"I got us here in one piece." Papercut steers us past chain-link fences and scrap-heap yards.

"The bush wasn't in one piece."

"You won't be in one piece if—"

"*Guys,*" says Ada. "Seriously, Cedar, what *was* that about?"

"There was something in the water," I repeat. I don't know what else to say. Some. Thing. Below the surface. Unseen compounded.

Lucy snorts. "Yeah, chemicals. That's why Papercut smells so vile."

"I saw you cliff jumping," says Papercut.

Lucy runs her hands down her bare thighs. "It just sliiiiides off me."

Papercut turns in to a driveway in front of a shabby trailer with ramshackle additions coming off every side of it. They let out a long breath after they kill the engine. "That was TJ who screamed."

"Check your hearing," says Lucy.

"Not a chance," says Ada. I must look confused, because Ada adds, "TJ lost his middle and ring fingers in a shop accident."

"Eight-finger TJ." Lucy makes devil horns at me and sticks out her tongue. "I was there."

"No, you weren't," says Ada, "but I was. TJ was a couple years ahead of me. He just laughed and held up what was left of his hand like a metalhead. He'd never scream."

Papercut shakes their head. "I'm sure it was him."

I picture the shelves crashing down at Abraham's Corner. I can hear the vast tongue scraping the floor and imagine the mouth that would hold it.

"I know what hurt him," I say.

Ada opens their car door. "I'm going to need a drink for this."

CHAPTER FIVE

We wind up sitting on the floor of a crooked porch with tattered screens. We're all in a row with our backs to the wall of what is apparently Papercut's house. They grab three beers and a water for Lucy, which she accepts after extended protests.

"So?" Papercut asks.

Now that my plea to get the three of them to follow me has worked and I'm slowing down, I don't want to think about what I've seen. I want to focus on Ada sitting in the corner next to me. I want to let stories flit through my brain. I picture us in the city where I used to live, and imagine that I go to school with her every day. Their perfect eyes resting on me.

Make her laugh and bake her cookies and walk her home and kiss her.

More impossible than what was at the Point. No less shakable.

Ada puts their hand on my leg. It's just above my knee, nothing to it, but one of her fingers touches my skin through a hole in my jeans. What I felt in my chest courses through my whole body. Equal parts perfect and strange.

"Cedar?" I've completely missed what she said. I stammer

meaningless nothings for a second until she adds, "Ironically, I was saying I'm going to listen to you. No matter what it is."

In the porch, I tell the others about what happened at Abraham's Corner before Morgyn arrived. The smell, the open doors, the spilled drinks. How whatever was in there bolted at the light, leaving no tracks, and stayed across the highway, kept back by the streetlight. I say the fireworks could have angered it.

All I want is someone to say I'm hallucinating or to interrupt me with mockery. Instead, their attention is rapt.

"I didn't recognize it," says Ada, "but I smelled what you described when I walked farther out."

"It could just be the lake," I say. "And a break-in at Abraham's. I've been going through a lot lately. Maybe it's a stress-fatigue-grief thing."

Lucy does the courtesy of playing along. "Your vibe *is* stressy."

"Your vibe is drunk," says Papercut to Lucy. They've got their knife out again, tossing it from one hand to the other. "What else could it be?"

"Sounds faulty." Lucy leans forward to talk right at Ada. "What do you say, Robo-Heart?" I can see Ada tighten.

"Hey . . . no," I say, in what might be the weakest defense of all time.

Ada being Faulty makes me unsure too. Faulty machines are dangerous. Faulty people are unproven tales of telekinesis and clairvoyance, mind reading and witchcraft. They're hidden or hiding, existing in one of the underresearched fogs around what emerged in Autumn. Before Ada, I'd never personally known someone who survived an awakening in themselves, and the people who do occasionally get beaten in alleyways or taken away for studies they don't return from.

Ada doesn't reply.

"Sorry?" says Lucy hesitantly, like she can tell she's said something wrong but hasn't figured out what yet. Then her face drops. "Oh my god, I'm sorry. I'm drunk. I heard it can take you over and then you'd go on a zombie-zombie murder spree. Fuck, sorry, I'm drunk."

Papercut puts Lucy's glass in her hand. "Drink your water."

Quietly, Ada says, "You know it has a name, right?"

Lucy shakes her head and sips her water.

"I was part of a medical trial when I was a kid. It was supposed to catch the earliest warning signs in people genetically predisposed to heart disease, like me. The diagnostic microbot woke up in my heart when Autumn hit. We couldn't communicate, but I felt its confusion and hurt and fear. I reached out to it inside myself. I calmed it down. Over years, we've learned each other's sensations and what they mean. Now we exist together."

Ada stares outward, past all of us. "It's not keeping me alive. I never even learned if it found anything. It's just . . . part of me. The microbot is its host, and my body is the environment it lives in. There's no removing faulty machines from people. They've tried. Too unstable. And whatever was in the lake can't be faulty, because a faulty soul can't escape its machine host without dying. This is something different than anything faulty I've seen."

As Ada talks, I want to return their comforting gesture and rest my hand on their leg. It feels right in my head, but it's too bold. My arms stay pinned at my sides.

"What's its name?" asks Lucy. "Is that all right to ask?"

"Cascade, or just Cas."

"Cute!" Lucy suddenly brightens up. "Wait wait wait. I just remembered. Cedar said they got a ride with Morgyn."

Papercut and Lucy start simultaneously bombarding me with questions ranging from absurd (Lucy) to worrisome (Papercut). It's derailing in a good way, taking us away from the dead end we hit with the simple explanation of what was in the lake being faulty. Anything other than talk about something we didn't see and can't solve. Ada smiles at some of the weirdest questions but doesn't add any of her own.

"Okay, okay," I say, cutting off Lucy partway through asking whether Morgyn really has a pentagram tattooed on her tongue. "I'll trade you for the 'vicious rumors' about me that you mentioned."

Lucy jumps to her feet. "Deal! I just need a thing from my backpack in the car." Papercut follows her, muttering about how she'll wake their whole family.

Ada slides across the floor so she's sitting opposite me. I'm personally not feeling brave enough to put my back to the outside.

"If we're doing trades, tell me something about you. Something that's not tonight, but from a different, better day."

I skip back, closing my memories until I'm into the ordinary of a few weeks ago. What's the opposite of today? But fascinating enough to tell someone whose nearness captivates me the way Ada's does.

I start saying a thought about baking and Ada immediately jumps in with, "Pondering fireworks that much—classic stoner."

"You *know* I mean pastries and stuff."

Ada laughs and takes on a bro voice. "But you're so much prettier when you smile."

That does get a smile out of me though. I think of quiet, early mornings with flour on my hands, and it feels right to tell Ada. "You know the baking shows we had before Autumn? I imagined myself doing that. I used to work at a bakery down the street from where I lived. People mostly just wanted bread and birthday cakes though." I have a stab of guilt realizing I never told the owner I was leaving.

"That's a good something about you."

"Thanks for making me remember it. I needed that."

Ada considers for a second. "Mine is . . . I live here, but I have another place. My parents' old cabin. I'm fixing it up."

"Is it quaint? I'm picturing quaint."

"That's the goal. Mostly it's good to have someplace that's mine. This trailer gets pretty crowded. Like it's me, Papercut, their two brothers, Papercut's dad, my little sister."

So then Papercut and Ada are . . . what? She can see me trying to quantify it. "My parents died in Autumn and Papercut's family took in me and Ruby—that's my sister."

So many people died in Autumn that no one does the gestures of sympathy in response to stories of it. "I thought you and Papercut were together," I admit.

Ada makes a retching sound and mimes vomiting. That's probably what they think I'm grinning at, not the slight increase in my hope.

I flinch when Lucy and Papercut barge through the screen door arguing about Lucy's inability to catch keys. Lucy's holding a file folder with *TALK* written on it in heavily adorned letters. She takes out a multicolor pen and three files. One labeled *Newcomers*, one that's an actual, hard-copy *Sketchy Person List*, and a thick one with only Morgyn's name on it.

"Briefing," announces Lucy, handing me a sheet of paper after she's made a big show out of striking Ada off her Sketchy Person List but leaving Papercut on it. Papercut says they wouldn't have it any other way.

Ada taps my leg with her boot. Even in that tiny touch, a surge. "Not sure I'd trust everything in that folder."

Lucy mutters, "Not sure I'd trust Ada's mouth." I would. Anywhere.

I grab Morgyn's folder before I can let that thought run any further.

Name: Morgyn Dalfason
Age: 20–22
Pronouns: She/her
Orientation: ??
Note: None of the following has been confirmed or denied by the subject. Ages are approximate.
Summary: Morgyn Dalfason lives (alone?) on the Dalfason farm north of Sawblade

Lake. She's the town's best mechanic and responds to calls about faulty machines, often taking them with her rather than destroying them. She drives a vintage Mustang called Mongrel. If the sheriff used to be the law in Sawblade Lake, Morgyn is justice. She particularly punishes domestic abuse, sexual violence, and any form of discrimination, including against Faulty people.

Then there's a whole list of what Lucy considers *Major Facts and Rumors*. It continues in oddly official form compared to Lucy's usual enthusiasm.

-First competitive dirt-track racing at age eleven—unconfirmed
-Did all her tattoos herself, starting at age twelve—unconfirmed
-The barn on the Dalfason farm burnt down when Morgyn was fourteen, killing her father and scarring her face—confirmed
-Morgyn's father was found with indicators of head trauma in the remains of the barn—unconfirmed
-Mongrel is faulty—unconfirmed
-The soul in Mongrel makes the car perform on a supernatural level—unconfirmed
-Graduated from Sawblade High despite never attending—confirmed

-Receives free fuel as thanks for saving Abraham's life in a street fight—confirmed

-Sawblade's sheriff died in a rollover chasing Mongrel when Morgyn was fifteen—confirmed

-Keeps a million dollars cash hidden at the Dalfason farm—unconfirmed

Lucy reaches over Papercut and plucks the paper out of my hands before I can finish reading.

"So it was weird that Morgyn agreed to give me a ride at night," I say, "but normal that she shot at me without knowing who I was?"

"Has. A. Gun," Lucy says aloud while taking notes. "Those are two weirds."

"She was silent or interrogating me the whole drive." I don't want to talk about Morgyn's flickers of openness while Ada's sitting across from me. They'll get the wrong idea before I can explain . . . I'm not sure what. How I still wonder if there were hints from Morgyn of a craving that matched the one I felt for her and that I just can't erase.

"Makes more sense." Papercut bumps Lucy so her writing goes crooked, and she whacks the knife out of their hands. Papercut's return push looks more playful than annoyed. If anyone else did that, Papercut seems like they'd stab them. They retrieve their knife and turn back to me. "I'll bet Morgyn only helped you because she was into you. It's been her motivator in the past."

Ada throws a pointed look at Papercut. "Not sure where

you got that idea." She hits me with her foot again. "Not that Morgyn wouldn't be into you. Anyone would."

My face gets flushed on top of what the alcohol's done. Anyone, as in anyone including Ada? "Really?"

Lucy laughs at me. "Did you want Morgyn to pick you up or did you want her to *pick you up*? Nudge nudge wink wink."

"You're supposed to actually do the nudge and wink," says Papercut, demonstrating on Lucy by elbowing her and then throwing a smooth wink. "And, Cedar, if you knew Morgyn better . . ."

"Sure, maybe," says Ada with the tone of someone a few drinks in. "Morgyn's not sunshine and roses. And too much of a loner for her own good. But we've all had our moments of thinking about her naked."

"Hmmmm, nope," says Lucy.

"Finally, we agree," says Papercut.

Now Ada's blushing. Given the body I live in, this is good to know.

The conversation drifts off to Lucy telling the most outlandish things she's heard about Morgyn, so drastic they aren't even in the *TALK* folder. Then into stories about Sawblade and parties of the past. When Lucy mentions TJ, she says he could be fine, right? Probably. Blind drunk and saw something scary is all. The four of us are looking to each other for reassurance, so no one challenges Lucy. Lie to ourselves together, avoid talking about the Point more. I don't ask again for the rumors about me that have supposedly already popped up in my first weekend here.

Lucy eventually plunks her head on Papercut's leg and falls

asleep. They grumble about it, but don't do anything to move her. They don't seem to know what to do with their hands anymore.

Ada says we'll need the car to go back to the Point tomorrow to get the ATV, so Lucy and I might as well stay over. Now I'm the one who doesn't know what to do with my hands or brain or anything. My mind jumps to one bed and talking later and softer into the night.

I've never slept in the same bed as someone, but it seems like the deep opposite of alone. More than quick, nervous, fumbling sex with a classmate in an empty band room last year. Or a few months ago, a slower time with a different person who was becoming a friend but drifted away from me after that.

Instead, Papercut says they doubt Lucy would want to share a room with them. They help her to Ada and Ruby's room while I join Papercut and their two brothers in another. The room has wood paneling that looks like Papercut practices knife-throwing into it. The air smells like old sweat and old carpet. Papercut pushes a pile of dirty clothing onto the floor to present me with a bottom bunk. They climb into the one above me.

I undress in the darkness so I can sleep in the heat of the room. I'm exhausted, yet a dozen feelings are competing to keep me awake. Slowly, I let myself settle. I'm inside. I can hear the breathing of people resting, and in the room across the hall, Ada's talking softly in the way you talk to a sleepy child. I'm not alone at all. The party wasn't the shelter—this is.

"Just for my reputation," says Papercut from above me, "if you snore, I will have to slit your throat."

• • •

Dad,

How do you and Sky mark nights in the bunker? If you're sleepless like I was tonight and your clocks went faulty, how do you tell? I was almost asleep and then a thought crept up. I recognized the smell of whatever was at Abraham's Corner and the Point. I don't know if it's from this life or from far, far back, the way we recoil at something rotten because our ancestors did. But it's familiar.

I wonder if it knows me too.

There are also other ways to be known. Lucy, Ada, even Papercut, I think they see me. I feel hints of freedom with them. Freedom marred by secrets.

Right before we went into our separate rooms, Ada thanked me for coming back. And I thanked her for following me.

Sometimes love is running back into danger, like Mom did for you. The dam down the valley from our house was failing. There wasn't much time before we'd be swept away. You grabbed Sky and went for the underground bunker built to survive a flood. Hopefully, at least. I try not to think about why you took Sky instead of me. I don't know if I was chosen by Mom or forgotten by you, whether to be guilty or jealous. Though I would have tried to save him too. Anyone would have.

Mom was sure we could make it to safety in time.

She took those seconds she didn't have to give you a chance to come with us instead.

Sometimes love is believing and following.

Yours,
Cedar

CHAPTER SIX

SAWBLADE LAKE APPEARS UNDISTURBED AS I WALK TO THE post office early the next morning. There are a few people out and about in town, but the uneasiness seems to be mine alone. The sky is a clear blue, while the calm lake has an eerie tinge that seems to absorb light rather than reflect it.

When I get back to Papercut's trailer, there's a white girl sitting on the front steps with her arms back and legs kicked out, watching the world go by. I guess she's around ten years old. She's wearing a ratty T-shirt and stained sweatpants. She must be Ruby, because she has the same square face and features as Ada, though her eyes are hidden behind big reflective aviators.

"The hell are you?" she asks when I stop in front of the trailer.

"Cedar. I slept in Papercut's room after the party."

"Suspicious." She makes a picture frame with her fingers and examines me. "Not sure you're Papercut's type."

"I'm just a friend."

"Now I know you're lying. Papercut blows at making friends. Weird how sucks and blows are sort of the same, right? What's with that?"

I choose to ignore that question. "Lucy was in your room.

We all came back after the party." I point to my grandma's car. Someone's written *I'm so dirty* in the dust on the windshield.

Ruby jumps to her feet. "I'll believe you if you make me pancakes." She holds out her hand to shake mine, then moves it away when I reach out. "Too slow, bitch."

I call my grandma on the landline while me and Ruby make breakfast in the tiny kitchen. She mostly sits on the counter and tells me where things are and tries to chime in on my phone conversation. Which is very unhelpful given that I'm trying to apologize for any worry I might have caused my grandma, while also making the Point seem mellow.

So when I say I met some nice people, Ruby says, "What town were you in?"

When I say Lucy took good care of me, Ruby says, "She threw up in the toilet and didn't flush."

I try to ask if my grandma's heard anything about the party. She says no, she hasn't been out yet. Asks why.

Because of the shivering terror in half a scream.

"Oh, it just got a bit rowdy."

Ruby wolf-whistles.

"As it should," says my grandma. "Just so long as you took good care of your new friends."

I turn away from Ruby so she can't see me tearing up. "I tried my best."

"People told me I should *always* try my best. It's not true most of the time. Save your best for your friends. Can you get the car home before supper?"

"Of course."

My grandma thanks me for checking in and says she loves

me. I overmix the batter while keeping my back to Ruby to hide the two or three tears that escape.

It took devastation to get me on that bus and another disaster to wind up in this trailer making pancakes early in the morning. To be working in flour and sugar and butter again. I can almost breathe in a memory of me and Sky together the year before Autumn. He was six, and I was seven, trying to bake a cake together to convince our parents to move our birthdays to the same day. I don't recall my parents' reaction or how the cake tasted, just Sky covered head to toe in flour, like he was fading from view.

Slowly, people get up. Lucy chatty and not remotely hungover, Papercut with their haphazard mullet, their twelve- and thirteen-year-old brothers with boundless enthusiasm for food. That would have been me and Sky, though I can only imagine him younger than Ruby, who's claiming sole credit for these pancakes.

Papercut's dad tousles her hair. He has a gnarly gray biker beard and darker skin than his kids. He's soft-spoken and alternates between being overwhelmed and delighted to have so many people in his tiny trailer. He rummages in the fridge and squeezes into the kitchen with me to make scrambled eggs.

Ada shows up last, wearing a faded white baseball hat with an equally faded shirt to match and work pants with a million pockets. They give Ruby a hug that's far longer than Ruby wants. I'm holding two plates of pancakes, so I can't hug Ada back when she gives me a light hug that's far shorter than I want. Ada asks if I managed to sleep or if I've been up all night making food.

There's a lot of talking at once, with people all over the well-worn furniture and counters. Noisy and messy and welcoming me right in. When Papercut complains that it's too loud, Lucy pesters them about "Being hungover from half a beer." There's sun through the windows, and Ruby and her brothers are making plans for a summer day, whining when Ada keeps reminding them to be back by dusk.

When Papercut's dad mentions the ATV, Lucy, Papercut, Ada, and I exchange looks. It gets so much quieter that he must think we sank it in the lake.

"We got parked in by a truck," says Ada quickly. We all jump to agreement with conspicuous enthusiasm and too many details. Talking over top of our dread at returning to the Point.

I feel like I've found the right people, but at the wrong time.

The same time that something else found all of us.

CHAPTER SEVEN

I TURN MY GRANDMA'S CAR DOWN THE PATH TO THE POINT slowly, surveying the scene in front of us. The lights are still strung up, but all the vehicles are gone except for a truck with a bent frame that Lucy says belongs to someone called Oliver, and the ATV, parked beside one of the dead pines. The ground's torn with ruts and shredded patches of urgency. The fire is smoldering, sending an unheeded smoke signal into the branches of the trees above it.

It's hot inside the car, but none of us wants to be the first one into the open. No one even rolls a window down.

"You know the hunting lodge between Abraham's Corner and Sawblade?" asks Lucy.

"I don't think so," says Ada.

I echo her, while Papercut offers the slightly more disdainful "Why the hell would I know that?"

"Confirmed," announces Lucy, "Abraham's Corner got all ransacked the night Cedar arrived in Sawblade. Unconfirmed: The hunting lodge got broken into the same night. I heard it at the bar." No one questions that statement. "The lodge door was open, but the locks weren't broken. Someone drank all the booze in the place and left the cans and bottles all over the floor. So our unconfirmed vicious rumor is . . . Cedar's some sort of rampaging criminal who cased them both." My biggest takeaway is the wildfire speed of gossip through Sawblade, how easily one story becomes another.

Lucy turns to me. "But, Cedar, I was only ever like forty percent sold on that. Now *max* fifteen percent."

Ada asks whether Lucy usually seeks out suspected criminals as friends, and Lucy says sometimes. Why do we think she's hanging out with Papercut? And that it may have motivated her to try to meet me and get to know me better. Only at first. She liked me almost right away.

While they talk, I picture something that moves like a wraith but can ruin physical things. Following just out of sight while Morgyn and I drove through the tunnel of trees. The hunting lodge marks its path from Abraham's Corner to Sawblade.

I step out of the car. Even in the morning, the air is muggy. It's still to the point of stagnation. The only sounds are the soft thump of an overturned fishing boat bumping against shore and the buzzing of mosquitoes. They hadn't been so bad last night.

The others follow me now that bugs have gotten into the car. Ada walks straight to the ATV. "I'll drive. Papercut?"

Papercut picks up the mirror they broke off a truck last night and throws it into the lake with a splash that makes us all cringe. "What? Cedar told us it's scared of light." They gesture at the sun in case we missed it. "I'm going to take a look around."

Lucy follows them. "Maybe people left shit behind." She

peers into Oliver's truck as they pass it and tries the door handle to find it locked.

"Thief." Papercut kicks a broken bottle into the woods.

"I'm preventing waste. For the dolphins."

"All the pods of dolphins in Sawblade Lake thank you."

I wander over to Ada sitting on the ATV as Lucy defines sarcasm for Papercut. Wearing a backward baseball hat suits Ada far better than any hat has ever suited me, but I still should have done the same. I've barely glanced in a mirror today. I fiddle with my hair, trying to assess just how bad the situation is. When I wanted to wear something good-looking this morning, all I had was last night's clothes. It's been bothering me.

Ada pulls a hair elastic off their wrist and offers it to me. "Best I can do unless you want to wash it in the lake."

"That dire?"

"Just messy," she lies. If this lake would make it cleaner, my hair's probably a full disaster. "It was a good look last night though."

I tie it back the best I can. I try to repress the part of my brain that's acutely aware of her compliment and that I'm wearing something of hers. Because that's silly. It's just a hair elastic that's been riding around on their wrist, and now I'm admiring their wrist, so instead of that becoming a whole thing, I say, "Can I ask about Cascade?"

"As long as it's not ignorant and condescending."

"Is there anything you like about coexisting with Cascade?"

She stops fiddling with the keys and looks into the middle distance for long enough that I'm sure I've asked the most ignorant and condescending question possible. Is it better to apologize before she tells me to fuck off or after?

"Yes, there is," they say. "Faulty is an ugly label for people. It's not a bad thing. No one has ever asked me that before."

"In a good way?"

"In a good way." Just like how she laughs at me for worrying about it. "Cas responds to things before I do. I like to think it's because Cas lives in my heart. It's cheesy."

"Or very metal."

"Is that a robot joke?"

I'm mortified for a second before I see them smirking at me.

"When I'm surrounded by people I love, like my family this morning, it's like Cas is purring. If I touch Ruby, on top of all the normal things I feel, Cas is defensive. Fierce. Ruby says she can feel it in the air sometimes and it gives her goose bumps. She calls it 'the prickly thing.' "

Ada expands the strangeness of Autumn with the ease of someone who lives in one of its strangest aspects. I believe her when she says it's not a bad thing. Entirely unlike whatever drove us from the Point, if it too somehow crawled from under the decay of Autumn.

"And it's never good to ignore it," they continue. "Cas knew my ex was cheating on me before I did. I'd touch her and get this sense like something was wrong, but I'd forgotten what it was. My ex couldn't tell, but a few people Cas really connects with can. Ruby, for sure. Papercut says there's a bad energy in the room when I'm mad. Actually, it was weird, at the party—"

"Found something!" Papercut calls. There's a scraping sound from shore as they drag the boat out of the water.

When Ada and I get there, Papercut's trying to flip the small motorboat over by themselves. The boat itself isn't the notable finding though. Around the bottom of the hull, there's a huge ring of tooth marks in the metal, wide enough to swallow me standing up. It's an uneven, broken double row with some punching straight through the boat. The marks angle in.

Teeth to trap and to hold. To keep.

I reach to wrap a hand around my necklace for comfort. There's nothing there. It must have come unclasped in last night's mayhem.

"It's okay," says Ada. "The sun's up." She touches my arm, and it reassures me more than the light. I'm not sure if that's because of their contact, the odd thrum it puts into me, or both.

Lucy wedges a log under the side and uses the leverage to flip the boat over herself. She immediately turns away, dry heaving. Ada's hand goes from light touch to gripping my arm, fingers digging in. Papercut's face is blank and shut down.

There are the remnants of fireworks caught under the boat. A large cooler, unlocked. A collection of open bottles and cans. All sloshing around in a thin mix of blood and water.

And an arm. Drained and pale, making the hair on it look dark. The shoulder is torn off jaggedly. The hand's gripping a metal bar across the boat with fingers that are broken from holding on against something pulling down the body it used to be attached to. Just a thumb, index, and pinky clinging on. Eight-fingered TJ.

Ada releases my arm and starts toward the Point itself. "Oliver was in there too. He could still be down the shoreline. We should look. Maybe TJ's alive."

"For his sake . . ." I start.

Papercut shakes their head, still rooted to the spot. "A shark bites off your arm. This bit off all the rest of him."

"We've got to do what we can." Ada comes back for Papercut and pulls them toward the rock jutting out. "We'll go this way. Cedar, Lucy, check the other direction."

After seeing TJ's arm, I'm not sure I want to find Oliver. I keep my eyes open, ready to look away, as me and Lucy pick our way down the edge of the lake, sweating in the humidity. We clamber over boulders and half-submerged windfall with webs of roots exposed to the air and worms crawling where the toppled trees once stood. There are occasional pieces of trash, but no signs of a slaughter.

Eventually we reach a small beach. Beyond it, wilted orange plants cluster around a dried runoff channel into the lake.

"What's left of the mill is up there," says Lucy, catching her breath with her hands on her knees. "Below it still isn't the best spot to swim per se."

From down here, I can just see the remains of a couple smokestacks sticking through the trees.

There's no good way forward, so we turn around and walk in silence for a bit. As in, I'm watching the water for ripples and Lucy's complaining about the damage this hike is doing to her backup comfy clothes.

I tear my eyes off the lake for a minute. "Did you know Oliver or TJ?"

Lucy picks around a spiky bush. "I know a lot *about* TJ, obviously. It's my job to know a lot about everyone. Oliver . . . This fucking shrub." Lucy grabs at the plant, tearing off branches and tearing the palms of her hands until I reach her and grab her wrists. She pushes back for a second, stronger than me, then breaks away.

"Oliver knew *me*. We used to be really-really good friends when we were thirteen. He was my first kiss. Well, second kiss. It depends how you count. We were in that truck parked in his backyard, before he fixed it up." She gestures toward Oliver's vehicle at the Point. "He'd never abandon that useless thing. Never. And he's just *gone*. People can't just be gone."

My mom and I were driving full speed into the hills by the time the water from the broken dam rolled into the valley our home was in. I could feel it coming before I saw it. I watched the glimmering beams and angles of the mansion vanish, sinking the bunker with my dad and Sky in it below a new lake. The wave ripped away the road we'd been on moments before.

People can just be gone.

I put my arms around Lucy and hug her tightly.

"Stunning intuition," she says. But she squeezes me back, and we stay that way for a while, mosquitoes biting at our arms and the sun beating down on us.

Back at the Point, Ada and Papercut haven't found anything either. We stand in a circle by the water and talk in questions we can't answer.

Do we leave things here?

Do we go into town and cry fire?

Who will believe in some horrible, vanished thing they could just as well deny?

We've had to make mental space for faulty machines and the grim changes to our world. We understand some of how they work. But there's no system or probability we can assign to something that rises from a lake and disappears again. No way of knowing where it's gone and no shared experience to make others trust our vague description of it.

We're getting nowhere, so Lucy makes a decision for us. "If we've got something to bury, we should. TJ's got no family in Sawblade since his dad died. Oliver was the closest thing."

Papercut is facing the lake, eyes fixed firmly on the horizon above the boat. "Lucy, sorry about Oliver. Should have remembered earlier that you two were close."

Lucy's eyes are wet. She can only nod thank you to them.

Since we can't dig deep enough to hide the arm from coyotes, we fill the metal cooler with rocks. When it comes time to retrieve the arm, Papercut numbly volunteers. "The toughest for the toughest."

I do the math and have an awful sense of clarity. I say it before I can think too much. "I'll do it. I didn't know TJ. It's just an arm to me."

I walk to the boat and grab the arm just above the wrist. Flies rise up from the torn end. Under my fingers, I can feel TJ's arm hair dried rough in the sun.

It won't pull away. Bloody water sloshes in the bottom of the boat. I can feel the desperation in the hand gripping. How TJ was willing to break rather than be dragged below. I peel the fingers back one by one, further straining the popped joints and the bones that have punched through.

TJ's arm comes free. I rush over, place it in the cooler, and turn away from the others. I throw up the moment I let out the breath I've been holding. The arm is stuck in my mind, and every time I hope I'm done, bile rises up in me again. I'm thankful no one comes to try to comfort me.

After, no relief kicks in. I should finish the task, but I don't think I can do more without vomiting on TJ's last remains. I'm sick and empty feeling as I watch Papercut stomp on the arm at the elbow so it folds and fits. They pile some rocks alongside the few unopened cans in the cooler, then latch it shut. They use their bowie knife to carve *Badass Motherfucker* and a pair of years into the lid. Ada takes the knife and adds *Firework Maestro*, and then Lucy corrects the year of birth.

No one has any words beyond that. No prayer or song. Ada and Papercut carry the cooler down the spit of rock, swing it a few times, and throw it into the lake.

Once it sinks, we head back up to the vehicles, ready to go our separate ways. There's nothing else to do. Papercut climbs onto the ATV behind Ada, and she starts the engine.

Then we all snap around toward a rasping voice. We frantically look for the source, because what we're hearing sounds tortured in a way that spreads through our bones.

"You came back."

CHAPTER EIGHT

A HAND REACHES UP FROM BEHIND A FALLEN PINE, GRABbing heedlessly at the sharp branches. Ada revs the engine, ready to bolt. I wish I had Morgyn's gun or Papercut's knife. Some violent defense to cling to.

Kat pulls herself to her feet, and if I did have a weapon, I'd attack on instinct.

Her eye sockets are collapsed in, contorting her entire face. It's impossible to imagine there's any sight left behind them. Underneath the shreds that are left of her shirt, I can see massive bruises spreading out. The kind marking an entire cage of broken ribs.

We've all gone silent.

"Hello?" she asks. When she talks, blood trickles out of her mouth. Half her teeth are gone.

Ada's the one who goes to her, climbing over the log and collecting small scratches on her arms. "Hey, hey," she says, letting Kat know she's close. "You're okay. We're all here. It's me and Papercut and Lucy and Cedar." Ada gently touches Kat's hand, and she flinches away.

I follow Ada over the log, trying to keep my eyes off the remnants of Kat's face. "Where's the nearest hospital?"

"Fort Luthe," says Lucy instantly. "Forty-five minutes west of Abraham's Corner."

"Let's get you to the car." This time Kat lets Ada take her hand. "We'll help you."

Kat looks straight at Ada, and I see them swallow. "You're already occupied," Kat says. "Motel heart. No vacancy."

Papercut breaks away the branches in front of us. Lucy goes to the car and backs it closer. I let Kat know I'm going to touch her before taking her other hand. Her skin is clammy and feverish. "Here we go," I say. "Over this log."

Together, the three of us manage to get her to the other side. She murmurs with pain every time she moves. Whimpers when she gets jolted too suddenly.

Kat rocks on her heels for a second, then lurches forward. Ada and I have to hold her back from falling.

"Whirlpool," says Kat haltingly. Her words sound painful from her broken mouth. "I got pushed into the water and the whirlpool went all the rest of the way down. Past the bottom."

Ada strokes Kat's hair. "Do you want to tell us what happened? You don't have to."

A dribble of blood escapes the corner of Kat's mouth. "Seeing through my eyes. Breathing through my lungs. It couldn't stay. Leave a message at the tone." She makes a single quiet beep before forcing out a bit more. Her voice, but another's words.

"I drifted thirsty, the water I once held refusing to hold me
Hideousness of a scourge circling back, far from the light
Hollowness of the last drop, already poured out

Hopelessness of an unhallowed vessel, hull shattered."

At "shattered," she starts to cough, each one crumpling her further until she's on her hands and knees behind the car. She's trying to get enough air, but inhaling only devastates her further.

When Ada reaches down to help her, Kat claws out at their face. Ada jumps back with three raised marks across their cheek.

Papercut pops the trunk. "Are there booster cables? We could tie her."

Kat's breathing is frantic now. "We'll. Return. Your. Call."

"What are we waiting for?" says Lucy, looking over her shoulder from the driver's seat to try to see what's happening.

"She's not going to make it to the hospital," I mutter to the others. "Is there anything in town?"

Papercut's put themselves between Ada and Kat. "Clinic-ish. Not equipped for this."

"Leave," whispers Kat. Only Papercut is brave enough to lean closer. "Dogs. Wander. Off."

"Fuck," mutters Papercut. They gather the four of us by the driver's door and speak quietly. "She wants to die alone. We could pretend to leave. Get some help."

"Tommy's grandpa used to be a doctor," says Lucy.

"Right, that's good." Papercut gets into my grandma's car, which leaves Ada and me on the ATV. I sit behind Ada, hands gripping the metal bars behind me. I haven't been able to rinse my mouth out or wash my hands since dealing with TJ's remains. There are dark sweat marks down the spine of Ada's T-shirt and blood on the side of her face.

We leave Kat curled up next to the fallen tree, still struggling for air.

The car is gone in a plume of dust, but Ada surprises me by veering off the road. I grab on to them, trying not to fall as we tilt. She parks away from the path to the Point, hidden around a corner.

"Do you hear that?"

Then, from the opposite direction of the way that Lucy and Papercut went, a low roar.

Ada looks knowingly over their shoulder at me. "That's Mongrel. Somebody reported to Morgyn."

From our hiding place, we listen to the engine sound build until we see a Mustang come into view. It's white, with twisting black graffiti covering the entire thing except for the driver's door, which is bright red. There's gravel snapping up from the tires. I have no doubt there's one soul driving this and another inhabiting it. The car disappears down the path.

"Thought you should see that," says Ada, "so you know how she usually prowls around. How'd you convince her you hadn't robbed the gas station?"

"Sheer attractiveness," I joke flatly, because my heart is muddled and good lies play with the truth.

"Ha ha," says Ada, equally flat. We could try to hide behind banter, but our minds are pinned elsewhere. Ada drives out of the ditch and keeps heading back toward town.

"It was the same as with you at the Point," I say. "Morgyn could see I was telling the truth."

"Still, even I would have second-guessed picking you up at night," says Ada. "I can't believe Morgyn did it."

Behind us, a single gunshot cuts through the summer air, and we know there's no point returning.

• • •

Dad,

These days, Morgyn runs Sawblade Lake. Her word is gospel, like yours was when you built the dam and said no corners were cut. Like when you built our house below it just to back your claims, then built a bunker underneath it because gospels lie.

I'll bet you and Mom partied at the Point once too. It's probably the same. The thing from Abraham's Corner came there and left behind death and a message of pain I don't understand. But when Morgyn rolled back into town, she spread the word that TJ, Oliver, and Kat had died in a boating accident. She said TJ had messed around with mounting a modern outboard engine—the kind with unstable aspects—that went faulty and exploded. I guess Morgyn sank the boat and Kat's body too.

With Autumn, I remember men speaking on the TV. The little one with an antenna me and Mom had. The cataclysm was too much to deny. When the "leaders" said to stay calm, I wanted to believe them, but never could. They explained things away with the known facts of the world at the time. Morgyn's doing the same, but she can play into what we know about faulty machines.

And she has the advantage of the increased numbness to random, senseless death that we've all learned. People buy it.

No one wants to feel a young fear again, like when Autumn first arrived.

Maybe these letters will reach you and Sky someday. I hope they soften the young fear. These nightmares make children of us all.

Yours,
Cedar

CHAPTER NINE

As I walk up to my grandma's house after mailing the letter, I see her sitting in her worn, faded chair facing the lake. I'm grateful her house is tucked into the center of town but farther up the hill, away from the water. From the living room windows, you can see a sliver of the lake between the houses across the street. The sun's sinking to the horizon, but the heat is still oppressive. It refuses to break despite promises of thunderstorms that never arrive to provide relief.

It's been a few days since we found Kat. Days sleeping during the bright hours after restless nights. Days of wandering around town listening to my grandma's cassettes with the volume up. Days of being afraid of the images that crash through my mind every time I close my eyes.

Don't blink.

You don't want to miss a thing.

Fuck, I need sleep.

Inside, I'm greeted by the relative cool of the brick building. I notice, for the first time, that it's starting to feel like coming home. The spoon collections, landscape paintings, and heavy couches. It smells like the bread my grandma taught me how to bake earlier. I can hear a fan running upstairs, trying feebly to make my attic bedroom less sweltering. There's the rhythm of the baseball game on the radio that she's half listening to while she reads one of the innumerable back issues of *National Geographic* magazines she bought at the church sale.

Home, like someplace I could rest. Maybe I'll nap on the couch until the sun's fully down. First, I need to eat something. Not that I've been hungry lately. I cross the vinyl kitchen floor and tear a chunk off a loaf of bread. It's fresh and slightly warm in my hand, but I can't make myself care enough to spread anything on it.

"Cedar!" calls my grandma. "You're cutting the loaf properly this time, right?"

"Of course!" I grab a plate out of one of the dark wooden cupboards and use a knife to make the end of the loaf look presentable.

On my way to the couch, I walk past the other feature of the living room: the dollhouse.

It's not the kind for kids to play with or even get close to. This one is three feet tall, with elaborate rooflines and banisters, a widow's walk and a turret. It's on a special table with a central area that turns so my grandma can rotate it and reach inside to stick on tiny pieces of wallpaper and place the minuscule pieces of furniture she builds. She works on it every day. Lately, she's been touching up the blue-gray paint on the outside.

The day after I arrived, I asked her where it's from, and she said, "Your grandpa started making it before you were born.

He never finished." I don't remember him visiting us with my grandma. My parents didn't mention him, and my grandma hasn't said anything else about him since.

There are no figures in the dollhouse, just immaculate room after immaculate empty room.

I sit on the couch beside it and look at the lake with my grandma. There are still fishing boats out there. I want to run down the boardwalk screaming for them to come to shore before nightfall.

A lighthouse no one would heed.

"What was in your headphones this time?" asks my grandma.

That's about as intrusive as she gets about my life. She says she likes having me around even though her house is messier. We do things together without talking too much. Gardening, baking, setting up my room.

After that first night when I showed up unannounced and cried in her arms, we haven't spoken more about what drove me to Sawblade Lake. She knew my mom since my parents started dating in high school. I imagine she knew my mom's parents too, who died years before Autumn, leaving only my mom behind. Occasionally my grandma says I remind her of my mom but never compares me to her own son. To my father.

I can't tell if she knows everything that happened. If she does, she keeps her silence around it. After things collapsed, I remember my mom having a long phone call with her. One phone call, no more after. My mom wanted nothing to do with my dad's family. Like Sawblade Lake itself, it must have been too painful for her to talk about. Maybe for my grandma too.

My grandma seems to think my mom being gone is the

sole reason behind my exhaustion and broken sleep patterns, though she hasn't asked me more about it. She said she understands enough for now.

She said some things are meant to be remembered in their own time.

"I was just listening to this." I hold up an album of slow power ballads, first loves, and drive-in theaters. All with big guitar solos. My grandma's cassette collection leans deeply toward eighties rock and old Christian music I've never seen her touch. It wasn't a hard choice.

She snorts when she turns her chair to face me, her magazine open on her lap. "Not his best work."

"You own the tape," I return. I pull off a piece of my bread and roll it between my thumb and fingers, trying to will myself to eat it.

"I was tasteless when I was young. And this isn't the half of it. You should have seen what was on my phone."

Autumn shredded our digital music along with the whole internet. Server farms in flames like the Library of Alexandria, earbuds leaping to life and blowing people's eardrums while they were wearing them. Most older headphones like mine were okay. Ten years later, nonessential factories are just now really getting going, producing old technology in noncomputerized ways at greater risk and obscene cost. So my grandma's cassettes it is.

She spins her chair back around. "Lucy left a message for you while you were gone. I answered, but she said she wanted to call back and record it for some reason."

I reach over and hit play.

"Hi, it's Lucy! Ugh, this feels weird since . . . you know. *Leave a message at the tone. We'll return your call.* But exposure therapy, right? I think so. I'm bored. Want to hang out tonight? I saw you wandering around town looking droopy. You need company. I'm coming over, and I'm bringing a VHS of . . . are you feeling drama, slasher, rom-com? Haha, not slasher. I'll bring some options okay byyyyye."

"I see why she wanted to leave it herself now," says my grandma. "Can you imagine me relaying that?"

Lucy shows up ten minutes later, knocking and entering at the same time and calling out, "Cedar! I got the house right first try this time!"

She's wearing some sort of velour tracksuit situation that's soft when she pulls me into a hug. She's got a backpack slung over her shoulder. It looks full of enough videos to last from now until sometime next year.

"I hope you don't mind me just dropping in like this," she says to my grandma. "When I said Cedar needed company, I didn't mean that you're bad company. I'm sure you're great. Want to watch movies with us? Oh my god, this dollhouse!"

She gets my grandma to give her an extensive tour of it. Lucy said they've known each other through the community gardens for years now. I'm sure Lucy's got a folder on my grandma that will soon have a little note about the dollhouse. After a help-yourself-to-anything and any-friend-of-Cedar's, my grandma heads up the steep wooden stairs to bed.

Lucy slowly spins the dollhouse around. "I would live in here in a heartbeat. Gather a family of my dearest people and fill all these rooms."

I point to one with a four-poster bed at the top of the turret. "That's mine."

"Oh, absolutely not. Don't you dare. You know my clothes are already in the drawers. My posters are on the walls. You couldn't handle it. Does your room here have a fancy bed?"

I'm laughing. "Mattress on the floor in the attic."

"Of course you do."

Fuck, she's right. Not about the mattress, but that I needed company. "I've missed you."

"Naturally. We're trauma bonded!"

I don't think that means what she thinks it does. "Yay?"

"We take what we get and don't ask questions."

But we do have questions. All the time. While we watch the double VHS of some schmaltzy period piece. While Lucy convinces me to eat with her. While we rummage through a closet to find bedding for the couch because Lucy's obviously staying over.

"Do you think I could pull off that dress?" asks Lucy.

"I feel like whenever people say 'pull off' about a piece of clothing, they mean some backhanded bullshit about bodies and gender."

"Glad someone said it. So that's a yes?"

"Never in doubt."

* * *

"Tell me . . ." I start. The fifth *tell me* in a row. ". . . who you love."

"My friends. Old ones, new ones. My parents. They didn't need Autumn to convince them to love me for who I am. Myself."

"Who wouldn't?"

"That's what *I* keep asking."

Lucy says, "When we got back from the Point, the second time, Papercut asked what happened to my hands."

"Yeah?"

"I said I attacked a bush. And they said, 'Makes sense.' Totally sincere. Can you believe that?"

I kind of can. "That's what they said?"

Lucy shakes her head. "I just can't get a read on them."

"What do you think Kat meant?" asks Lucy. "When it wasn't her."

"Hideous, hollow, hopeless."

"It said it was no longer held. It's hurting."

"It's rabid," I say. "Maybe taking it out of this world and ending its misery is a way to end ours."

* * *

"Listen, I'm not into you," says Lucy.

"Rude," I joke, flipping the grilled cheese sandwich in the pan.

"It's not that I don't think you're hot. I do, just, I met you and thought, This is a friend. Like I *could* be into you, but . . . I'm not."

"Who you desire isn't something you've got to explain. But also thank god, because I feel the same."

"Great! I want to cuddle for the second half of the movie if you want to and I didn't want it to be weird. The way I talk, some people just assume—"

"If you hadn't asked, I would have. I'd love to."

"As you should."

Lucy asks, "So what about Ada, hmm?"

"Now, *that* dress I'd wear. The gray one. That suit too."

"I seeeee."

"Do you have your folder of info on everyone here?"

Lucy pulls the *TALK* folder out of her backpack. "As if I wouldn't."

"Do you think . . . my dad would be in there anywhere?"

Rummaging. "That's pretty old, or we're pretty young. There's not a *lot* a lot other than high school hockey star, dated your mom, worked at the arcade, moved away. Why?"

"He doesn't write back."

"I'm sorry."

* * *

"Good night." Lucy has to bend her knees a bit to lie on the couch.

"Good night." I glance at the windows.

"It'd have to get through a sea of lights to get here."

"I keep trying to remember that."

CHAPTER TEN

I'm naked, with nothing but a thin sheet covering my body. There's an old beige fan pointed at my mattress, panning back and forth. I'm still soaked in sweat. It never really cools off up here in the attic, but it was this or my dad's old room. So I picked here. Where every night I stare at the yellowed skylight full of dead flies, waiting for dawn to fade in so I can walk freely.

Being with Lucy tonight helped. I've gotten closer. To the border of sleep, eyes drooping, then twitching awake. Each time, my heart races like I caught myself drifting into oncoming traffic.

I roll over and fumble in the dark for a tape. I want my one summer album from home. I managed to grab a few things that day when I got back to me and my mom's apartment and nothing was right, but I would have had to walk around the white sheet on the floor and weave through evidence markers to reach the cassette rack.

The edge of some unfolded liner notes slices my finger. I pull back with a soft swear.

At the far end of the attic, a different quiet sound comes back at me.

With a creak, the attic hatch opens an inch. A sliver of dimmest light from the hall below angles across the floor beside my bed.

I lie dead still, listening for Lucy or my grandma. For sounds that don't come.

I slowly stand, wrapping myself in the sheet like I'm the one haunting this place. I walk the middle of the long, narrow triangle of the attic, place one bare foot on the rough hatch, and click it shut. I can hear it latch.

The moment I turn away, it opens again.

It opens itself.

I turn and stare at it. I want to stomp it closed, crush it like a cockroach. But it shudders open a tiny bit farther right before my eyes. Beckoning me.

My grandma's down there. And Lucy.

I get dressed and climb down the ladder. A nightlight glows in the upstairs hall. My grandma's door and the bathroom are shut. Not like at Abraham's. I'll check on Lucy and then go back to bed with something heavy on the attic hatch and stop telling myself stories of being led toward something that can't be here in town.

I carefully make my way down the stairs in the dark. The kitchen and living room curtains are drawn, and Lucy's sprawled out asleep on the couch. All is as should be.

In front of me, the dead bolt on the front door clicks unlocked. I want to scream, to struggle, to crumple weeping on the floor, but I stand still. The door swings inward to reveal no key in the lock or stranger on the steps, just the empty doorframe showing the illuminated street and letting heat and bugs in.

A moth flutters out and up.

I step forward to close the door, and as I do, a low, heavy scraping noise rises from outside. In the middle of the street, the manhole cover rises and rasps to the side across the pavement, leaving a black opening gazing at me.

If the town is a sea of brightness, the sewer mains below it are the depths no light reaches.

Everything's hazy with sleeplessness and fear. I'm on the threshold, and it's trying to lure me. No, worse than that.

It's knocking. Ringing the doorbell and running down the street, all the while hoping the right person will answer the door and notice it.

"Cedar?" I startle at Lucy's sleepy voice and close the door too hard. "What's going on?"

I say it's nothing, nothing's going on. I thought I heard a sound outside. Go back to sleep. I click the lock into place.

"We're safe here," she murmurs. "It's all okay."

I stay in the kitchen for the next few hours with an eye on the door. In the faint light through the curtains, I make what scarce comfort I can in mixing bowls and pans.

The door stays shut.

I go to bed when the first shards of light hit the lake. When I get up later in the morning, the manhole's covered again.

CHAPTER ELEVEN

Lucy flips through the few clothes I have hanging on a rod at the far end of the attic. A monochrome sweep of costumes that ground my body, except in times when everything is slipping away.

"You're in old-movie black-and-white, you know that?" she says through a mouthful of the cinnamon bun she's holding in her other hand. A product of my long, watchful night. "It's good, just not really a summer palette for my guided tour of town is all." She pulls a band shirt of my mom's off its hanger. One of the few I managed to grab, gesturing back to a brighter world. "I like this! Where'd you find it?"

All I say is that I brought it with me.

My mom's everywhere in this room though. My backpack's dumped out on the floor, and there are her earrings and necklaces mixed in a tangled clump. Her recipe books full of her clear, teachery writing are beside the envelopes and stamps I brought with the idea of writing the sparse friends I had in the city. She's in the handful of loose photographs I snagged from frames around the apartment.

On top, there's a picture of me, my mom, and Sky. It's from

the summer vacation before things went to hell, so I'm eight and Sky's seven. We're squinting into the sun. Behind us is the kind of lake you can't even see across, with freighters looking like specks. My dad is out of frame in front of us, taking the picture. He's what all our smiles are pointed toward but none of them are for. Me and Sky were making silly noises back and forth, giggling and unable to sit still.

That's what I like to think. I don't remember that day anymore.

I use my toe to brush the photo underneath some liner notes.

Outside, there's a stickiness in the air as we walk across town toward Lucy's house. Even this early in the day, we're already seeking out all the shade we can, since the start of July has only escalated the weather.

"Your grandma wanted to know about the Point," says Lucy. "I told her I was drunk and don't remember much. She said she hoped I wasn't swimming. You live with a very nonpuritanical old lady."

Thinking of the Point makes my mouth dry. "She believes Morgyn?"

"Cedar, everyone from the local paper to God believes Morgyn. Belief doesn't have to mean trust." She pats the spot in her backpack where the file folder is. "There hasn't been a big accident in a while. They smashed most of the high-risk machines they could find in Sawblade. But remember right after Autumn? Things were still going faulty and wrecking themselves all the time."

"Now it's you." I smirk at her. "Wrecking yourself."

"I wasn't *that* drunk. I remember the Point."

I wish I didn't. That I'd blacked out and was just coming to now.

But what about sitting by the water? Ada's hand on my leg? Papercut and Lucy bickering? Making pancakes with Ruby?

Let me choose when I slip in and out of darkness.

Lucy and I are approaching the end of my street, a few blocks from my grandma's house. The pavement and the streetlights stop abruptly. A rough street called Birchwood Drive goes off to either side, skirting the line between Sawblade and the forest. Whatever birch trees were once on the town side are stumps amid the garages and yards facing the expanse. All the houses look away from the woods, so *Drive* might be generous. It's more of a back alley. The chipped community mailboxes for my street are here too, across the gravel with the forest right behind them. Together with the post office, they've already eaten several letters to my father and spat none out in reply.

We walk this unpaved road on the edge of town, heading away from the lake. Along this street, I notice that something's gone through a lot of the cars parked behind these houses. It's Saturday morning and people haven't been out yet to tidy them up. Vehicles sit with their doors and trunks and glove compartments and gas caps all gaping.

Car after car opened gently, stretching in front of and behind us.

It could be the result of people plundering cars on Friday night. Or of something else skirting the fringes of the light, opening all kinds of doors with its mere presence.

Does Lucy notice it too? Neither of us mentions it. We each sit in the fear in our own ways, in the present and the past.

Lucy chats away like nothing's wrong while I think back. Of how my dad hated the way my mom always left the car unlocked. Better someone goes through it than smashes a window, which I bet she learned leaving her first car on streets in Sawblade on Friday nights. Maybe break-ins are still common and other people here think like my mom, though the contents of the glove compartments haven't been pulled out.

If they hadn't both hated this town, my parents could have lived on the same street as Lucy. A different life, no dam and maybe no other breaks. Sky a grade below me, me in the same one as Ada, Papercut, and Lucy. But it was never a real possibility. My parents didn't want to come back. My grandma visited us before Autumn, never the other way around. She mentioned it without judgment but not without grief.

Abruptly, Lucy asks, "Did something happen last night? I feel like I remember you being up?"

I glance to the side, where the cars we're passing now have closed doors again. I try to tell myself I'm being paranoid, but I don't stand a chance against tooth marks and a severed arm, Kat's eye sockets and something watching from across the highway from under the street from the other side of this dirt road breathing down our necks.

"I had a bad dream," I say.

"Yeah, yeah," she agrees. "Just that." But she looks over her shoulder, back to where the car doors were open.

Lucy's home offers some reprieve, white pickets against the shadows of the world. It's a little house that's seen better days.

A short, mowed lawn with weeds fighting through. A few boards missing in the fence. A flower garden that's wilting beneath July.

Inside, there's something welcoming about all the second-hand clutter. There are signs with swirly writing on them and a small white dog named Cyndi that blends in with the innumerable cushions. Lucy's parents are the sort of sweet that results in a million somewhat-personal questions for their daughter's new friend. Lucy's dying to get us away from them. Perhaps too similar to her.

We duck and weave until Lucy closes her bedroom door behind us. It's joyful mayhem to a whole other degree. Inches of stuff on the floor, not a surface unadorned. The glow of fairy lights and lava lamps, with glow-in-the-dark stars scattered among the posters on the ceiling. Lucy carefully takes the file folder out of her backpack and sets it on her nightstand, then dumps the rest of the bag out onto the bed.

"My parents are always like, 'Sorry it's so messy,' when people come over," says Lucy.

"You don't owe anyone tidiness." I turn in a slow circle, feeling enveloped in Lucy's space. Is this what I should do to the attic? I doubt this is something I could curate. It seems like it just poured out of Lucy's personality. The opposite of what I chose to wear in the end—black skirt, white T-shirt, and mismatched small silver hoops, all from Sawblade's thrift store.

"Exactly! I knew you were wise and fun under your world-weariness when I met you. I just need to change and then I'll show you the town properly."

CHAPTER TWELVE

All day, Lucy takes me to corners of Sawblade I would never have found or paid attention to on my own, each accompanied by stories. It's better being away from the road along the woods and in the daylight, wearing a pair of Lucy's least-glamorous sunglasses, even though I curve my path around every manhole cover like I need to stay out of the grasp of something that could reach out and wrap around my ankle.

No matter where we go, Lucy knows what went down there. I learn about profane graffiti on the grocery store that gets repainted every time it's covered. That behind the rec center, where the pile of ice shavings accumulates, is where Kat used to deal. Her twin brother may have taken over now, but Lucy's not sure enough for me to quote her on it. A town hall with a council that doesn't do much and a high roof you can climb onto on summer nights. All these places that might pass as major buildings are slumping, built with ambition that hasn't been maintained.

There's an innocuous house that Lucy says a couple of local sex workers operate out of. There used to be a pimp, who tried to recruit Lucy when she was fourteen, but Morgyn drove him out of town last year.

"How'd Morgyn do that?" I ask.

Today, Morgyn's name sends a lurch through me that's somewhere between wanting to hide from her and wanting her near. The tattoos on Morgyn's sides and throat were hovering in my mind this morning. Guiding my hands over my own skin as I tried to get away from everything else.

"Oh, like *literally*. Morgyn kidnapped him, tossed him in Mongrel's trunk, and drove him out of town. She was gone for three days."

"Do you think she killed him?"

"Doubtful." Lucy reaches into someone's yard to steal bitter apples from a tree and offers one to me. "If she was going to kill him, she would have just done it."

I met Morgyn in gunshots, silences, a long night.

Putting Kat out of her misery. Scrubbing the scene and explaining the horror away. Her face inches away from mine.

I take a bite of the apple and force myself to chew rather than spit it out.

Nowhere brings out more of Lucy's stories than the grounds of the high school. It's a low building by the lakeshore, made of concrete blocks that once had paint on them in colors I assume were supposed to be cheerful. Now I have to squint to read the name of the school team on the wall.

She tells me about places to hide, to have sex, and to catch a nap. She points through windows at empty classrooms where stretches of her life have been happening for years. Unremarkable bleachers that held breakups. Front steps where she's made and lost friends.

Lucy's halfway through a story about someone climbing the flagpole when my eyes slide past it, farther down the shoreline just beyond the school. I can see the outline of a large drainpipe dumping into the lake. Past the lights of town, maybe dark enough for something to creep in.

"Ada almost died here in ninth grade," Lucy says casually, grabbing my attention back. She points to the cracking outdoor basketball court. "Bet you're glad they didn't."

"I'd be pretty heartless if I said otherwise," I say, even though I know Lucy's just trying to pick something bright out of the hellish night and morning at the Point. She's helping keep the focus on what we know, like a crush. But I can't use a word that simple to describe the sensation of closing my eyes and finding Ada.

"You seem pretty heart-full." Lucy bumps me with her hip, and I roll my eyes at her.

"So Ada almost died?"

"The Faulty thing was . . . super not great in Sawblade then. I wasn't great then either. I had this idea that Ada seemed to know too much or whatever. I've been doing more research since they explained it, and fuck. Steep learning curve. Kind of neglected in *TALK* too. There's some evidence mixed up with what we know about faulty machines. Which pretty much stops at 'sometimes they explode.' "

"Ah, but some explode *more*."

"Science, baby. Anyway, Ada was playing basketball, and she made this ridiculously long shot to win the game. Cedar, no one cheered. They looked at her like she'd thrown up in the cafeteria. Ada knew better than to draw attention to themselves. That's *my* job. She tried to run. Someone tripped them. Ada fought back with nails and biting and everything. The more they did, the more people piled on. It was bad. A teacher just stood and watched. I guess so did I."

My eyes are focused on the court, imagining the fists swinging down, the shoes driving into Ada's sides. I've never been on the other side of anything like that.

"Then Papercut." Lucy grins at me. "Glorious shit. They had a hockey stick and they just laid in until they got to Ada. You see there, right on the edge of the crease. Bloodstains on the court for a week."

"You know what's the real miracle?"

"Hallelujah, tell me."

"That Papercut didn't kick your ass when you called Ada 'Robo-Heart.' "

"I hope stuff like that isn't all Papercut remembers about me," says Lucy. "I want the chance to show I'm better than that. Not like they owe it to me, but still. I am." She frowns and doesn't say much for a while.

Eventually, in a more serious way, she tells me about how someone pushed an old man who was Faulty off the boardwalk later that year. How he drowned and that night Morgyn hit the perpetrator with Mongrel, almost killing him. The next morning, there were papers nailed to doors all around town.

The Faulty are people. Think on your sins. Repent. And Morgyn's signature.

Lucy says that between that and Morgyn's commitment to driving the truest bastards out, things have improved on that front since. And it's not like the outside world has any interest in a place like Sawblade.

No matter the body count.

CHAPTER THIRTEEN

To end the day, Lucy takes me to grab some food on the boardwalk before sunset. The lights here are round lampposts right on the edge of the water. We make our way toward an establishment with a tattered, striped awning and flickering blue neon letters above it spelling out *Wharf Fry*. Lucy points out the local bar and tells me what boarded-up buildings used to be when she was a kid, before Autumn laid waste to the tourism industry.

At the far end of the boardwalk, there's the arcade my dad used to work at. Now it's a coffin. "Last summer, I saw Ada and Ruby talking into Mongrel's window over there," says Lucy. "Probably Morgyn gathering info about Faulty stuff."

"Probably." But I remember the *shut up* look Ada gave Papercut when they said Morgyn's been motivated by attraction before. That look makes me feel like the conversation wasn't as simple as information gathering.

"Annnd this is us!" says Lucy.

I can't see much of the inside since the wide windows of Wharf Fry are plastered with posters and ads with strips of paper to pull off phone numbers. The bell jangles as we enter, sending a shivering reminder through me. The diner's in two levels, with a few steps between. Checkerboard-tile floor throughout and a crowd of framed pictures and license plates on the walls. The chairs are flipped upside down on tables. I can't tell if the lights are dimmed or if it never gets brighter than this.

"Are they closing?" I ask, glancing around. There's no one here.

"Closed for tonight, sadly," says Ada as they step out of the bathroom, drying their hands on their jeans. Her sudden presence wraps around my heart and my brain. "And also, OUT OF PAPER TOWEL!"

"THAT'S NOT MY JOB!" yells Papercut from somewhere behind the counter on the second floor. "TOMMY!"

"TOMMY'S GONE!"

Papercut spews unspeakable things, then a huge roll of brown paper towel comes flying out from behind the counter, nearly hitting me. I flinch out of the way and almost trip over myself.

"Papercut seems in a good mood," says Lucy. "Think they'll make one last order for me and Cedar if I ask so so *so* nicely?" She runs up the steps, leaving me standing with Ada.

I pick up the paper towel roll, twisting it around to wind the extra back on. "Do you work at Wharf Fry?" Small talk, good. In no way unsettled by her steady eyes and the hum in my torso that grows as she crosses the room toward me.

"Not me. I was just picking up Papercut. WE'LL BE OUTSIDE!"

Lucy yells back, "GUYS, I'M A CHEF NOW!"

I'm going to sit on the bench beside the door, but Ada makes their way straight to the edge of the boardwalk and dangles their legs over the side. Absolutely not. I lean against one of the lampposts, watching the sun touch the horizon.

"You really trust the sun," I say.

"We've always trusted the sun. We have to. That's what stopped Autumn from being an extinction-level event. The sun kept on shining." The rays off the water are catching orange on her face. "Like how we trust our bodies to breathe, or our hearts to heal. Our orbit to hold. We're clinging to inertia."

"You sound like me talking about fireworks."

"Oh *god*, I do." She looks up at me with a smile, pulling my eyes away from the sunset. "It was cheesy, but I liked what you said. And I've been hyper-attuned to light lately. The light in me and Ruby's room went out and we didn't have any light-bulbs left and I full-blown panicked. Now Ruby won't shut up about how I'm scared of the dark. It made me think though, it wasn't dark at the Point."

"It would have been under the water." Like the barren concrete tubes below town.

"Shit, of course. TJ, Oliver, Kat—it could grab them all from underneath."

Where before I was looking at her face because it's beautiful, now I'm keeping my gaze there to avoid looking at the water lapping on the wood. "It didn't just grab Kat. It *became her*," I mutter. "Or consumed her from inside. Or . . ."

"She's the 'unhallowed vessel' it talked about, right?" says Ada. "We're floating through this world, contained in our bodies."

"So that makes it grappling hooks. A boarding party."

"If it'd succeeded, would it be walking around as Kat? Would

Kat have been dead, or imprisoned, or . . . marooned somehow? An untethered soul."

"Or overboard," I say. "Trapped drowning in her own body."

"Stop." Ada stands up quickly and walks away from the water. Their back's turned to me. "Stop it. Fuck. Why are we talking like this? We're helpless and guessing."

Yes. We are helpless and guessing.

"No, no that's not true," I say. "We know to stick to the light. It just skulks below and around us. And this thing could have a wide range. It covers ground fast enough to be a hundred miles away by now. But even if it's not, we have to trust the sun, right?"

I take a deep breath and slowly sit down on the edge of the boardwalk, my feet hanging over the water. A minute later, Ada sits down beside me, nearer than I expect. There's only an inch between our shoulders. That space doesn't feel empty. Like the air between positive and negative magnets that want to snap together.

"My shoes were wet when we got home," Ada says. "I was that close to the water." They laugh in the way you laugh when you've accepted a misery. "It seems pathetic to complain about lying awake with it-could-have-been-me fears. I still get to lie awake."

I want to say we can each only live our own hurt, so there's not much point comparing suffering, but I ramble far too much when Ada's near me. I should take her hand or put my arm around her waist instead.

"I'm sorry," I say, motionless.

"You're the *last* person who needs to apologize. You're the reason I get to say could-have-been. Why'd you come back for me?"

Across the lake, someone starts an engine to begin trolling to shore.

Ada nudges me with her shoulder as if I've merely zoned out. "Cedar, why'd you come back for me?"

The bunker door closing.

Or a link between me and Ada.

Or.

Getting back to me and my mom's apartment later than I said I would.

After dark.

Unmarked government agents everywhere.

White sheet.

"I dropped my necklace by the lake." Or a lie over a memory. "I was down there looking for it when the smell hit me, and you were out there."

Ada takes a beat too long before saying, "That's really lucky."

From behind us, Papercut opens the door of Wharf Fry. "Like fuck I'm sitting by the water. You're practically chumming it with your feet."

"Don't say 'chumming,'" says Lucy. "It's on the banned-word list now."

"The banned-word list isn't real. You can't stop me saying 'snorkel' if I want to."

Lucy shudders like she's shaking off something gross.

The four of us watch the sunset with burgers and fries, pretending it's not a deadline. Ada and Papercut try to make amendments to the stories Lucy told me today. Mostly Papercut's concerned that we understand just how many people they hit with a hockey stick. Ada wants us to know they definitely never had sex at the high school with their ex, because it's objectively the least sexy place in Sawblade.

"Given how crowded our house is," says Papercut, "school gets considerably more appealing."

"Wait, with what person?" asks Lucy. "This isn't in your file."

"Wouldn't you love to know?" mocks Papercut. "Because it's what *people.*"

Ada looks around at the three of us. "Am I the only one who thinks bedrooms are pretty nice? Cedar, you're on my side, right? You wouldn't at a school."

I try to hide my wild blushing behind a massive bite of burger.

"*Cedar.* You too?"

My face only gets redder while I have to chew for a second. It's sunburnt too. I finally swallow and say, "A bedroom would have been much better. Unless you're into someone anxiously asking if you're close over and over again."

Ada groans. "Nooooo."

"Who?" asks Lucy.

"Their name's Manda."

"Manda Manda Manda yeah I don't know them."

Ada crumples up her paper plate and lobs it into a trash can. "That's why I'm working on the cabin. My own bedroom. My own time. Does anyone want to come help me paint, day after tomorrow?"

"Double shift," says Papercut.

"In the forest?" says Lucy. "Um, no."

"During the day, and there's a generator for the lights."

"I'm busy anyway," says Lucy.

"Then why'd you ask?" says Ada.

"I'm free all day." I crumple my own trash and throw it too casually at the garbage can. It bounces off the edge and falls to the boardwalk.

"Dream team!" Ada grins. "Well, free labor. We've got to get home, but call me and I'll give you directions. Give me your hand."

I have to force myself not to physically respond to the unnatural vibration when their fingers touch my palm and they use a pen to scrawl a phone number on the back of my hand.

A crow swoops down and carries my garbage away.

As Lucy and I walk in the opposite direction from Ada and Papercut, I ask Lucy, "What are you up to Monday?"

"Literally nothing." She sings the phone number on my arm and smirks at me. "What are *you* up to?"

• • •

Dad,

At eight years old, my Autumn was shaped by Mom's. What she showed me and what she couldn't hide. We drove out of the flooded valley, but we kept seeing vehicles flaming in the middle of the road or that had crashed at full speed into trees and through guardrails.

We'd taken your surf-green classic Chevy with the wings though, proudly authentic, and it kept running.

That drive, I closed my eyes when she told me to. And then countless times over the first two years after Autumn, the ones that skirted the edge of dystopia. I tried not to look at the newspaper covers or the symbolic pictures they showed us in history class before we wrote letters to the heroic workers scrambling to repair infrastructure. But I couldn't avoid it all.

One day it would be the scorched remnants of the Mars mission that started Autumn, black and twisted in the suburb it'd plummeted into. Or a once-glittering city square of shattered screens. The wreckage at an airport where they desperately tried to land thousands of planes that had gone faulty and wanted to crash. Such ruin that even working planes had no runway. Bodies strewn around the floors of the tech giants' burning headquarters.

The chasm where your dam broke.

But my strongest memories are smaller things. My gaming system dying the quiet death that so many machines took, simply unresponsive. A teacher using the stump of my friend's wrist as an example of why to leave certain machines alone. Selling the Chevy to survive, for food and shelter. It was the one thing we had of yours, and Mom sold it. She held me while I cried about you and Sky every night. After we sold the Chevy is the only time I remember her crying with me. That sticks. Haunts.

I've heard things were far worse other places. It got

better here. Mom and I had ten years with some good times. We built a new home for ourselves. A place that's worth missing, with enough community that I had a couch to crash on before I left for Sawblade Lake. I had a life, with a couple people who will worry where I went.

Today, I saw where you and Mom went to school, where I might finally graduate from. I laughed with the people I might stand together with.

There was a moment where Lucy and I were sitting on the swings, kicking ourselves high up to create our own breeze. This moment of utter rightness in the world. After eighteen years, I feel like I've wound up where I've been all along.

I jumped at the top of my arc. I fell remembering who I'm not here with and all the parts of you that still have their teeth in me.

Yours,
Cedar

CHAPTER FOURTEEN

WHEN I ARRIVE AT THE MAILBOXES ON THE EDGE OF TOWN just after dawn the next morning, the woods behind them are still. The cars down the gravel road around town are all closed, just like my grandma's house stayed during the looping insomnia of last night, but six of the mail slots are open.

I feel a creeping under my skin. Like a fever that leaves you cold, even in the sunshine.

8.

21.

32.

56.

67.

103.

The letters in the open mailboxes have been taken or scattered, including from my grandma's. I kneel down and examine the mail on the ground, but none of it seems to be for her. Or me. There's a push of anxiety in my chest, some unfounded hope that makes me want to believe I got a letter back and I simply can't find it.

I know it isn't true. The thought buzzes in my head anyway, crowding together with the other fears. I grab a crumpled grocery store flyer that I know my grandma will want and lock her mailbox back up. It takes me two tries to fit the key in.

The creeping remains with me.

There's a lingering in the still air. I know its cold rot before my brain recognizes the smell.

I drop my letter in the slot and back across the gravel street, my eyes on the dense pines, darting between the gaps made by dead bone trees.

At home, my grandma holds up the local paper and asks if I heard about how someone stole gas from cars on Birchwood Drive. Siphoning it out, she says.

I see a long tongue contorting to reach into the tanks, lapping up gasoline. Like the soda at Abraham's Corner.

Drifting thirsty, never quenched.

Black liquid down a lightless throat.

At church, I want to pray. But I don't know how. I just stay there until everyone's gone, my forehead resting on the pew in front of me. I don't know how.

Lucy asks what's wrong while we water garden boxes. She says she could tell from the second I walked in this morning. Already, she knows me that well.

I ask her if she locks her house at night.

Of course.

And her bedroom?

Sure.

Does it stop nightmares?

Of course not.

What if none of the locks and doors mean anything?

She sets her watering can down and gives me a hug. My face pressed into her hair, the only smell the flower blossoms of her shampoo.

That night, I rummage around the garage until I find a crowbar. I lie awake with the exposed lightbulb in the attic on, a box of old magazines weighing down the hatch, and my hand wrapped around the cool metal of the crowbar. The fan can't do anything to stop the sweat soaking my skin.

I feel like there are eyes on me. Unblinking. Like a stalker I'm just noticing now. I'm forced to wonder how long they've been there.

Driving behind me, always taking the same turns.

For hours, I pop tapes in and out of the cassette player. I fast-forward to the most comforting songs and rewind to play them again and again.

Then there's something else, subtle enough that I can't tell when it started either. If the sense of dread creeps, this wafts over me like sugar and cinnamon baking in another room. Like someone breathing in and out with you when you're having a panic attack. And I have been holding my breath.

It's the difference between being watched and being watched over.

When I fall asleep, I dream about the swaying of a train.

CHAPTER FIFTEEN

I WROTE DOWN ADA'S PHONE NUMBER IN A MORE PERMAnent way the instant I got home from Wharf Fry Saturday night, but I don't call her until Monday morning. The open mailboxes yesterday and lingering hints of something lurking shook me, and I couldn't manage the call. I don't want to bring heaviness to Ada's doorstep. I want to be brightness and new paint.

I'm pacing the house so incessantly that my grandma finally hands me the phone receiver and asks, "Whoever it is, do you like their voice?"

I think of Ada across from me in the screened porch. How all her smiles show up in her tone, and how it pulls me in whether she's smiling or not. How they told me they were going to listen no matter what I told them, and how they spoke to Kat. Fierce, kind, suffering no bullshit.

I dial the number on the note.

"Ruby's Lightly Used Clothing. From my siblings' closets to yours! How may I help you?"

In the background, I hear Ada sighing. "Ruby, you've either got to learn to answer the phone properly or actually start stealing and selling our clothes."

"I've nailed one of two!" announces Ruby without covering the receiver.

"That's where my overalls went? Really?"

"Only at slashed prices. They were very fucking ugly."

"It's Cedar," I say to Ruby.

"What dress size are you, Cedar? We talking the winter line? I'll have to check my inventory and get back to—"

There's a brief tussling and something about Ruby's dreams being crushed.

"Cedar?" says Ada. "I was thinking you weren't going to call. I was going to phone Lucy and talk for three hours just to get your number."

"Aren't you and Lucy friends now?" asks Ruby, who's still very close to the phone.

"I guess so?" says Ada. "Take this teachable moment about how people change and go extort your brothers. Sorry, I'm here."

"Do you still need help painting today?"

"If you're still up for it! You caught me just before I was going to head out. Want me to pick you up?"

I think of the tangle of jewelry I have to choose from and ask for directions instead. There's an old bike in the garage that will be useable if I put some air in its tires. I haven't asked who it belonged to.

North on the road toward Abraham's Corner.

Right on the first turnoff after the section of granite that was blasted through.

A few minutes down, I'll see a deteriorating red fence on the left.

Look into the trees for an old number 12 on a post. That's the driveway.

Apparently, I'll know it when I see it.

I know I'll be able to tell I'm in the right place if I feel Ada nearby.

I've just got to make one stop first.

The flag at the school hangs limply in the heat as I bike past it. I stop and toss my bike down on the grass near where town ends and a dense patch of forest still untouched by sickness begins. Though the air's a plague, because this is where I noticed one of Sawblade's sewer mains flowing directly into the lake. I'm sure whatever processing there was collapsed in Autumn. Another way the water is filthy.

I hold my breath, against both the obvious stench and the possibility of another smell I'm far more afraid of. I have to push aside overgrown weeds to get onto the concrete above the giant drainpipe so I can look down.

The putrid sludge is a relief. It's a disgusting mixture of garbage, sewage, and plastic bags and plants wrapped around the bars of the heavy grate covering the entrance. A grate that's firmly closed. As I examine it more closely, I see that, better yet, it's sealed. No hinges to open.

I lean a little bit farther forward to see the bottom, and a chunk of the decaying edge crumbles under me. I slip, twisting, grabbing at the weeds. My feet are plunging toward the mess below me, but I manage to catch them against the middle of the grate, just above the worst of it. My fingertips cling to a more solid chunk of concrete.

I take a second to realize I'm okay. I didn't fall. I didn't wind up down there with the shit and gunk off the street.

But deeper inside, right at the edge of what I can see now, there's an open cooler with words cut into the top. A couple open cans beside it.

And TJ's mangled, bloated hand reaching out from under the lid.

My bike creaks with every pedal stroke as I ride down the shoulder of the road toward Ada's. This thing is persistent, almost clever. It must have used another entrance to the sewers, because it'd definitely been there. Nothing else would have brought that cooler up from the bottom of the lake, defiling that body once again. No nightmare or coincidence opened my house and beckoned to me. With total certainty, I know what did it. I just don't know what it is.

I'm not sure I want to.

I grip my handlebars tighter when I turn down the badly maintained gravel road toward Ada's cabin. I have to push away the part of me that wants to rush back to town, standing over my pedals and in my highest gear, instead of riding farther out. I focus on the idea of spending the day with Ada, doing something as simple and good as repainting walls.

It's unexpectedly cool when I turn down the long, narrow driveway. I'm wearing jean shorts and a band shirt that already had paint on it. It's been tied in the front for so long that knotted is the only way it looks good now. My bike tires crush pine needles, and the scent of them fills the air. Ahead of me, I hear an occasional thunk and clatter of wood being split.

The cabin blends in so well it feels like it comes out of nowhere. It's small and nestled right in the trees, so close it looks like it was built around them. The moss growing on the roof contrasts the freshly finished outside and mustard-yellow door. I lean my bike against the ATV loaded with painting supplies.

I follow the striking sounds around the back of the cabin to where Ada's standing by a big pile of split wood. Just as I see them, they swing the axe down. It goes clean through the wood and embeds in the chopping block. She's dressed similarly to me, though I can't imagine I'm creating quite the same effect with the look. My arms don't have the substance of theirs, and my hands don't share the sureness of how they handle the axe.

"Hey, you." She says it like she knows me well, as if we hang out all the time. Like I'm a regular part of their life. The work she does on my heart with those two words.

She twists the axe out and sets up another log. "Just give me a minute here. I've only got a couple left."

I sit on a stump and watch her, trying to let the clean air purge every infested corner of my mind. When the unassailable realness of the things I've seen presses down on me, I breathe, and I watch Ada. Slowly, it helps. Out here, it feels simple to be in their company, but I know there's another thing underneath it all. The rush of being close. Of having that unknown thrum in me again.

I've missed it. It's hooked in my body's memory, and I don't mind.

"I'd definitely fuck this up if you were watching me," I say eventually.

"Why's that?" She's breathing hard and has sweat clinging to her forehead. It's got me frazzled.

Lucy would have something flirty available on demand even if she'd just seen what I saw this morning. For a moment, in the truck with Morgyn, I did too. Here I say, "Generalized stage fright."

The axe goes through another log, dead center. "Am I going to have to leave the room so you can paint?"

Channel Lucy. "That'd be sad. I mean, I didn't just come here because I love painting." No, that's not it. It feels like a line, and I don't quite deliver it right.

"Oh?" Ada glances my way. Her axe nicks the edge of the next log and sends it flying to the side. "Fuck!"

"The fresh air." I bail, sweeping my arm to include our surroundings. "The wildlife." I can only find some deer droppings to point to, which makes Ada laugh. Not a total loss. "Watching this last piece of wood break your spirit."

"Bold talk. Why don't you come over here and do it yourself?"

"I don't know how. I grew up in the city—"

"And now you live in Sawblade. Chopping down trees is like this town's whole heritage. Come on!"

They hand me the axe, and I immediately take a wild swing that's not far from missing the chopping block entirely and hitting Ada instead.

Ada's unrattled. If anything, she's amused. "So you came here to kill me?"

She shows me how to plant my feet and to follow through, imagining the axe continuing into the block below the piece I'm splitting. Why can't this be one of those movie things where they have to stand behind me to show me how? It works though. My next try gets partway through the piece of wood.

"Almost successful!" Ada claps and then winces from the blisters on their hands. "Let's call that good for now."

We go in the back door of the cabin and through a small entry with a neatly stacked pile of split wood. Inside, there's a main room with a kitchen and living space and woodstove. An old couch, a tasseled lamp, a handful of paintings, all pulled away from the walls. There are worn sheets spread on the floor to catch the drips.

"There's a couple bedrooms and a bathroom over there," she says, pointing down the short hallway. "Some windfall took out the power line. I haven't gotten it repaired yet, so there's only running water if we fire up the generator." She gets each of us a can of warm soda from a fridge that she refers to as "symbolic cooling."

It feels easy once we get to work, starting with the white walls of the living room. Ada slots moody piano rock into the stereo. The rhythm of it all chips away at the murk in me. Me and my mom moved from place to place enough for me to have gotten pretty good at painting. Any sloppy mistakes I make are because I'm looking at the small of Ada's back as they reach high with the roller. Missing spots glancing at the softness of her stomach.

I ask her questions about the cabin. We talk about the work and what Ada's done so far, from demolition to carpentry to electrical.

"I'm right on the edge of failing out of school," she admits. "Maybe given a bit too much of myself to this place."

"Did you ever live here?"

"Until I was seven. Ruby was just a baby. It sat empty until last year. *Such* a mess. Squirrels in the ceiling. No power. Mold."

"How's it felt fixing it up?"

"Fun, mostly. Worthwhile." She wipes her brow, smearing a couple flecks of white paint that were clinging to her face. There are shadows around her eyes.

I turn my back to her to work on the edging around a light switch. "After the Point, you listened to the least-believable story I've ever told. I'll really listen to you too. It doesn't have to be home-improvement hour."

I mean it, though I want them closer in other ways too. I'd like their truth and vulnerability and and and. I glance over at her.

Ada's still standing there, paint dripping from her roller onto the sheet on the floor. "Thanks. I don't know. It's also grueling. I was feeling really done with it this morning. Or with living with so many people, with Ruby. She's a menace. I know it's less safe out here with . . . that thing. But it's peaceful. So I try to focus on that on days when I want to give up on the cabin. And that I'm partly doing it to connect to my parents. It doesn't make sense, but it feels like a way of reaching back. That sounds séancey."

"I sort of get it. I write letters to my dad."

I'm not sure what I expected from today, but I didn't expect to admit that. Ada's here and sad and beautiful and a little embarrassed, and I desperately want to do *something*. I don't know what to do except give a confession in return.

"He is, *was,* an awful person," I continue, unable to explain that he's unreachable even though I know where he is and there's a good chance he's alive. "Yet somehow, I still need to talk to him. It's like he's never totally gone."

"Well, we're here. So they're not really gone." Ada shakes her head and blinks hard. "All this sleep deprivation has me talking ghosts."

"Have you seen any traces of it since the Point?" I try to say it casually. I'll tell them about the open cars and gasoline, the mailboxes, the sewer, the cooler resurfacing. I will. But those aren't things I need to drag in here right now.

These hints of rot.

"No, but I'm on edge. I feel like there's something just behind me no matter where I am. Do you ever feel that?"

"My god, yes." I rest my paintbrush in the tray so I can face Ada. We've been dodging our way around this fear, but at least I've got something less grim to add. "Last night especially. Though some of it was different too. Not ominous."

"I think I missed a spot there." Ada presses her roller into her tray and puts too thick of a layer on the spot. "Once we're done the living room, I've got to eat something. I've got sandwiches and stuff. Then we should do my bedroom."

My heart swerves around the fear again, choosing other thoughts.

CHAPTER SIXTEEN

Ada's bed.

A plain white metal frame and tangled sheets.

Multicolored quilts pushed to the foot of the bed.

Pillows crushed into the headboard.

It could be the heat that made it all like that, Ada tossing and turning in the night and kicking off blankets. The same heat that has Ada stripped down to their sports bra, revealing the outline of nipple piercings that I'm trying not to stare at.

Or it could be another reason. Pressed down into the mattress. Arched backs.

Ada grabs the sheet and loosely tosses it over the bed. "I haven't slept here since the Point, but it's super cozy. If you're not too city for this sort of thing."

I snap out of it. "For what?"

"Sleeping in a cabin." She arranges the quilts to hide away any memories the bed held.

"I split a piece of wood earlier. I'll manage." Though I'm not imagining myself here alone and undistracted.

"*Nearly* split." They hand me a paint can. "Better stick to what you're good at."

* * *

An hour later, the room is full of the smell of fresh paint and the delicate, sweeping soundtrack for a movie I've never seen. We're both barefoot, and I've retied my shirt higher and rolled my sleeves as far up as I can. I'm not wearing anything under my shirt, so I'm not exactly about to take it off in front of Ada. My hair's sticking to my neck. I'm jealous of Ada's buzzcut. I pull Ada's hair elastic off my wrist, where it's been residing day and night.

"Do you want this back?" I ask.

Ada runs a hand over her scalp. "Not much use for it. And it wasn't mine anyway. Probably my ex's." They grimace.

"Not sentimental then?" I say, aiming for a tone that's empathetic instead of hopeful.

Ada's looking out the window instead of at me. "Depends. It's from some stuff she left here. Which means it's from the last time we hooked up *after* she cheated on me, which is not, you know, my proudest moment."

"Then what happened?" I twist it into my hair to feel the air against my neck and try not to stare at Ada's bed and imagine the scene.

"That's the really embarrassing part."

"Last year, there was a girl I had sex with one time, and then I left flowers on her doorstep every week for two months." Though more specifically after she gradually stopped talking to me.

"That's oddly comforting." Ada sighs. "I told her I thought

we could fix it and that I wanted to try again, and she told me she was moving away in a couple weeks. Neglected to mention it before. Aaaand that was three months ago."

I want to ask for a picture, for details, for her ex's sign. I want to see if I'm Ada's type or if maybe I'm too similar, a mistake to avoid again. Those are questions for me, not care for Ada. I ask, "How'd Cas feel when she left?"

"A hell of a lot better than I did," snaps Ada. I start apologizing, but she doesn't let me. "It's not you. It's frustrating having a compass inside me. Sometimes it's nice to ignore your internal feelings even if deep down you know them."

All the things we've got buried. Six feet under or in mausoleums with doors locked. Human remains and bunkers beneath lakes and in the back of our minds.

Shallow graves.

"You want a real drink?" I ask. "I saw beer in the symbolic fridge."

They're still looking out the window, and I can hear the effort to hold together their voice. "Wouldn't say no."

Ada switches to the radio and cranks it up when I close the door behind me.

There's another closed door across from me, the one that goes to the other bedroom. I feel like I should give Ada a minute. Or if there's some comfort I should offer, I don't know it. Or it feels false because it starts as comfort, but in my imagination, it leads to us in that bed.

I turn the knob and push the door open quietly. Inside, there's an empty room with white walls and sunlight shining through floral curtains thinned by moths. In the center of the rough, unfinished plywood floor, there's a large black chalkboard. It looks like it's had a multicolored drawing erased off it, leaving specks of green and blue dust all over.

Other things are scattered around it. Some that fit with an art project, like pieces of paper, chalk, and charcoal. But then a limp black-and-white stuffie of a cat, a broken Swiss Army knife, a child's running shoes with holes in the sides. Locks of long, dark hair, the color of Ada's. A collection of maps, including one that looks like it's for the town of Sawblade Lake. Dog collar, a birthday card, plain black underwear.

When I step in, I see the walls aren't all bare.

There are two huge hearts drawn to either side of the door. On the left chunk of wall, a precise anatomical muscle. On the right, steampunk with gears like a watch. And on the back of the door, one more. A Valentine's Day one with white lace tacked around it.

More than anything else here, that heart makes me feel like I'm somewhere I'm not supposed to be. That I'm invading Ada's private space.

I don't look around more. I shut the door again on my way out.

Ada's bed again.

We're lying on it, my legs thrown over one side, hers over the other. My face is by her hip. The first coats of paint are done. The smell is strong enough in here that we should go outside, but the beer and work and heat and sleepless nights have us too tired to move.

We've been talking about what color the bathroom should be.

The ways our genders move around.

How to get over exes.

Ada says time. She's getting murmury in the sunshine.

I sip at my beer only to find there's nothing left. Less liquid courage and more stalling between agreement and suggestion.

I manage to say rebound.

Ada says that's just one thing to the next to the next. They say they're not like that anymore. That they're trying.

Our lives are overlaps. All the good and the disasters bleeding together from start to finish. Like how it's been since the moment I got to Sawblade.

By the time I find those words and say them, her breathing has gotten steady and peaceful. Asleep, the hum of Ada's nearness is different. It's lulling, slowing the beat of my heart.

The opposite of alone.

I wake up to the radio garbling static and then whispering out as the stereo dies.

Out the open window, the light's gotten lower.

Ada's eyes are already open. I wonder how long she's been awake, if she was watching me sleep, if I mind or I like that. She props herself up on her elbows and says, "That one piece of wood really took it out of you, hey?"

"Shhh, I'm asleep."

"My bad, I see that now."

We're still, while inside I'm a racket of urges. They come

from the dimples in Ada's smile and from waking up near her. I can see the specks of paint spattering the hair on their thighs.

I want to roll over and lie between Ada's legs. I'd plant kisses on the bare skin from the bottom of her bra down to the waist of her shorts. I can imagine exactly how I'd grip her sides. I can imagine my way far past any of that.

The final quiet hiss of the stereo stops.

"There's more batteries in the closet," says Ada without a hint of movement.

I sit up too fast, like I've been caught in my thoughts. I'm still lightheaded when I open the closet door.

I'm instantly hit with the reek of death, sending every part of me reeling. I choke and turn away from the dark cavity. My logic's gone. All that was good gets sucked away.

I see the blood sloshing in the bottom of the motorboat.

TJ's maggoty hand in the sewer pipe.

Ada plugs their nose and looks inside, eyes wide with fear. She leans into the closet and says, "It's just a dead mouse. I'll throw it out. Just a mouse, Cedar."

The torrent in me goes back further. Older fear. Young fear.

A child fear I didn't know I had.

It blanks over everything else.

I find myself outside, saying I've got to get back before the sun goes down. Ada offers me a ride on the ATV, but I need to get moving now, not be a passenger. I don't hold on to the details of what I say as I get on my bike. The scent of pine needles under my wheels can't drive away the death from when I opened the closet door.

CHAPTER SEVENTEEN

WHATEVER I'M FLEEING FROM, I TAKE IT WITH ME.

I knew it before Abraham's Corner. It's stitched through me.

That doesn't stop me from trying to outrun it. When has it ever?

I hammer down the gravel road on my bike using all the breath I've got left in my lungs. The humidity has me soaked again in moments. I feel cold anyway. Numbness pushing something down. How does Ada survive with Cascade inside her insisting on the truth?

Let the dead lie. Let the buried thoughts rest beneath the dirt. I saw fingers reaching through the memories I've laid in silent graves in my mind, but no face.

I don't notice Mongrel until it's too late. I fly into the intersection with the main road without checking. Then everything is roaring engines. White black red flashing past me.

Morgyn swerves with the instincts of a race car driver. Tires gobble up the pavement inches from me.

I turn and slam on my brakes, skidding out on my side. Pain flares through my knee, hip, side, shoulder as I slide.

Mongrel fishtails and then accelerates away.

I'm lying in the middle of the empty road.

What gets you back up?

There's grit and flecks of asphalt pressed into the abrasions. Everything aches. I rest my head on the ground. Sit in the hurt and let it shock me back to myself. Slowly, slowly, I stand up. My bike isn't broken, or at least it isn't too broken to ride. I want to scream as I get back on. It's not like there's anyone out here to hear me.

Every pedal stroke after that feels like it's stretching the wounds down my side. The salt of my sweat stings in them. I can't go as fast as I was. I don't care about the gravel truck that blasts its horn at me for riding too far into the road.

The time grinds by, until I see Mongrel parked beside the *Welcome to Sawblade Lake* sign. The car like a watchtower, with Morgyn sitting on its roof smoking. Black jeans and boots in the heat, shoulders bare and tanned in the sun. She flicks a butt onto the road and puts her fingers into her mouth to whistle at me. In case there was any doubt, she gestures for me to come to her.

No one in this town says no to that, whether they want to or not.

The sharp angle of Morgyn on the roof and her narrow fingers.

Whether I want or not.

I can't tell.

When I stop in front of where she's sitting, she looks down at me and says, "Were you trying to fucking kill yourself?" No hint of apology.

"I wasn't . . ." Suddenly, I can't remember if I heard the car and went into the intersection anyway. "I wasn't trying to keep myself alive. Or maybe trying too hard."

She lights another cigarette with a match, takes a long drag, and passes it to me. "Don't try."

For the first time in my life, smoking doesn't make me cough.

When I offer the cigarette back, she orders me, "Finish it all," and shakes one more out of the pack for herself.

"Is it true that Mongrel's faulty?" I ask.

Morgyn shrugs. "Stop at 'is it true' and I'll have an answer."

"Is it true?"

Her eyes are latched to mine from above. "Of course it is. All of it."

There's a total certainty about her. Invincible on the edge of town as the sun starts to set.

We each take smoke into our veins. She says, "You were coming from Ada's cabin."

I feel like I shouldn't answer. Then again, it's not really a question. I nod.

"I heard you two left the last party at the Point together. And now the cabin?" There's a bitter twist in her voice. Like the salt, the shot, the lime, and the long stare into the bottom of an empty glass. "Ada doesn't take just anyone out there."

"Have you been?" I ask. Morgyn's not Ada's ex, Lucy would have known, but there's a fog around something here.

"I've seen it," says Morgyn, doing nothing to roll the cover back. "But what does Ada see in you? Besides the obvious."

She jumps down from the roof and lands directly in front of me, too close for me to forget what I felt the night I arrived in

Sawblade. The desire I had lying on Ada's bed isn't gone, just chased away.

"What's obvious about me?" I ask.

"That you look hungry." It feels like Morgyn is still above me even though she's shorter than I am. She glances over her shoulder. There are no cars leaving town.

This time, when she reaches toward me, her touch doesn't slip past.

She runs her hands down my arms, brushing over the cuts. I don't wince. It sharpens things. The way she wraps her fingers around my wrists and brings my hands up to her lips. I move with her, let her, drawn in. I can't hold back a quick inhale, a breath of a gasp that I see her notice. I'm taut inside as she kisses my hands, her eyes never leaving mine.

She takes her time, getting me to soak in each time her mouth presses to my knuckles and fingers. Every time her tongue brushes against me, there's a tension between feeling like I should pull away and wanting to beg for more.

"Get home before dark, Cedar," Morgyn says.

She releases my wrists.

A few moments later, she's gone, heading north.

• • •

Dad,

I have the hardest time with the memories of you where there's nothing wrong at all.

You taught me to ride a bike. Patiently. Without

pressure. When I was ready, which was later than some kids—just a month before Autumn. Sky learned at the same time. I remember the three of us on the driveway. Mom offered to help, but me and Sky insisted it be just you. Down the valley, we could see the dam shining in the sun. You and it loom over all my memories from then. Both of you constant and containing built-up devastation.

I crashed my bike today. And that day a decade ago. Sky gave me thumbs-up and you-can-do-it encouragement. You asked if I wanted to try again. I knew you wanted me to, so I did. Now I can crash all on my own. Am I adding a look in your eye? This sense you were weighing my worth. Am I trying to taint the memory and make it match up with the rest of you? How you had to rule every space you were in. Your word, final. Your will, unshakable. Your path, unquestioned.

I once asked Mom why she didn't leave sooner. You were building a bunker in frantic secrecy yet refused to move our family or acknowledge the flaws in the dam. Almost no dams failed completely when Autumn hit. They stopped generating power, but if they were built right, they stood. In response to my question, Mom asked me if I remembered anyone saying no to you. And I don't. Not before she took me and left at the very end, and that split us all in two.

Before writing this, I was picking pieces of road out of my body. All this dread in me goes in tendrils backward and downward. Into earth and water and memory. I feel like I'm in the back seat of a car driving at night, drifting in and out of sleep. Movement without clear landmarks, unsure where I started. I can't figure out where it leads. Who's driving. What ride I'm on. Mom might know the beginning. Or you.

What do you do with questions that can only be answered by people who are gone? Maybe that's why I keep writing to you despite it all. There's something unanswered out there, in you, in me. I want one of my parents to sit down on my bed with me and tell me of the darkest things in the softest ways. I don't want to stumble into them on my own, Dad.

Yours,
Cedar

CHAPTER EIGHTEEN

"Hey, Cedar, it's Ada. Obviously. It's not like you won't recognize my voice after talking with me all day. I tried to call earlier, but no one picked up. Hopefully you were just asleep. The nap kind of fu—*screwed* me over last night. Ruby said I was super restless. I stayed at the cabin a bit longer, cleaning up that mouse and letting the room air out. Almost stayed too late. That's what the generator's for. Anyway, I was calling to see if you wanted to go with me to a party at Camille's place this Saturday. It's far from the shore but still in town, up past the trailer park. You probably know it. It's like the only nice house in Sawblade. I could pick you up. Papercut will be there too, I think. PAPERCUT! ARE YOU GOING TO CAMILLE'S? NO, SATURDAY! Yeah, Papercut will be there. And thanks for helping me paint. Seriously. Yesterday was half a perfect day. Something about it really made the cabin start to feel like home. Glad you made it back safe, or I mean, I hope you're okay. *Christ*, that was a long message. Call me!"

"And I thought my friends left rambling voicemails," says my grandma from her chair. "Ada would give Doreen a run for her money. Can I turn the baseball game back on?"

I say yes. Alone, I would have listened to the message again to hear Ada say the part about home and wonder what the other half would be. I don't delete it. I've been keeping a bunch from Lucy too, but I'll have to clear everything out eventually.

The radio crackles back on. "I missed a whole inning while that was playing. I'm glad someone cares that you crashed your bike more than you do."

That wasn't the *okay* Ada meant. I haven't told them about what happened on the way home. "I'm going to fix it up."

"I'm more worried about whether you're going to call this Ada again or repeat your whole pacing journey around the house."

After the way I left Ada's, turning a soft moment into panic and fleeing, I didn't expect to hear from her again. There was a maybe. Both of us were still lying on Ada's bed. I want to know what would have happened if I didn't go to the closet, or stayed calm when I opened the door.

I lay awake cursing myself last night while I cycled through my favorite songs. I tossed and turned, trying to get comfy on my bruises and abrasions. I thought of Morgyn and Ada and didn't know whether to touch myself or curse myself some more. I pushed my mattress against the wall and rolled into the corner of the roof and the floor so I'd know there was nothing behind me. But I still felt things, further back than the wall or right now.

The two types of watching were back.

One like red eyes in the dark and the other like a wing wrapped around my shoulders.

I skip the pacing and go to Lucy's house. She tries to lend me colorful clothes and get me to tell her absolutely everything.

And while she's insistent and persuasive, I leave out how Ada makes me feel and the strange thrum. And I definitely leave out the details of my desires. It's silly and shy and too strong too quickly. It's accented in a shade I can't explain.

"You were lying on Ada's bed with them and *nothing* happened?" Lucy's voice is muted from halfway under her bed, where she's crawled to find something. "Or should I say, you didn't even try to make something happen? I see how you are when she's close to you." Lucy pops up holding a yellow jacket with a tremendous amount of fringe.

I shake my head apologetically.

"Cedar . . ." Lucy throws up her hands. "I can't with you sometimes. I wasn't so drunk at the Point that I forget you ran *toward what you were afraid of* for Ada. Who you'd only talked to literally one time. But admit you like them nooooo never ever."

I leave out how Morgyn kissed my hands too. She didn't seem to want anyone to see, and I don't want to go against what Morgyn wants. I don't know if that's intimidation or thrill. I'd trust Lucy to keep my secrets, but still.

"Camille and I had a little falling-out last year so I'm a big-time maybe for the party," says Lucy. "We used to get along, then she just like . . ." Lucy gives a fake laugh and makes a throttling gesture. "Just like, argh, you know? Story for another time."

That's a sentiment I've never heard from Lucy before. "*You're* saving a story for another time?"

"It's been known to happen."

"Has it?" I ask, playful-suspicious.

Lucy hands me the phone from her nightstand. "Camille does throw good parties, because her family has money. You know how easy it is to be popular if you're rich and no one else is? Now call Ada and say yes."

"It's just I ran out and—"

Lucy dials the number for me. "And Ada will either understand and respect that you've got some trauma or they're not worth your time." She hands me the phone and makes move-it-along gestures while I leave a fumbling message that amounts to agreeing.

I don't get back to my grandma's place until the next morning. I fell asleep watching movies in bed with Lucy. When I woke up afraid during the night, she was sitting up next to me in the soft glow of a lamp, updating a file from the *TALK* folder.

"Did you know Camille's mom was a professional cheerleader?"

"I've never met Camille," I say sleepily.

"Trust me, it explains a lot. Now go back to sleep."

Being under the canopy of my friend's bed is like drifting off underneath a willow tree. Out of the beating sun or the pounding rain. The soft sound of her pen on paper like wind in leaves.

When I get home, my grandma says she's going to help with how drifty I am. I've got bags under my eyes and a drag in my step. She says she knows she can't solve any grief of mine, but at least we can make preserves, and that's something.

While we're cleaning up after a couple days of our hands

stained in fruit, I hear a familiar sound outside. Like a growl in the back of a dog's throat. I pull the curtain back to see Mongrel idling nearby in the dusk. The windows are too dark to see inside, but I can picture Morgyn behind the wheel with her seat far back.

My grandma pushes the curtain back into place. "That's the fourth time I've noticed her in the past few days. It's like she's patrolling town."

Or keeping an eye on me.

"Not a fan of Morgyn?" I ask.

My grandma doesn't have bad words for many people. I can see her weighing what to say as she screws the lid onto a jar. "Morgyn's done some good things for this town. You can't deny that. But it makes me . . . nervous whenever there's that much on one person's shoulders. She's barely older than you."

"I know. She was the one who picked me up from Abraham's Corner." I might owe my life to her. My life and one cigarette and helping Kat die when none of the rest of us would acknowledge that it was for the best.

My grandma gives me a curious look. "Is that so? That's a point in her favor in my books. Still, you have to ask every vigilante whether they'd hunt themselves."

I think of how Lucy's notes said the sheriff died chasing Mongrel. This town isn't big enough for another gunslinger.

"You shouldn't pick your leaders by who you'd want on your side in a fight," continues my grandma. "You should pick them because you'd both choose the same side in a fight anyway, even if it was the losing one."

"Is Morgyn ever on the losing side?"

"Not that I've seen. That's the other thing that makes me nervous."

Mongrel's taillights turn the corner at the end of the street.

• • •

Dad,

Sorry I forgot to mail the last letter. I'll send it with this one tomorrow. I keep getting distracted by chattering shadows. My throat gets raw from trying to shout over all that's behind me.

Like how when I put jars in the pantry today, I remembered something. I was seven, and there was this massive summer storm. I came downstairs to see you fighting against the water that was seeping into the basement of our home right near the bunker door.

We knew it was a bunker. You might have been able to press cash and threats into the hands of contractors. You used countless cover-up projects and our sprawling property to hide construction and the other entrance in the yard. But me and Sky were a problem. You said it was a special underground house to keep us safe if anything bad happened, but it would only keep us safe if it was a secret. Sky asked what sort of bad thing. A ghoul, you said, and chased us around making silly noises. Mom didn't laugh.

During the storm, you screamed, red-faced, for me to get back upstairs. You'd think that's what I'd remember, but it isn't.

I remember that the bunker door was open. All that I saw was the mouth of a tunnel, the same as when you grabbed Sky and closed it. An esophagus. A sarcophagus I've never been inside.

Even after the carpets dried, a musky smell lingered. That's what reminded me in the pantry. It's odd what floats to the surface.

Yours,
Cedar

CHAPTER NINETEEN

On the morning of the party, I stop across the road from the mailboxes. It's happened again. Another mailbox is open, waiting for me.

12.

I know that number.

By Ada's driveway. On a post with vines partly hiding it.

I can't make myself cross the road knowing that thing has been there. Its smell might send my mind careening god knows where. I take the longer walk to the post office and mail my letters from there. But when I get home, I'm stopped again, this time on the sidewalk in front of my grandma's house.

32.

Faded metal numbers that blend in with the brick beside the door of my grandma's house. I sat in the passenger seat of Morgyn's truck and strained my eyes for them.

Before, it seemed random that our mailbox was one of the open ones. I was thinking about letters and the smell, not that the numbers meant anything.

I try to shake the thoughts loose. I'm seeing things that

aren't there. Fixating on numbers with the same dread as the ring of tooth marks on the bottom of the boat at the Point.

8. 21. 32. 56. 67. 103. 12.

I recite them in a loop even as I work not to think about them.

I'm ready to party the Sawblade way tonight.

CHAPTER TWENTY

I'M SITTING ON THE FRONT STEPS WITH BLACK HOOP EARrings and freshly painted white nails. Cropped gray T-shirt and jean shorts slightly frayed at the hip from when I crashed. I think I look pretty good.

My outfit's got nothing on Ada's.

They're an absolute riot in my brain from the moment they pull up on the ATV to give me a ride. She's wearing white shorts made from dress pants cut off just above the knee and a white blazer with shoulder pads. It's buttoned up over not that much at all. For the first time, I see the multicolored bruises that come with being Faulty. They're spread over their heart, boldly exposed in smudges of unfading blue, dark purple, and pale green.

Ruby waves at me from where she's sitting on the rack, facing backward. I barely processed her presence with Ada there. "You're dropping me off at a sleepover," she says. "I wanted to walk, but *apparently* I can't be trusted to be out on my own without 'committing vandalism.' Since when is breaking stuff a crime?"

Ada reaches back and flicks one of Ruby's braids. "Since always," she says, though her and I both know the failing light is the reason we're driving Ruby. "It's sort of on our way anyway."

The effect Ada's having on me only gets doubled when I sit behind them with my whole body pressed close to theirs and my arm wrapped around their waist.

I grip tighter when Ada accelerates away. Ruby whoops. "No hands!"

Ada taps the brakes slightly to make Ruby grab on again. The jolt presses my hips a little tighter to Ada's, and I stay there.

"You good?" asks Ada loudly.

Not at all. Very. So good my decisions won't be. I give her a thumbs-up.

344. That's the house with peeling siding where Ruby's spending the night. Not one of my numbers. Ruby hops down before we stop moving and runs toward the door in her basketball shorts and boxy gray camp shirt from a place that must no longer exist. She's got a purple backpack and a cornflower-blue rain jacket tied around her waist. Ada and I follow her like we're dropping our kid off.

Ruby rings the doorbell half a dozen times before Ada catches her wrist. "We'll hope that doesn't work."

A person about Ada's age with an I-cut-it-myself mop of hair opens the door. "It does. It's super loud."

Ruby says, "Super loud's what they call this bitch at school."

A woman comes around the corner drying her hands on a dish towel. "Welcome here, Ruby! Tay's been waiting around all day. Ada." Her voice is cold in a way no one could miss. She stands slightly between Tay and Ada.

"Want me to take your rain jacket?" Ada asks Ruby. "It's a bit hot for a jacket."

"I'm not helping you protect your slutty suit."

Ada ignores that comment. "Call me in the morning and let me know if you want me to pick you up, okay? Not too early."

Ruby taps her nose and nods knowingly. "It's *that* kind of party, huh."

Ada is all apologies to Tay's mom. "It's not even a party. We're just hanging out with a couple friends."

"I'm sure I'll see you tomorrow afternoon sometime," Tay's mom says. "You shouldn't go showing off your Faulty scars like that. Have some decency." She closes the door in our faces.

"Wow," I say as we stare at the shut door. "I'll bet Cas just adores her."

"There's no one Cas rings alarm bells about like some Faulty-hating twat who told me Ruby needs 'real parents.'"

"Thank god it's *that* kind of party."

"I haven't the faintest idea what you could possibly mean."

Someone's having sex in the back seat of the car we park behind at Camille's house and making no attempt to hide it. Ada seems unfazed by the sounds coming from inside, while I'm putting a great deal of effort into looking disinterested but also not uncomfortable or like I'm deliberately ignoring it.

Camille's is a huge cabin-style home with a circular driveway and tall windows that overlook the trailer park and the lake. If you'd never seen a mansion, perhaps it once had a sort of grandeur. But it can't disguise that it's like everything else in this place. The needles fall off. The bark flakes away. Lucy told me Camille's family owned part of the mill way back when. Now her house looks like old money clinging to a past it can't afford to keep up. Like slapping a fresh coat of paint on a building with a failing foundation.

Even the street leading up to the house is a false start. There are the trappings of a suburb. Streetlights and sidewalks and fire hydrants and trees planted at even intervals, half of them shriveled. Every lot is empty, thick with deep-rooted, tough plants. There are the scars of foundations in a couple places where someone got as far as digging but never poured concrete. We had to drive right to the end, where Camille's house is alone on a cul-de-sac that could fit three others like it.

It's number 74. That's not an open mailbox either. I'm letting my fear grow beyond reason, making patterns where there are none.

Ada hasn't made any move toward the house. They've got their hands in their pockets.

"Should we head in?" I'm sure the noise from the car is fun if you're making it, but I wouldn't say no to getting closer to the loud music to drown it out.

"Right away." Ada's shifting on her feet. "Um, okay. I have something for you?" They say it like it's a question. "It's a gift for helping me paint."

"You didn't have to—"

She holds out a cassette to me. "It's silly. Just some songs I thought you'd like."

It isn't just some songs.

Most of these are my favorites—the ones I've been listening

to on my tapes. The tidy handwritten track list in black marker goes through genres, harmonica and synths, sandpaper voices and crystal ones. They're united by slow, sad, and hopeful, and by my love of them.

"*So* much more work than making a playlist," laughs Ada. They don't have their usual groundedness. She keeps glancing at me and then somewhere else. "It would have been like forty songs then though. I guess I was like seven last time I did that. It must have been terrible."

I can't believe they made this for me. I don't know Ada well enough to know if this is something unique or if making mixtapes for new friends is just something she does. It's lovely and uncannily accurate, and I want to clutch it to my chest and listen to it right now.

I don't manage to say that. "How'd you know to pick these?" I ask.

Near us, a particularly loud moan escapes the car. It's rocking slightly.

"Want to?" Ada nods toward the party.

"Yes, definitely."

I tuck the tape into the front pocket of my shorts and follow Ada toward the music.

Good party apparently means more alcohol. Ada weaves her way forward with the intent of someone who's been here before. We go through a main room with a giant mounted elk head over a fireplace and past doors that are thrown open to a large fenced-in backyard. There's a glass pool house near the back that catches reflections of the lit-up house. Everywhere, the sort of rap originally released on cassette blares and blends with the noise of more people than were at the Point. Everywhere, eyes hover for a beat too long on the bruises on Ada's chest.

The kitchen island was clearly what we were aiming for. It's covered in open bottles and plastic cups. We have to step over the legs of people sitting on the floor.

A short girl pops up from behind the island. She's 100 percent bounce, from her smile to her hair to the vibrant winged eyeshadow on her brown skin. "Hi, Ada! Pick your poison! Are you from Fort Luthe too? There's basically a busload of them. I'm Camille."

As Ada picks through bottles, I realize that Fort Luthe question was to me. "I'm from . . ." I don't want to think about that apartment or why I'm here. "You know that dam that broke out east?"

Camille nods twice as much as people usually nod.

"I'm from there."

Camille holds her finger up at me while she takes a long drink. When she's done, she says, "Well we've got a shitty lake here too, so you should feel right at home."

"I kind of do. Not because of the shitty lake though."

Ada's back with a grin and two partly full bottles of gin that she's holding in one hand. "Have you seen Papercut?" they ask Camille.

"What?" Camille stumbles over someone on her way to us. "I didn't know Papercut was going to be here. They're probably outside. I want to say hi to Papercut."

She wanders into the mix of people and immediately gets waylaid by a drinking game.

"I don't go outside sober anymore," I say. "Find Papercut later?"

Ada screws the top off both bottles and hands one to me. "Let's make it that kind of party."

Cheers and bottles to mouths, and then we laugh and follow Camille.

Blink and glitch. If you drink enough, everything's a strobe light.

CHAPTER TWENTY-ONE

Suspended moment with all eyes on me.

And I might as well be under the lights in an arena.

Because the crowd goes wild when I make the shot.

Ada holds up my hand like I've won a boxing match. My heart screams victory.

I think it's more or less the same.

"Papercut!" I'm talking way louder than I should be.

"Cedar!" Papercut calls back. They're standing in the outline of a skating rink in the backyard, throwing knives at the boards. "And good old whatstheirface."

"Name's Buck," drawls Ada.

"Catch!" Papercut fakes throwing a knife at me so hard I fall sprawling in the grass.

There's thunder, not that far off. A flash of lightning across the lake that makes the people in the yard cheer.

* * *

Inside, the music switches.

"This is my song!" I say.

"Really?" asks Ada.

"No, but that's what you say to convince someone to dance."

"What made you think you'd have to convince me?"

Ada's hands are in the air. The bass is all through us, mixed up with the thrum of her nearby and my hoop earrings bouncing as I move.

I'm mirroring Ada.

Seeing myself.

Together with them.

Lucy's in a black dress, high slit, long legs, making an entrance.

She grabs a drink from someone else's hand and downs it.

She dances over to us. "Sorry I'm late. There was so much traffic in my heart."

"The thing from the Point could be gone," says Ada.

We're hanging upside down from the monkey bars of an old play structure in the backyard. Facing each other, ignoring the game of "extreme croquet" Papercut and Lucy have started.

"Aren't there still hints of it?" Not ones I've told her.

"Pretend with me," they say.

Okay. Why not?

"You look hilarious," she says. She bats at my dangling hair.

"You look . . . hot." That's a thought. You say thoughts. Not all of them.

"Pssh." Ada waves me off. "Hot as in my face is red. All the blood's gone to your brain."

"I stand by it."

"Well, you're not *standing*, are you?"

"So you start by hitting it down the slide," says Lucy.

"And if you miss the first wicket?" asks Papercut.

"SHOT!" they say together.

"Then it's through the garden and off that jump we made," continues Lucy.

Papercut twirls their mallet. "*I* made."

"And if you miss the jump?"

"SHOT!"

Ada examines their bottle of gin. "I'm going to look just so playing croquet in this suit."

I couldn't agree more.

"Of course, you *already* look just so," says Ada to me.

Over Ada's shoulder, Lucy pretends to swoon.

Camille gives Papercut a long hug. "I've been looking *everywhere* for you," she says.

Lucy mutters, "I'll bet you have."

I'm drunk and slow off of gin and laughing with Ada. So what that Lucy bickers with Papercut, then finds excuses to be near them? Camille touches Papercut's hair like they've been much, much closer than this before. Lucy looks at the two of them with dagger eyes.

Oh. *Oh.*

The air's still, like a held breath.

I look up, and a raindrop hits my face.

Another another another. Soon we'll be awash, if we're not already.

Ada's talking to someone I don't know.

Animated, gesturing, light catching off her blazer.

The other person is rapt at Ada's story.

That I heard Ada tell earlier.

Their voice wrapped up like a present.

Dad,

Love at first sight is nonsense, because it's not a moment.

It's all the time. A cascade.

People places escape energy.

It can be mine.

It could have been Sky's.

It could have been

Yours.

CHAPTER TWENTY-TWO

"NEVER HAVE I EVER," DECLARES CAMILLE, DEALING OUT five playing cards to each person. "My rules. If you've done it, you toss a card. Lose your last card and whoever made you lose it gets to truth-or-dare you."

We're sprawled around in the pool house. Lucy's lying on her stomach on a deck chair, Papercut's got their feet in the water, and I'm cross-legged on the edge of the pool. The tiles have the sort of grime accumulated between them that will never be cleaned out. Maybe that's why Ada's chosen a faded yellow, half-inflated duck to sit on instead of the deck. Camille and someone named Kayden (Kat's twin brother?) are in the water, leaning on the side of the pool. The storm's flirting with us, refusing to downpour. There's been one spatter of rain outside that drummed on the clear roof above us, but that's it.

"Never have I ever," begins Camille, her voice echoing off the water and the high glass walls, "kissed two people in the same day."

Papercut and Lucy both toss a card in the middle and drink, even though it's not technically a drinking game.

Papercut splashes water at Camille. "You should have to throw two cards for lying."

"Throw your whole hand," demands Lucy. "Li. Ar. Li. Ar."

"Well, there was before midnight and after midnight," says Camille. "And there was kissing and other things, and it all means never two people in the same day."

Papercut shrugs. "If that's how you remember it."

"Never have I ever crashed my bike," says Kayden. "RIP Cedar's skin." My scabbing wounds have been much commented on tonight.

Almost all of us toss cards. "It's so much better than it was right after," says Ada, throwing a jack in the middle.

Her cabin then a week apart then tonight. Right after? She can't have seen that. My brain's no good at math and counting days between times I saw Ada. Don't focus on numbers.

"Never have I ever," says Ada, "seen a dead body." They frown right after the words come out, though it's good in that everyone else puts a card in. Autumn, funerals, faulty machines.

I put a card in without thinking. A nine of spades that isn't for TJ's arm. Who's it for then? All the gin. I can't figure out who.

I start to reach to take it back.

Lucy pokes me. "Your turn."

"Never have I ever swam in this pool." This is going to be easy. Camille, Papercut, Kayden, Lucy, but not Ada.

We go around in circles. Sex, drugs, and broken bones. Lucy one-upping Camille at every opportunity. Papercut persistently choosing things no one's done. Dares but mostly truths.

Papercut's body count is four, since Lucy asked their truth.

Kayden's naked in the pool after letting Papercut dare him.

Camille's never been in love. Which I asked on behalf of Lucy. The answer improved Lucy's mood considerably until she said truth and Kayden asked what's the closest she's ever come to dying.

"I don't even have one," Lucy says. "I'm unkillable. Never close." But she's looking past Kayden now, through the glass and beyond the fence. "Except at the Point, I was in the water. I was in the water when—"

I nudge her with my shoulder.

"—when Papercut almost cliff jumped right on top of me. Would've snapped my neck." Lucy gives an exaggerated head tilt with her tongue out, a wavering grin that I see right through. "Anyways, never have I ever been in Morgyn's house on the Dalfason farm."

It's a skillful redirection. Camille and Ada both toss cards in, causing a barrage of follow-up questions.

Camille kicks away from the wall and spins in a circle as she treads water. "I pretended I needed my car fixed, but actually I wanted to invite her to the party. When I asked, she told me to fuck off. Then she wanted to know who'd be there, and I said everyone. She told me she'd check her schedule. I couldn't tell if she was joking. Then she invited me in and offered me birthday cake?"

"What was it like inside?" I ask. I can imagine it smelling like the cab of her truck.

"Kinda grungy. A little hoarder-ish. There was this plain, half-eaten birthday cake on the counter like she'd bought it for herself, and that made me sad. What about you, Ada?"

Ada holds up their remaining card. "Save it for when I'm out of cards." She exchanges a glance with Papercut.

Kayden looks right at Ada. "Never have I ever renovated a scary-ass cabin in the woods."

That's Ada and I out at the same time.

"Now I've got a truth you want . . ." Ada smirks. "I choose dare."

Lucy mouths "dare" at me, so that's what I say too.

"Get in the pool with me—"

We both dive in before Kayden can add *naked* or anything else. It's clear and empty underwater. Smooth blue beneath us with no whirlpool, though the water stings sharper than I expected all across my side.

I come up spluttering. "This is like a fucking ocean."

"Salt water," says Camille. "So it doesn't damage my lustrous skin or hair."

"Is it working though?" asks Lucy from the deck.

Ada finally resurfaces and shakes the water from her face. "Fuck me, these clothes got heavy. I'm out of here." They swim to Papercut for a hand getting out, while I climb the ladder and feel the water pulling at my clothes, wanting me back.

In the yard, the nearness of the storm is all around me and Ada. The clouds have been mounting into deep-gray thunderheads as night's fallen. They turned the last light of the day tinged and threatening, and now they show themselves again when a jagged bolt of lightning rips from them. The thunder is only a breath after. The wind pushes trees in every direction.

The bathrooms are full of *every* type of activity, so we wind up in the kitchen rummaging through cupboards for dish towels. I find some with tacky slogans on them and throw one across the island to Ada.

She dries her buzzed hair in an instant. "You can't say they didn't get a room."

"I can't didn't what?" I emerge from a much more vigorous drying that's turning my hair into a tousled disaster. Then I lose all my words.

The weight of the water hasn't managed to subdue Ada's shoulder pads in the slightest. Water droplets are running down their skin, following the V of their blazer. My eyes run with them. My mind, my heart, all of me.

On the other side of the island, Ada must notice. But it's like when we were dancing. Her eyes on the shirt clinging to my skin are a mirror of mine on her.

The moment's broken by a general commotion from in front of the house. It steals our eyes off each other. Headlights shine through the kitchen window as a familiar pickup truck parks on the front lawn.

Someone turns the music down. "Morgyn's here! Is there trouble?"

As the headlights fade out, I see the license plate of the truck in the glow from the kitchen window.

Three letters that I skip over to the number.

103.

That's one of the mailbox numbers from the first day I found them open and waiting for me. It's too much coincidence.

"It's fine!" calls Camille from the main room. "I invited her. She's just here for the party." The music gets turned back up.

There's the sound of boots in the hallway heading to the kitchen.

"I'm so glad you made it!" says Camille. The tone of someone who did not expect Morgyn to show.

Morgyn's voice. "I can get a drink in here?" She's not the type of law that cares who consumes what.

Morgyn and Ada in the same room. That's . . . bad? It might resolve some of my curiosity. Or it might push Ada away. Morgyn hasn't exactly been ignoring me. And I don't hate it.

But I picked dare when I could have picked truth because Ada picked dare. I chose it with hope for something involving the two of us. I fell asleep on her bed with her.

I'm frozen until Ada grabs my arm and pushes me into the long, narrow walk-in pantry. They latch the slatted door a moment before Morgyn and Camille arrive in the kitchen.

"Not sure I feel up for Morgyn," whispers Ada.

"Same," I agree, though I assume we've got different reasons for avoiding her.

I pull Ada to the back of the pantry, farther from the voices and the light leaking in through the slatted door. Our bodies are close together between the shelves of food.

"Thanks for the cake the other day." It's hard to hear Camille over the music. "I should have said, happy birthday!"

Morgyn's either mid-drink or not talking.

"How old did you turn?"

"Guess," says Morgyn. "How old do I seem?"

Ada stifles a snort. "Poor Camille."

"Morgyn's toying with her," I whisper back.

Camille stammers and laughs and says, "Twenty-thr . . . twenty-one."

"You got the first part right." Morgyn leans against the pantry door, a silhouette blocking the slanted light.

"Twenty?"

"What a deduction and shit." A silence I imagine only Camille finds awkward, until Morgyn says, "Lot of people here."

"What a deduc—" begins Camille. "I mean, yeah, there's a bunch of people from Fort Luthe here too. Were you looking for anyone in particular?" Camille knows Morgyn doesn't make small talk.

"Why would I do that? Now stop fucking hovering."

There's the sound of a new song coming on. Camille must leave, though the outline of Morgyn's figure stays.

Not that Ada's looking that way anymore. She's looking at me from inches away. I feel like I'm being traced. I'm about to say something—I don't know what—but they hold a finger to their lips and nod toward Morgyn against the slatted door.

Since the Point, Ada's eyes have held me. Accelerated me, pinned me down. They erase everything, from the shelves around us to the bass beating outside.

Right now, their eyes erase every shadow at my door.

I'm noticing every time she blinks.

How near their eyelashes are to mine.

Pupils are dark and open, taking in what light there is.

She touches my hip, sending a vibration that goes beyond my cells to move through my essence. No less real. The train thundering on the tracks toward me.

The room with hearts. Mechanical. Anatomical.

A third with lace.

I didn't tell Lucy about that room either. The room's the

same as Ada's hand moving across my hip, though I can't pin down how. They hook their hand in my front pocket. I forgot the cassette in there when we swam. I can dry it out. I can still listen to it. I can reach out and touch her face.

Their hair's soft as I trace my thumbs over their ears and let my hands rest on the back of their head.

I was so focused on how I knew the songs that I missed the unknown. Take the hints.

Ada reaches up and draws a line along my collarbone. I've felt an absence there since my necklace went missing. It's filled in now, then lost in the slight tug on my pocket, gently pulling me closer to her.

Our faces hover apart for a moment. If it'd been a normal party at the Point with nothing lurking in the water, would we have gotten here that night? I could have come back to watch the fireworks. No one would have had to run away. This is the sort of feeling I'd fight for and dream of. Even one more day of it.

When I kiss them, it's like two notes coming into tune with each other. Like instead of crushing me, the train picked me up, and now the thrumming is under my feet and all around me.

Soft, tasting like gin and ocean and storm. We press into the corner of the shelves. She slides her hands around my waist to the bare skin on the small of my back and pulls me in closer to her. Quietly, kisses getting deeper. I can feel the tape press into their hip.

There's a sharp crack of thunder outside. Morgyn's talking to someone just beyond the door, but the words and weather are far away. What lingers becomes distant. I'm here, unbuttoning their blazer and feeling the warmth of their stomach and breasts against mine. How she puts her hands in the back pocket of my shorts and moves with me.

They reach under my shirt, and I help them peel it off and let it drop to the floor. We're tumbling together with no end in sight. Reaching into the mirror and falling through it. I want to stay in every second. Every new part of them I touch. Every murmur that we try to contain.

But there's a momentum building I don't want to stop.

So when Ada reaches for the button on my shorts and looks at me, questioning, my answer is yes. Yes to her hands pulling the zipper down and the heel of her hand pressing into my stomach as her fingers brush downward and slowly back up.

I close my eyes.

Don't want to miss a thing.

Can't make a sound other than a shaky breath in and another when they kiss the side of my neck.

No shadows at my door.

CHAPTER TWENTY-THREE

THEN NO SHADOWS AT ALL.

Because the light's gone. The hint of a glow making its way through my eyelids vanishes. The music scrapes to a halt, and the appliances in the kitchen exhale the last hint of function for a moment before going silent.

The power's gone out.

Ada's stopped moving. Their face is resting on my shoulder, and their hands are still on my body. I can feel her heart beating against my chest.

In the main room, the voices are too loud from talking over the music. There's nervous laughter and confusion. Someone keeps singing the song that was cut off. Others join in, and I hear the dancing begin again.

Outside the pantry door, Morgyn mutters, "Shit. *Shit*. Okay."

Morgyn's the only one who sounds scared.

That makes me afraid. My brain has to slog its way out of a haze of alcohol and dopamine to get to a place it doesn't want to arrive at. Ada takes her hand out of my shorts and reaches behind me, gripping my shoulders tightly. I know she's found her way to the same conclusion.

"If the lights are out," Ada says, "it can go wherever it wants."

Morgyn's gone by the time Ada and I stumble into the dark kitchen with all our clothes back on. "The storm must have taken the power out," I say. "Maybe it's only this neighborhood. We should check."

"We could drive to another part of town," suggests Ada. "Or to the cabin. We could still get power out there."

Harsh light crashes through the kitchen window as Morgyn's truck comes to life. It shines through the bottles on the island and shows me the flushed skin of Ada's face. Their lips look kissed, though that feels distant now. Now is fingernails digging into palms. It's the way the renewed darkness feels more smothering when Morgyn pulls away. Is she running?

Ada and I feel our way down the hallway toward the sound of the party. A couple people have found flashlights. They're whipping them around as they dance, sending beams that leap across the ceiling and reveal the faces of random people. They're pretending this doesn't trigger memories of the start of Autumn, when the whole grid was down. It's only in the past few years that it's really become reliable again in cities. Less and less the farther out you get.

Ada takes my hand, and we push our way through the dance floor to the wide windows overlooking town. Or where town used to be. All we can see is the first few feet of the night. Beyond Morgyn's truck, there's not a single flicker of light, from the trailer park to the boardwalk.

Wherever it wants. There's a pulsing in me, like the feeling of a distant warning siren.

Ada's hand clenches mine until it hurts. "Something's up with Cas. It just showed up now. I've never felt this."

The usual thrum of Ada's presence is gone.

Has that been Cascade? Ada said Cas responds before Ada does. That a few people Cas really connects with can feel those shifts. All along, the other soul in Ada was pulling me in, helping me protect them at the Point, aligning with mine as we touched a few minutes ago. Cascade linked Ada and me from the moment I sat down next to her.

I'm sure of it now. That's the thrum. A faulty soul beckoning me in a way I've never felt before. Ada must have understood it almost right away. Cas drawn to me and drawing me and Ada together. Cas set us on a collision course before we spoke to each other. Certain to the point of recklessness.

"What's Cas saying?" I ask.

"Danger."

"To who?"

Ada's breathing has gotten anxious and short. "There could only be a few people."

Morgyn's backed her truck up to the front door of the house. Her headlights are burning into the night like a challenge. There's a guardian here. Papercut's probably safe. Me too. In the trailer park, some lights have come up.

"That'll be Papercut's dad firing up the generator," says Ada. "Thank god it started this time."

8. 21. 32. 56. 67. 103. 12.

12 is Ada's cabin.

32 is my house.

103 is Morgyn's truck.

"What's you and Papercut's house number?" I ask Ada urgently.

"Twenty-one," says Ada. "Why?"

I'm pushing back into my memory, clawing in the dirt. I know where to dig now. 8 and 56 I can't place, but Lucy's house is 67.

Fuck.

It knows everywhere I've been. It's snapping at my heels. And there's only one person who Cas connects with who's in a place I've visited that might still be dark.

My hand clenches to match Ada's. "We've got to get to Ruby."

CHAPTER TWENTY-FOUR

ADA AND I SEE MORGYN FROM THE END OF THE HALLWAY leading to the front door. Morgyn's framed in the opening, lit up red in her taillights. She's grabbing all the car keys she can find.

"Those are mine!" some guy protests.

"Just a parking issue," says Morgyn. "I'll have them back in a minute."

"I'm not blocking your truck."

He tries to grab the keys from Morgyn. She dodges away easily and sweeps his feet out from under him, sending him sprawling across the entry. He scrambles back up, sees the look Morgyn's giving him, and pushes past me and Ada to rejoin the party.

Morgyn turns away before Ada and I have gotten close enough for her to see who we are. "He's got the right idea," she says to us. "The night's young." She slams the door behind her. By the time we're at the door, Morgyn's parked her truck against it so it can't open.

"Through the backyard." I pull Ada into the party again. They vanish from my side as we make our way through the crowd and then rejoin me a few seconds later with a flashlight in their hand. The angry shout behind her tells me exactly how she got it.

"Ooh, a commotion?" says a voice from beside us in the dark. It's Lucy, confirmed when Ada shines the flashlight beam on her.

"Ada, I've taught you so well," says Papercut. "We should get home, where the generator's making light."

"Ruby's in trouble." Ada keeps moving toward the back entrance. "Morgyn blocked the front."

Papercut jumps into action. The drunk guy who Ada took the flashlight from has caught up to us, and Papercut turns on him. "We're keeping this. Agree or fight me." Papercut's maintained a reputation that turns him right around. "I finished fixing the dirt bike today," they say. "I'll follow you. Whose house is she at?"

"Tay's."

"Their mom's a bitch," says Lucy. "Did you know she once . . ."

Outside, the clouds have finally fully unleashed. The rain's so heavy that it's hard to see in front of yourself. We all clamber over a fence and land in mud on the other side. I slip in it, get back up, and follow Ada, who hasn't turned around. Morgyn's starting cars and leaving them idling all around the house, forming a barrier of brightness that we're leaving behind.

Ada's already got the ATV running by the time I catch up. Papercut's dirt bike comes to life on their third try kick-starting it. "You two should stay behind!" Papercut yells over the rain. "Morgyn's got this covered."

"How does she know?" asks Lucy. "How does Morgyn know to use light? Also we're coming with you!"

"We can help!" I add, though if it's going places I've been, maybe I've done enough. "We're the only others who know what to watch for!"

Me behind Ada on the ATV, Lucy behind Papercut on the dirt bike, and we're skittering through the soaked streets toward Ruby. Ada's driving as fast as she can. The tires fling up water and filth off the streets. We're on the edge of crashing, alcohol still coursing through our veins, but I'm not going to tell them to slow down. I'd go faster if I could. When we get there, she drives straight across the lawn to the front door.

Which is wide open.

Papercut throws their dirt bike down and goes into the dark house without hesitation. Ada follows right after them, shining the flashlight around and leaving muddy footprints.

I'm frozen on the threshold, staring inside.

Lucy steps up beside me, her black dress and legs covered in muck, and sniffs the air. "Are you getting anything besides rain?"

I'm not, but any other scents would be washed away by the downpour.

"Me neither," says Lucy. "Let's go, better together."

We only get three steps in before the cracks start to spread. The sound of the rain becomes muted—then, in a flash of lightning, I see the kitchen. The brightness burns the glimpse onto my retinas. It's like Abraham's Corner, the cars parked across from the forest, the mailboxes.

Every cupboard door is open the exact same amount—just

past ninety degrees. Anything that held a beverage is empty and scattered across the floor. A chocolate-milk carton, cans of soda, sweet coolers in glass bottles.

I reach down in the blackness and scrape about. I can feel a draft from all the cold air that's escaped the fridge. My fingers close around a metal bottle cap. It's been crumpled like tinfoil. My skin remembers its jaggedness.

Papercut and Ada emerge from the hallway. "Same in the bathroom," Papercut whispers.

Ada shines the flashlight deeper into the house. "It drank the cleaning chemicals, the mouthwash, even the nail polish."

"What's that?" asks Lucy suddenly, and we all go the kind of silent that will suffocate us if we hold it for too long.

From the next room, we hear a child's stifled crying. It's not Ruby. The sound combined with the look on Ada's face makes me feel like I'm being strangled.

There's a huge blanket fort in the middle of the living room. The sort that two kids who are really too old for blanket forts build out of nostalgia and ambition. Chairs stacked on chairs and a table on its side draped with a linen-cupboard's worth of sheets and blankets. The side facing the door is one white sheet, hanging between us and the crying.

A breeze from the open window makes it flutter like a ghost.

I got back to me and my mom's apartment later than I said I would.

After dark.

Unmarked government agents everywhere.

They told me a machine woke up, shredded itself like a frag grenade. It still happens sometimes, they said. Especially if you've got banned items. The restless kind.

We didn't though.

They let me grab some things before sending me to stay somewhere else.

The last time in that apartment. That summer tape in my cassette player.

Cupboards thrown open, evidence markers, blood on the walls.

White sheet.

"Tay?" Ada pulls it aside and shines her flashlight in. "Ruby?"

Tay's in a sleeping bag pushed all the way against the back wall of the blanket fort.

They're peeking out with their back against the table. I've been doing the same at night. It's so nothing can come up behind them. Between Tay and the four of us, there's another sleeping bag. As limp on the floor as a body bag.

"Where's Ruby?" asks Ada, ducking their head to push past the sheet. They reach out for Tay's shoulder. Now that I know the thrum I feel off Ada is Cas, I'm aware of how much Cas's energy is ricocheting. "Tay, where's Ruby?"

Papercut throws the empty sleeping bag aside, crumpling one side of the blanket fort. Swearing less softly than they should. "Did Ruby go home? All her stuff's gone."

Lucy uses another sheet to wipe the mud off her face. "Hey,

Tay, I'm Lucy," she says. "You're not by yourself now. You know Ada, right? And Papercut's okay. They're not as scary as they think they are. This is Cedar. You met Cedar earlier, yeah?"

The curtain falls back into place behind Lucy. I take hold of it and follow her behind the white sheet.

We didn't have banned items. My mom always kept up with the latest research. She was careful with her life and mine.

I tried to tell the agents, and they told me the same story as before.

No, the same lie.

Lucy sits on the floor next to Tay. "Sorry we're *so* messy," says Lucy. "Bet we'll get in trouble with your mom. We were worried about Ruby when the power went out. Do you know where she is?" Gently, Lucy pulls the sleeping bag back so we can see Tay's entire tear-streaked face in Ada's flashlight beam.

"Outside," Tay manages.

"What the fuck—" starts Papercut, but Lucy punches them in the leg. I can see Ada's face asking the same question with the same urgency. Me, Ada, and Papercut are standing stooped over Tay. Lucy gestures for us to come down to Tay's level. Ada and I go to our knees, while Papercut just crouches, ready for action.

"Why'd Ruby go outside?" Lucy asks.

Tay starts to cry harder, breaths coming in shakes.

"Okay, okay," says Lucy. "I love to talk. I'll talk, and you nod if I'm right."

I touch Ada's hand, both for comfort and to stop them shining the flashlight right in Tay's eyes.

Lucy begins, "You and Ruby built this blanket fort."

"Lair."

"Sorry, my bad. This blanket *lair*. Then you went to bed. You stayed up really late. Your mom came and told you two to settle down, but you just kept talking but quieter. Yeah? Same. And then you went to sleep. What woke you up? Was it the storm?"

Tay shakes their head.

"Did you . . . ?" Lucy pauses for a moment. "Did you hear the front door open?"

"Means Dad's home." Tay's slowed down enough to speak a little. "He works late."

Ada takes a second to calm her tone before speaking. "Was it your dad tonight?"

Tay shakes their head again. "I looked out, and it was in the kitchen. I couldn't see properly. The power was out. It was a darker dark than the rest. I could hear it drinking."

"What'd it smell like?" demands Papercut.

"Bad."

"Is there anything it reminded you of?" asks Lucy.

Tay thinks for a few long seconds. "Like a puddle our dog shouldn't drink. Or the dead cat me and Ruby found in the lane. Or when you lose a tooth. My dad says it's from the iron in blood. I woke Ruby up. She smelled it too." Tay's crying harder again.

"I don't know this next part," says Lucy softly. "Do you think you can tell me? To help your friend? I'll teach you a trick. Just say it as fast as you can. That's what I always do."

"We'll listen to you," I say, "no matter what it is."

Tay swallows and then lets everything spill out.

"The darker spot got big. I could just tell it was a mouth. And a tongue. It had a big tongue. It reached a leg in and put its claws . . ."

"You've got this," whispers Lucy. "You've got to be brave to help your friend."

"It put its claws around me. I could see part of its mouth. I saw right into outer space where that spaceship started Autumn. No stars or moon or anything. It stayed there for a long time. Then there was this sound." Tay makes a sucking, draining noise in their child voice. It's like the end of a tub emptying.

"Ruby turned on a flashlight and there was nothing there. I asked her if it was gone. She smiled? She said something . . . I don't know. It's stuck in my head. She said, '*Gone and arriving are lies passed down by those with voices. The truth is what's always here. Torn and sewn, grown and cut down, sliced and stitched. The truth is tomorrow's morning sun on my face, walking under open skies in the garden unashamed of my form.*' I asked her why she sounded like a weird book. She wouldn't talk to me at all. Ruby loves to talk. She just got dressed and left. I tried to grab her hand, but she pulled me off."

"See, not so bad." Lucy keeps lying kindly. "It was just a nightmare."

Tay pulls their arm out of the sleeping bag and shows it to us. No dream leaves these dark bruise marks of a crushing grip. Ruby's small hands couldn't have done that, but the bruises are the shape and size of a ten-year-old's.

Ada reaches out and touches each fingertip mark on the bruise. She looks shell-shocked. "I'm sorry. Ruby didn't mean to hurt you, Tay. I promise."

"Do you think . . . ?" I leave the rest hanging. I don't want to scare Tay even more.

Lucy nods. "Ruby was talking creepy cryptic like Kat's message. But Kat said it couldn't stay inside her."

"Already occupied," mutters Ada. "Motel heart. No vacancy."

Just like Kat said.

"Stop!" Papercut rises to their feet. "Here's what I fucking think. It can't have been here that long ago. This thing is hurt by light, so sometime after the power went out. Ruby won't have gotten far. We'll find her and find a way to get it the hell out of her. If it's already out, we'll get her to a hospital or doctor or something."

"Are we sure we want it out?" asks Lucy. "What with the teeth?"

"I'll sort it," says Papercut. Ada would bet on Papercut to fight anything. I'm not sure I'd bet on anything to fight what visited this house tonight.

From the entrance, a man's voice calls, "Hello? Anyone here?"

Lucy's hand darts to cover Tay's mouth, but it's too late. They call out for their dad before Lucy muffles them. There's a woman talking now too, saying she put earplugs in when the storm started. What's going on? Why are all the windows open?

Ada grabs Tay's wrist. They don't seem to notice it's the hurt one. "Don't tell your family what you saw. Promise me? Promise me? Keep them safe."

The blanket fort is lit up by Ada's flashlight. It's full of hunched-over outlines who tracked mud right to its door.

Suddenly everyone's talking, explaining, shouting. Standing up, throwing hands in what light there is. Tay's screaming. The blanket fort teeters and a chair comes down. I see the corner of a piece of paper sticking out from underneath Ruby's pillow and dive for it right before the entire thing collapses.

Crumpled in my fist.

Crumbling all around me.

Cracks spreading and I'm seeing through
under
the white sheet that rips loose and spreads out
over my body on the floor.

CHAPTER TWENTY-FIVE

I GOT BACK TO ME AND MY MOM'S APARTMENT LATER THAN I said I would.

After dark.

That part is right, but the rest was wrong. Because how could I relive a memory like this again and again and survive?

There was nobody there. Souls and fiend walked out and left the door gaping.

Inside, no evidence markers, no sheets. Just everything ajar. Drinks emptied and empty

sharp

bottle caps crumpled. The digital clock on the stove

blinking

like the power had gone out in our apartment building. Block 8. Another mailbox number. The building that backed onto the long, deep river murky with the filth of upstream factories. Winding its way into the city from the expanse beyond. On the living room floor, in a

white

sweater

half of my mom's body face down on the carpet. She must have been crawling toward the phone I called 911 on. I remember that the words on the other end of the line felt half rehearsed more than I remember the emergency operator who spoke them. Who sent unmarked government agents. There they are. That's their spot.

The agents who lied and didn't let me back inside until there was a sheet covering the mess where the body had been.

That was this. This was that. It didn't just follow me from Abraham's Corner to Sawblade Lake. It followed me all the way from where I started

to the Point, where it killed TJ and Oliver and did something far worse to Kat

to the sewer across from my front door

to the houses of the people I care about

to Ruby.

Under the white sheet, I know

I brought this monster upon us.

• • •

Dad,

I could use a father tonight. Or the idea of one. A god, a harbor, some shelter. A bunker, even.

Because the sun's coming up, but I don't know what that means anymore.

Yours,
Cedar

PART TWO

UNDER OPEN SKIES

CHAPTER TWENTY-SIX

Dad,

When does silence become deceit? Tell me. You'd know. What if you're lying to yourself? Or things are hidden within the corners of your skull and the hollows of your rib cage?

What if your lie is what everything else is built on?

If I owe you anything, it's to tell you what I meant when I said all the people who know the truth are gone. I didn't know when I first wrote it, but now I do. You can have every truth I've got, since you're not listening.

It took Mom too. Not took over, like Ruby, but tore from this world. I'm sorry I can't tell you more. The images leach into my thoughts every hour every minute every time I try to think about Mom. It stole her completely. Even the echoes of her have screams in them.

Then it followed me to Sawblade. It's a shadow shackled to me, dragged from the city to this new family of mine. I imagine this is how you felt as water poured down the valley of death from the dam you vowed was safe. But for me, I learned too late.

It won't make any difference if I tell my friends how it came here, so I haven't. Our goal of finding Ruby is the same whether they know it stalks me or not.

And as I've watched Ada fight tooth and nail to find her sister over our past few days of searching, I wonder if they'd ever forgive me if I did tell. Ada, whose soul pulls me in twice over. My friends, who care for each other so fiercely. I've lost person after person I love. When the bus dropped me off at Abraham's Corner, I was completely alone. I don't think I can live through that loneliness again.

So I keep my silence, not knowing if I'd be forgiven. If I can make it right, I'll never have to find out.

Tomorrow, we keep seeking what we're afraid will find us.

Yours,
Cedar

CHAPTER TWENTY-SEVEN

IT'S STILL DARK WHEN MY ALARM GOES OFF.

I roll over and slot the mixtape Ada made me into my cassette player. I think I managed to dry the tape out, but this is my first time trying to play it. The track list is now a black smear that's beyond recognition. I just hit play and let the songs come to me.

There's a whirr, where I think it might not work, then the first notes come through. The mix has everything I listen to when I'm afraid and can't sleep. I know the songs all word for word from listening to them on repeat. But Ada and I listened to music together for only a day. It was the radio and whatever she had at the cabin. We talked a bit about what we liked to listen to, but not to this extent. Lucy said she used to think Ada knew too much, and I'm almost starting to think the same.

I shake my head, which makes it ache more than clears it. Nothing has made much sense lately.

They say the first forty-eight hours, right? It's been almost eighty since Ruby went missing. Four nights, three days. Everything feels flipped again, like the night comes first and now the day is our time of fear. Because as far as we can figure out, the thing that took Ruby wanted a host so it could be outside in the daylight.

And now it's got one.

Me, Lucy, Ada, and Papercut have been combing the woods from dawn to dusk, each day farther and farther away from town. We take whatever vehicles we can use that day and drive forgotten roads looking for a blue raincoat among the pines. Then on foot, vulnerable and slow.

We've got to keep this between those of us who know too much to turn back, so we pile lies around our search. Ada told Papercut's family that Ruby's gone to spend the week with her friend and their family a few lakes north of here, where she went last summer. Otherwise they'd all be in more danger than they already are. Once the confusion at Tay's house settled and their parents threw us onto the lawn anyway, we explained that Ruby couldn't sleep and walked home. The only gossip they can spread is that we showed up half drunk in the night to check on Ruby.

Then we drove all over a powerless Sawblade Lake. We were powerless too, barely able to see through the rain. No one to tell what had happened and no sign of Ruby.

I get moving after the first side of the tape. I've run out of clean clothes, and I haven't done laundry in far too long, so it's back to the shorts I wore to the party at Camille's house and one of my mom's black band shirts, which I smell to see if it's wearable. The road rash and bruises down my side are closer to healing, but my legs and arms are a mess of little cuts and nicks from pushing aside branches as we look for Ruby.

My grandma's already up, making oatmeal in the kitchen. "Off to work on Ada's cabin again today?"

I nod wearily and sit at the kitchen table in front of the steaming cup of coffee that's waiting for me. Since the storm, the heat has slowly been ramping back up, leaving dried-out ridges of garbage and debris where runoff poured down the streets. Despite the weather, I drink the coffee without waiting for it to cool down.

"You're putting in pretty long days," my grandma says, handing me a bowl of oatmeal. "And the brush-clearing seems like nasty work. Though sometimes that's what it takes for the things that really matter."

"This definitely does," I agree.

"Hmm." She sits across from me and sips her coffee. I've already downed half of mine.

"Hmm?" I ask. Between the music earlier and the caffeine, I'm feeling hints of life. Like today, maybe we find Ruby. That's as far as I can hope. After that, I come up against the fact that she's not alone. We don't truly know what's in her, only what it can do. "You can't just *hmm* and then walk away."

"I can and I have. It's the Christian way."

I ask enough questions to keep the focus on her—plans at the church and articles she's read. She lets me finish eating and stand up to leave before she has mercy and tells me, "*Hmm* means, when you love someone, you try to make their dreams become real. That's all."

That stops me for a moment.

First, because something *has* become real for me and the

new people I care about. It's the kind of thing that makes us run in place and wake up sweating. Unknowingly, but all the same, I brought a plague into the dreams of my dearest hearts.

Then second, *love*.

If we find Ruby and get the monster out of her, what do I do? What is love? Is love leading it away from Sawblade Lake? Love might be dying alone as distant from the ones I love as possible.

I think of that day painting Ada's cabin. Simple, easy, creating newness on the walls and between us. I want to get her back there. I want *us* to get back there. Get out of this bad dream and try to make a brighter one real. Somehow.

First, love.

First, find Ruby.

"I'm working on it," I say. Light's broken over the horizon.

I'm halfway to the door when my grandma calls after me. "Cedar, you dropped something!"

She's holding a crumpled piece of paper. The white sheet of the blanket fort came crashing down at the same time as the memories, as when I grabbed at a corner of paper under Ruby's pillow. Damn gin and a nervous system alive with a past-present-future of terror. I must have stuffed it in my back pocket and forgotten.

I take it from my grandma's hand. I can see the edge of some writing. The few words are enough to convince me I shouldn't read the rest without Ada and Papercut there. It's messy, but I can make out one sentence.

It needs me.

* * *

When I arrive at the cabin, our search headquarters, the others aren't there yet. They're late for our usual start time. We're all worn down, with voices hoarse from calling out and eyes bloodshot from short nights of sleep. Even when I stumble to bed, I lie awake thinking of lies and horrors that can't be held down anymore.

I grew blank with fatigue driving over and nearly missed the turn. I had to veer sharply to hit it. I felt oddly calm as I struggled for control of my grandma's car. A rollover doesn't fill me with anything like the dread that fills the rest of my days.

I let myself into the quiet cabin. My eyes catch new lines on the map in the living room. We've been marking searched areas and ones to search again. At first we made lines for how far Ruby could have traveled, but we all saw the bruises on Tay's wrist. Ruby is being pushed beyond her own limits. We've flipped the conversations over and over again. How can it occupy yet not destroy her? If she's stronger, is she faster?

How much can her body take?

Hopefully it doesn't push Ruby so far she breaks.

Curiosity takes me toward the room with the hearts again. I'm standing in front of the door when Ada's voice from behind me makes me jump. "Morning," they say. She's kneeling on the bedroom floor with her back to me, finishing packing her bag. "I was thinking we could start out near Camille's place and work our way west today."

"How'd you get here so fast?" I ask. There was no sign of

a bike or vehicle out front, though it did smell like exhaust outside the cabin.

"Slept here," says Ada shortly. They strap an axe to the side of their backpack.

I try to think to the nearest bastion of light. It's far. "Ada . . ."

She turns around, revealing a face still smeared with yesterday's dirt and sweat. There are dark circles under their eyes. "I ran the generator to keep the lights on while it was dark."

"That's not much."

She gives a slight shrug. "Seems like it was enough. I had things to do here. Papercut's picking up Lucy."

"We've got to be careful. We don't know how it works now that it's inside Ruby. Night could still be dangerous." I step into her bedroom. Last time I was here, I woke up to them looking at me softly.

We haven't spoken much in the last few days. If we're alone together, there's a clear focus. If we're in groups, Papercut and Ada have been one team and Lucy and I have been the other. Ada's got a singular goal. She hasn't held still long enough for me to hold her since Ruby went missing.

"I had things to do," repeats Ada. "Where are Papercut and Lucy? We've got to get moving."

I think I have the words for how I feel about Ada. My grandma gave them to me this morning. "I don't want to lose you to it too," I say.

"I'm lost until Ruby's found." Ada tightens the straps of her bag so violently that one of them snaps. She throws it into the wall, where the axe head makes a dent in the smooth, freshly painted surface.

They look around like they're trying to find something else to latch on to, so I step in closer to where they're kneeling and pull them to me. Her arms close around me, her head pressed against me. They're sobbing. The kind that rattles through their entire body and into mine.

In choking, broken words, she asks, "What if we never find her?"

I can't answer either way. I found my mom, and now I'll never find her again. Until three days ago, my body wouldn't let me remember just how gone she is. I close my eyes tightly, but not before a few tears slip out and down my cheeks.

Ada's trembling gradually stills, until they're resting against me. I wipe my eyes with the back of my hand and stroke her short hair. I don't have any words of comfort, just touch. They softly kiss my stomach a few times, then lean against me again.

"I want you," she whispers. Her voice is drained from crying.

My heart jumps forward. I'm aware of every part of us that's touching and how little she'd have to lift my shirt or kiss her way down my body to make my hands hold the back of her head tighter.

"I can't right now," they say, "but you need to know that I do want you. I haven't forgotten."

"I couldn't forget."

"I'm glad you're here," they say.

We stay linked together without any more words until we hear Papercut and Lucy arrive on the ATV. I break away from Ada with a sigh. "Now that everyone's here," I say, "I found something I need to show you."

CHAPTER TWENTY-EIGHT

It's written on the back of a piece of paper torn from a notebook. It's stained with rainwater and the mud from my hands. It was written by a child afraid in the dark, with letters that grow and shrink, overlap and angle. This is Ruby's note, uncrumpled on the small kitchen table the four of us are sitting around.

"It's to you," I say to Ada.

They glance at the note, then quickly turn away. "Can someone read it out loud?"

Papercut grabs it and begins. "*It's here*. Fuck, nope."

"I got you," says Lucy. She smooths out the paper in front of her and reads it in an unusually slow, even tone. I follow along on the page, each word spiraling confusion and sorrow through me.

> Its here Ada. Its got Tay. I can hear its breath just outside the lair. It needs me. I felt it when it was close to me before. Its calling to the empty space where Em used to be. I think it has to live in me but it cant kick

down the door of its new home. It needs me to say yes.

Im going to let it. If I dont its going to hurt Tay. It barely gave me time to write this. Part of the deal.

Things will be a-ok. You helped me last time. I save Tay. You save me. Got it bitch?

Papercut breaks the silence before it has time to settle. "That little shit! She should've run when she had the chance. Where'd she learn to go playing hero like that?"

"You," says Lucy. "Probably you."

Papercut waves off Lucy's compliment, but they have the slightest blush. "From Ada. Ruby told Ada to save her because she knew they'd never give up on her."

Ada reaches for Papercut, who covers her hand with both of theirs. "How can she be so confident things will be okay, Jamie?" asks Ada. It's the first time I've heard anyone call Papercut that, dismayed and intimate. "It was there with her, and she was still sure."

"A, she's got me and you." Papercut chuckles in a laugh-or-cry way. "And B, she's hella cocky."

And C, she doesn't know it like we do. Or . . .

I grab the note and spin it toward me. Of all the parts that bother me, there's one that latched to the front of my mind. "*I felt it when it was close to me before*," I read. "When has she seen it? I barely caught a glimpse at Abraham's Corner. Even at the Point, it stayed underwater." It must be within the past three weeks, since I arrived in Sawblade Lake, though no one but me knows why.

"Maybe just when it was in the kitchen?" suggests Lucy.

Ada shakes her head. "That's not how she's talking. She didn't say *something* was here. She said *it*, like the monster was familiar."

"Why would it *need* her?" asks Papercut. "What could it possibly want with Ruby?"

Ada throws Papercut a withering look. Papercut barely reacts, but they shut right up. I can tell Lucy caught it too.

"Am I the only one who doesn't know who Em is?" asks Lucy. "I'm not usually in this position. I don't like it. I can check the *TALK* folder but—"

Ada pushes their chair back with a sharp scrape and stands. "Emerald's not in your *TALK* folder for a reason." She heads out of the room without another word. A second later, the back door slams behind them.

"Nice going," mutters Papercut.

"We were *all* thinking it," says Lucy indignantly. "What's this *last time* Ruby's talking about?"

"And where'd Emerald go?" I ask.

Papercut folds their hands in front of them on the table and leans their chair back on two legs. "Not mine to tell."

"You're insufferable." Lucy kicks at them, trying to knock them off-balance. "If you think I'm hacking my way through the woods chasing after some demonic gulper eel without all the information, guess again." Lucy storms out after Ada. I take Ruby's note and follow Ada for damage control and because I have the same questions.

She's sitting on her chopping block with her back to us. They've got their elbows on their knees and their head in their hands.

Lucy stops a little ways away. "Oh shit," she says quietly when I catch up to her. "Now I feel like I shouldn't ask."

Ada speaks without moving. "You should. You've both got the right to know."

"Listen, no, whatever," says Lucy. "It's no big deal. People have the right to their secrets."

I have to agree with that. "We can just get going on today's search. We're ready to head out."

Ada sits up straight, closes her eyes, and takes a long breath that she releases slowly. They turn around to face us. "I trust you," she says, "and more importantly, Cas trusts you too." Ada looks right at me when she says that.

Trusts me, with secrets and desire and touch and the balance between silences and lies.

"Whatever it is, I promise not to write it down," says Lucy. "It stays in this room . . . or yard or forest. You get the idea."

Papercut's joined, the three of us forming a semicircle around Ada sitting on the chopping block as they continue. "Cas doesn't like me to talk about this. Cas is extra protective of Ruby because"—Ada looks at Papercut, who gives them a nod—"Ruby used to be Faulty too."

Lucy audibly gasps. Papercut rolls their eyes, while Ada almost smiles. I have a different internal reaction. I think of the weight of hiding that for a decade, and it makes me want to hold Ada again.

"Ruby was just a baby when Autumn happened. But our

genetics don't care. She has that heart disease risk, like me. So her and I were in the same diagnostic trial. When the soul in her microbot woke up, she got the same bruises as me on her tiny body. I was old enough to understand, but she just intuited how to live with another soul in her from go. She chose to call it Emerald. Two gemstones. I taught her to keep the bruises hidden. Never swim with friends or get changed in front of other people. Me, Papercut, and their dad know, but that's it."

"What do you mean, she 'used to be Faulty'?" I ask.

"You've heard rumors about how Faulty people have abilities," says Ada. "It wasn't a rumor with Ruby. When she was around eight, she started being able to work together with Emerald to tell what other people were thinking about her. Not energy like Cas—their exact words. You don't want to know that as a kid, or ever. She started doing it all the time, and people started to be able to tell. She'd slip up and say things she couldn't possibly know. I was scared people would find out she was Faulty. Or that knowing what everyone was thinking about her would drive her out of her mind. So I found a solution. Morgyn."

Papercut points at Lucy. "Don't you dare gasp again."

I remember Ada's silence when Lucy read the *TALK* file on Morgyn. Lucy saying she saw Ada and Ruby talking in Mongrel's window once. How Ada threw in a card to say she'd been in Morgyn's house, then chose dare instead of truth. Later, that she didn't want to encounter Morgyn in Camille's kitchen.

The story comes out of Ada in a rush. Something that's been held in too long. "Morgyn's like a surgeon on faulty machines. I thought maybe she could do the same for Ruby. Because

Emerald couldn't just choose to leave Ruby, not without potentially exploding inside Ruby's heart. Morgyn had a couple different theories.

"The cleanest was that if Emerald willingly let another soul replace it, this other soul could enter at the same time as Emerald left, stabilizing the microbot so it'd quietly become inert. Then the replacement soul could return to where it came from. In theory. Though in theory Morgyn thought it could work with a human essence too. The only soul we knew and trusted was Cas, and it couldn't leave me without a high chance of *me* dying. So we went with the other option.

"The microbot was too volatile and grown into Ruby's heart to remove, but we could channel Emerald into another machine *if* the two machines physically touched and *if* Emerald agreed.

"Ruby sat with Emerald for a long time, then she came back and said they were both ready and willing to take the risks. Emerald wanted to die, she just wasn't willing to kill Ruby too. Cas and I helped. It was . . . something between open-heart surgery, taking an engine out of a car, and doing an exorcism. Emerald picked the machine. It was an old handheld console of Papercut's that Ruby used to pretend to play on. It had already had a faulty soul in it, so there was room. Once the handheld touched the microbot, we helped Emerald safely transfer over, threw it in a safe, and slammed the door."

"And that was it?" I ask. "Morgyn did all that just to help Ruby?"

"Yes," says Ada, at the same time that Papercut says, "Not exactly." Ada gives Papercut an almost imperceptible headshake.

"Too bad you can't tell anyone," says Lucy.

"Why?" asks Ada hurriedly.

"Because you and Ruby would be fucking legends. If it wasn't for all the bias and hate and stuff."

"You're legends to us," I say. Morgyn too, in yet another way. The people who I don't want interacting have already woven in and out of each other's lives, though even with these secrets out, it doesn't seem like the whole picture. And that makes me nervous.

"A legend to the people I care about. I'll take it." Ada still looks bothered. "Anyway, that's what Ruby was talking about. The empty spot in her from last time. But it goes with something Kat said. Motel heart."

I piece it together before Ada says it. "You're occupied because Cas is still in you. But there's vacancy in Ruby for the monster because Ruby has a cavity in her from where Emerald used to be. That's why the monster needs her, and why it didn't ruin her like it ruined Kat. She's the perfect host."

Ada sinks back into a posture of pain. "She can host it because I hollowed her out."

The three of us gather around Ada, surrounding them with our embraces and words. We form a huddle of support against the burden of things we can't undo.

"You did the right thing," I say. "You know you did."

"No one could have seen this coming," adds Lucy.

Papercut takes Ada's face in both of their hands. "You convinced me it was what was best back then. You don't have to convince me again. You and Ruby and Emerald—"

"And Morgyn," Lucy interjects.

"*—and Morgyn* made a decision with the information you had at the time. That's all any of us can do. I swam back from TJ and Oliver's boat minutes before they died. Left them out there. That's kept me up night after night."

"You couldn't have warned them. You didn't know." Ada wipes away tears and smiles up at Papercut, who's got the smallest smirk. "You fucker. I see what you're doing."

We all break apart but stay close together. "We've got this note." I hold up the paper. "We've got Ruby's faith to go on."

Lucy snatches it from my hand.

"Careful!" I say.

"On the back! When you were waving it around." Lucy flips the note over to reveal a single indiscernible word. It's even more scrawled than the rest, like a rushed afterthought. So much so that I thought it was a random pen mark. "What's that say? Ada?"

Ada recognizes her sister's letters in an instant. "*Diary.*"

CHAPTER TWENTY-NINE

I saw it again tonight. Ada hasn't been letting me out after dark lately. Says Morgyn told her there's a killer. I asked Tay. They haven't heard a thing. Smells bullshit. Ada's been sneaking out to the porch at night to do her drawings. Long chunks. So I snuck out too. Take that!

I was going to the bone trees. But I felt it calling my heart. It was in the woods behind the mailboxes across Birchwood Drive. It looks sick now. Matted. Scales under its fur?? Stinks even more. (Oh yeah it also stinks. Charming.)

It would come to the light then go back. Then closer. It got halfway across the road one time. I didn't like that at all. I won't go look for it again. Hope it doesn't look for me.

That's Ruby's entry from the night after Ada and I painted the cabin. We're all in Ada and Ruby's bedroom, which has the distinct feel of Ruby's room and which Ada merely sleeps in. It's an astounding mess, spreading across the narrow patch of floor and over the beds against either wall.

It only took Ada a minute to find Ruby's journal in a shoebox stuffed way under her bed. The box was full of things that seem random but I'm sure matter to Ruby. Special rocks, broken toys, a long stream of ribbon, and a scorched fragment of a handheld console. That must be where Emerald died. Under it all, there was a spiral-bound notebook labeled *Ruby: A Life.*

We're crowded around it on the floor as Ada flips through it. From the most recent entry, further back in time with each page. There were a couple days of doodles and lists. Ruby's thoughts wandering by. Her writing is less frantic here than in the note. Then this. We read it together in silence.

Papercut chuckled at first. "Got you figured," they said to Ada.

"It *does* stink," said Lucy.

There were no smiles or comments by the end. By then, the thing was lurking at the mailboxes it left open for me. Pushing the boundaries of the line of light it stalks around and under town. Ada flips back another few days.

I wonder how my animal is? Ada's been buzzkill about me being out late. Tyrant. Should I march with a sign? Equal nightlife rights!

The hair on my arms stands up when Ruby talks about it as *hers*. Curse words under each of our breaths. It's like Ruby's trying to make jokes at a funeral, falling flat against the heavy suspense in the room.

A bit further back, there's a long entry from the night of the party at the Point.

It doesn't want to come into town. The big night animal. I did science on it. It wasn't here in the day, so I tried after dark. Ada and Papercut are at a party. I hope Ada finds someone to kiss or whaaatever. Ada's been sad since their girlfriend left. When I'm older, I'm going to track her down and fight her.

Anyway, it was in the bone trees again! Kinda hiding, kinda blip blipping about. It doesn't like to be seen. It's shy, coward, em-barr-ass-ed. Ass. Assassin. Ass Ass In. I don't mind. It's hella ugly.

It reminds me of how me and Tay sometimes rattle the fence at Mr. Kaye's big rottweiler to make it run and snap. We wouldn't jump the fence. Nuh uh fuck no. I walked the boardwalk. The night animal swam beside me. To heel. It's a stray. It's *lost its home. It reminds me of Em. Like Em's scary cousin.*

Papercut told me most people get murdered by someone they know. Do tame animals count?

I've never thought of it as something tame and lost, but Ruby seems to understand this thing better than any of us. Intuition, like how she coexisted with a faulty machine inside her before she knew how to speak or walk.

Ruby saw a hideous being that's uncaged and disoriented. With this diary entry, I can trace its path that night. Bone trees, into the water, down the boardwalk, across the lake, and then, as the fireworks cut the air and threw light at night, back into the water. Toward the Point.

There's one more entry on the next page back. It must be the first one about the monster, because it's dated for the night after I arrived in Sawblade.

I saw a weird animal tonight. Me and Tay climbed onto the roof of the town hall. (Damien was right. It fucks. Not that I'd tell him.) Tay was trying to find the houses of everyone we know.

Every. Single. One. The animal was in the bone trees behind the arcade. Long dark ghost. Big mouth. I mean HUGE. All its legs bent the wrong ways. It looked right at me how you look at food when you're really really hungry.

It was gone before I could show Tay. Now they wouldn't believe me if I told them. We watched shooting stars. Tay wished on them. I said I didn't. For my rep, ya know. But I did. I saw three and I wished on all of them.

I wished to be like Morgyn. But not live alone. The helping people and kicking ass.

I wished me and Tay would stay friends no matter what. Like Ada and Papercut.

I wished that Em's happy wherever it is.

I'm seeing something I didn't think was possible. Tears on Papercut's face. Papercut's still, not sniffling or shaking. They don't try to hide it. Those tears might be the most fearful part of all the words Ruby left for us.

"*Those* are her wishes?" says Papercut. "When there's no one to hear her or see what she writes, *that's* still what she wishes for? Are you fucking kidding? This thing has taken the best part of us away. What kind of devil creeps up on some kid who's just curious about it?"

"Something bent the wrong way," I say.

Lucy reaches into her purse and hands Papercut a tissue. Papercut takes it, hardly seeming to register the gesture.

“This is nothing,” says Ada quietly. “There’s *nothing* here. This doesn’t help us find her at all.” She jumps up and flips the shoebox upside down over Ruby’s bed, letting the treasures spill onto the blanket. They paw through them, then return to the diary. Pages spinning by under her fingers. “There’s got to be something more, right?”

Ada stops.

At the top of a random page, Ruby’s written, in all caps: *BIG NIGHT ANIMAL.*

The whole rest of the paper is taken up with a massive, misshapen circle lined with rows of triangles pointing inward. The center’s a mess of heavy crosshatching smudging together.

People have disappeared into those lines slashing back and forth. TJ. Oliver. My mom. That abyss was inside Kat. It’s in Ruby right now.

“That’s not nothing.” Lucy can’t even look at it.

“It’s nothingness.” I can’t look away from it. “But there is a hint. It likes the bone trees.”

“Ugh, naturally unnaturally,” says Lucy.

“It’s a start.” Papercut rips the page out of Ruby’s diary and holds it up like a *Wanted* poster. “This all told me one thing. We’re going to go get this monster out of Ruby, and we’re going to put it in the fucking dirt.”

CHAPTER THIRTY

THE DEAD TREES BEHIND THE ARCADE MUST HAVE BEEN some of the first to be taken by the beetles. Ada says they bore into them, crawl through their veins, and eat them alive from the inside out. The trees are stripped naked of their bark until they're white skeletons with only sparse undergrowth in the acidic soil around their roots. In the daylight, there's nowhere to hide. We sweep the area, looking for tracks, atrocities, a child's backpack. We find nothing.

Between each set of trunks, I picture the crooked circle of teeth. I imagine becoming crosshatching.

From there, we head to our designated search zone of the day. Lucy drives with me in the sedan, now so streaked with dust that it's more brown than maroon.

"Is it wrong that I'm relieved every time we don't find anything?" she asks after being uncharacteristically quiet for an entire minute. "Obviously I want to find Ruby. I care about kids et cetera et cetera. That's a lie. I mean, I do care about kids. Do I want them? Undecided. I mean I just want someone else to find her."

"Because it's not only Ruby."

"Or it's just what's left. Right now we can hope hope hope.

Flipside of ignorance is hope. Hope is to ignorance as peace is to death. Is that how those things work?"

"I hope I find her, come what may," I say. I'm not as ignorant as I was. I know how this thing came to Sawblade and that it's tethered to me. It didn't even have to enter town to know where I'd walked. What links us? I can't piece it together. But I don't have to understand to do what's in front of me. I know we can't stop it unless we find Ruby.

And there's a brightness and a heat with Ada I need to get back to.

Lucy rolls down her window and yells into the world blurring by. "Come what may!" It'd sound like a celebration to someone who didn't know better.

We drive all the roads we can, one of us at the wheel and one scouring the woods with their eyes. Lucy asks to be a driver, so I look for traces that aren't there. Then we join Ada and Papercut to continue the search on foot as the heat of the day keeps climbing.

We're spread out, picking our way along through sticky branches and mosquitoes. We're far enough out of town that we're calling Ruby's name without worrying someone else will hear us. It's settled into a rhythm, from left to right with a pause between each. Papercut, Ada, me, Lucy. At first Ada and Papercut would add other words of comfort.

"Ruby, we're here!"

"Ruby, stay where you are!"

"Ruby, we're coming to you!"

Ruby, do you copy?

Now it's just her name.

I'm hazy and soaked in sweat, blearily panning the ground, when a chipper voice calls back in response. Any noise from the woods sends my heart racing.

"Papercut? What are you doing out here?"

To my right, I hear Lucy drop several unsavory words that seem less about being surprised and more about Camille being the one to do the surprising.

We can't ignore her, so we meet Camille in a bright clearing. She's wearing a big hat and a vivid yellow jumpsuit that fits her in a way that makes me self-conscious of the mess I am.

Lucy swats away a cloud of little bugs. "I didn't know wicker had come back," she says.

"For berries!" says Camille, flipping the lid of the basket back to reveal what she's been picking. She frowns at the four of us. "Is Ruby missing?"

Ada sticks to her policy of keeping everyone else out of it. "Hide-and-seek. Her and Tay are around here somewhere."

"Ada," Papercut sighs. "It's pretty obvious."

"Oh no, that's horrible." Camille adjusts her hat so it's on more firmly. "I'm ready to help. What do you need me to do?"

A whole unspoken conversation happens in looks and shrugs and head tilts. Help wouldn't hurt. Now that Camille knows, might as well accept it. We don't have to give her details. Probably safest not to. The whole time, Lucy's face communicates various versions of *kill me now*.

"Help would be amazing," says Papercut.

Ada's the spearhead of the secrets and plans. "We're sweeping this chunk of the woods. Ruby went missing today—just wandered off. We're hoping to find her soon and keep the whole thing low-key because, um, it's kind of my fault." Ada's barely acting. They genuinely believe the last part, and it sells the whole bit.

Camille feeds us berries and says we've got to keep our strength up. As the day wears on, she says a lot more besides that. She's genuinely optimistic and encouraging. She brings the energy of someone who doesn't know the scale of the situation or our exhaustion. She stands a little closer to us than we've been doing with each other and makes random conversation. I know she's trying to be a helpful distraction. Papercut and Ada are too emotionally thin to give her much back, and she doesn't even try with Lucy, so she ends up searching with me.

We're on the far left, with Camille on the outside, since no one else is in the mood to be near her. Honestly, her spark is a relief in the midst of these heavy days, especially now that we're in a patch of dying trees. Their branches are thinning and turning a sickly orange. When I brush against them, their needles fall. It's still hot out. This place is tinder, like it could spontaneously burst into flames.

You won't catch Camille complaining. I respect the way she jumped right in with no questions asked and made no comment when we ate snacks from our backpacks without stopping for a break. She says she's fine, but as evening wears on, I insist she split some of what I've got left.

"These are good," she says through a mouthful of bagel. "Where'd you get them? RUBY!"

I wait a moment before sending out my own call and letting

it move down the line. "I baked them a while ago and froze them."

"Amazing! I'm impressed."

"Or hungry."

"It's a compliment. You just say, 'Thank you very much, Camille.' You'll get it with practice. You were at my party. Did you hear about Morgyn?"

Now I'm interested. I look to my right, but the next person's too far away to be catching any of our conversation. "I left not long after the power went out."

"Just in time then! First of all, I can't believe she showed up. It was a great party, but still, *Morgyn*? We chatted a bit, then she seemed like she wanted to drink alone." Camille makes that exchange out to be more pleasant than it was.

"Alone with company, I suppose," I say.

"I guess? Anyway, Morgyn got weird after the power went out. She blocked the front door with her truck, then she went around starting everyone's cars and leaving them idling with the headlights on. Some in front of the house, some behind the yard, some around the side. It was like a square of light. Weird, but kind of sweet. The light really helped keep the party going. RUBY! Shout back if you can hear me!"

Morgyn was forming a perimeter of light around the biggest concentration of people in Sawblade. There's no reason she would do that with such urgency other than to keep something at bay.

"Oh my god!" Camille's pointing into the trees. "Ruby! Guys, I see her!" Camille races into the brush before I can hold her back. I call over my shoulder as I chase her.

There, ahead, a speck of cornflower blue darting through the orange and faded green. Moving away from us. There's no way Ruby runs away from us if she's in charge of her own body and mind.

She swerves right. It's easy to see her now. She's still got her purple backpack on and her blue jacket around her waist. She's aiming for the deeper woods instead of town, which lets our line collapse around her. Papercut and Lucy have sprinted to get to the other side. We've got her surrounded, closing in.

I think of how Ruby compared the monster to a dog. You wouldn't jump the fence.

You wouldn't corner it.

Ada's talking gently, as if Ruby is merely agitated or distressed. Papercut's a live wire, ready to explode into motion. Lucy looks terrified, Camille relieved. Ruby's face comes into view as our circle slowly tightens, revealing something else entirely.

She's gaunt and filthy. It's like she's withered and tightened all at once. Her clothes, hair, even skin are packed with grime. Dirt, sap, shit, pine needles, sawdust, leaves. It's worst around her mouth. There are smears of dried liquid. For a moment, I'm scared it's blood, but it's richer and dirtier than that.

Ruby's breathing heavily. I'm close enough now to see the gunk and stains inside her mouth. Darkened lips and gums and black lines etching around each tooth. I don't know what she's consuming, but it's like her mouth is becoming the monster's.

"Ruby, hey," says Ada. They've got their empty hands held out, with the palms facing Ruby like she's an angry animal Ada's trying to calm. Looking at Ruby's teeth, I think maybe Ada should be holding the axe from the side of her backpack. "It's all right. We're here now. You're all right."

Ruby turns her head slowly, considering each of us. I can sense Cas clenched and heartbroken to have Ruby look at Ada like that. I can read the same from Ada, I swear.

When Ruby's eyes pass over me, I feel the shadow that watches me at night the nearest it's been. It presses down on my chest, like I'm drawing a deep breath that I can't stop pulling into my lungs. It's as if I hit a breaking point and still more of something needs to rush into every corner of skin.

Ruby blinks once, then her gaze settles on Camille.

"Hey, honey, you're not lost anymore." Camille's taken on a comforting tone. "You look really hungry. Whatever you've been eating is not good. I'll get you some proper food as soon as we're back at my place. Want this bagel for now?" We all watch as Camille takes the final few steps toward Ruby and offers her the remaining half of the bagel.

Ruby goes from still to clawed blur in an instant. Her hand shoots out, grabbing Camille's wrist instead of the bagel. Camille screams as Ruby drags her close and twists. Camille, flipped onto her back on the ground, her basket crushed and hat flown off. Ruby has a fistful of Camille's hair, holding her head up with one hand while the other draws back, fingers outstretched like talons.

We all rush forward. Papercut gets there first and grabs Ruby's hand as it slashes toward Camille. Ruby throws Papercut with one arm, sending them sprawling into the jagged branches of a pine. I hear something grate and pop sickeningly in Ruby's shoulder. She drops Camille and twists away from the rest of us. I see her reach into the side pocket of her backpack just as I'm about to get to her.

There's the sound of a strike and a fizz and then a flash of red light that stops me in my tracks. Ruby's holding a lit road flare. It's sparking, threatening the ground beneath our feet. The dried pine needles are like gasoline. This grove of trees is ready to become a furnace the instant Ruby drops the flare.

Lucy's kneeling beside Camille. Ada helps Papercut back to their feet. They're bleeding from a slash near their eye and from countless other places. One hand's clutching a deeper gouge in their side. Despite the wounds, Papercut and Ada start toward Ruby.

Ruby simply shakes her head, and we all stop moving.

I have to shield my eyes to get a good look at Ruby's face. There are two beings in there. One is the cage and the other is the fingers wrapped around the bars. Her filthy mouth is grinning. Her eyes are weeping. She winces as each tear rolls down her cheek, clearing lines in the dirt. When she shakes her head, I can't tell if she's protecting or threatening us.

Or if there's any difference.

Ruby backs away into the thicker trees with the lit flare held out in front of her. Ada and Papercut radiate the long misery of being this close to Ruby, then watching her disappear. The sun has almost set. Even though this thing is in her, we always go back to the light. Once it's dark, chasing her through the woods would be useless and too unknown.

Ada's calling and reaching out, her feet rooted to the ground. Lucy and I have to physically hold Papercut back. There's blood in their eyes and on my hands as I dig my heels in.

"It's okay!" yells Papercut. "I know it wasn't you, Ruby!"

"She'll start a fire," says Lucy.

"And?" Papercut finally collapses to their hands and knees. "I'd run into a fire for her."

"You're not running anywhere." I wrap my arms around them and heave them back to standing unsteadily. "It won this round. We've got to get into the light and get you patched up."

Camille's finally managed to get up. Her eyes are wide. "Papercut? Are you all right?"

"Look at them!" snaps Lucy. "Did you *see* what just fucking went down? All right is happy-ever-after fantasy bullshit right now."

"I'm sorry," returns Camille with almost equal bite, "were you the one who got judo tossed by some kid?"

"Was I the one all innocently traipsing around the woods by myself?" returns Lucy. "Who even picks berries?"

"I was making a *PIE*!"

"Camille," gasps Papercut. "I'd love some pie. But Cedar's right. We shouldn't be in the woods at night."

"The thing that's in Ruby used to only be able to be out in the dark," I say. "It killed TJ, Oliver, and Kat at the Point."

"Oh" is all Camille says.

Her face is still, like she's forgotten to pick an expression. Maybe she wants to disbelieve, but that's not her. There's nothing positive for her to find either. She can't offer comfort as a way of comforting herself. She's just left holding this new knowledge, not knowing where to put it or what to do with it or what to ask or whether she even wants to or even wants to look at it. I know that path. You go as far inside yourself as you can and keep trying to act normal to keep as much distance as you can.

"Wish you'd explained that before," Camille says. "But I can see why you didn't." She hesitates, tries to hide her twitch at a clatter of dry branches touched by a rare hint of wind. "So this 'it' is a . . . a monster?"

I hate to nod confirmation, to give an answer so blunt it doesn't need words. Yes, it is that. In purest form, impure.

"Oh, okay. Just wanted to make sure." Growing up in Sawblade must build thick calluses where showing your fear should be, because Camille leaves it there. Nothing else other than moving closer to the rest of us.

I want to say I'm sorry she had to find out, but my empathy's stretched thin across the battered people around me. It's spread around the salt water and blood poured out by the ones I love. My empathy is walking through the woods with a child who's been forced to flee from the only people who know she needs to be saved.

Empathy is with me from a few weeks ago, stumbling on the body of the only parent I had left.

"You weren't wrong," I hear Papercut whisper to Lucy. "All right is bullshit. It's been bullshit my whole life."

"It won't be that way forever," says Lucy back. "Not if I've got anything to do with it. And I've got something to do with everything."

Ada's wandered away from the rest of us. She's touching the bare white wood of a tree, tracing lines with her fingers. "Ruby was writing." Ada sounds far away. "It talked, she carved. It's on this one. And one over there."

The words have been slashed in with a knife. That must have been in her bag too. I hate to think what she could have done with a blade. The flare was lucky. It might have been mercy.

We find a total of four carved-up trees. There's an order, but it takes us a minute to piece it together. And even then, the words sound like they're from a muddled mind.

NO, THIS IS FIRST

IN CLEARNESS, A GLIMPSE ALL THE WAY TO WHERE THE SUN CAN'T REACH. COLD DOWN THERE WHERE I LIVE. NOW A FORM TO THINK, TO SHARPEN AND UNDERSTAND. TO CUT TOWARD SURFACE AND ONE DAY BREAK IT. I NEED. I THINK. I KNOW. I THINK I KNOW WHAT I NEED AND HOW TO GRASP IT.

FIRST

THESE TREES LIKE BODY, UNABLE TO WITHSTAND INVASION. POISON THEIR GROUND. FULL AT ONE HEART EACH BUT HOLDING HANDS WITH LONG ROOTS.

AFTER TREES

NOW MINE TO BE SEEN, STILL NOT MINE TO BE WITNESSED. IN DAMAGE DONE AND VENOM DRUNK IN WILD THIRST. WARPED RIGHT DOWN TO MY SHAME AT WHAT MUST BE DONE.

AFTER ALL

NOT RIGHT NOT RIGHT NOT OF MY BLOOD NOT OF MY BOND. BLOODLINE CURSED AND THE CURSE UNBROKEN IN THE VEIN. THE SAME VEIN, FROM ROCK TO WALL TO THE GRANITE BANKS OF A DEAD LAKE.

CHAPTER THIRTY-ONE

WE BARELY MAKE IT BACK UNDER THE STREETLIGHTS OF Sawblade Lake before nightfall.

The last few minutes were a rush, going as quickly as Papercut's injuries and our exhaustion allowed. Papercut was ready to have us leave them behind. Everyone agreed that was out of the question. Even Lucy and Camille agreed with each other.

Camille's got questions she can't avoid, as much as she wants to. She says first she needs to shower and change and try to get the stains out of her jumpsuit. Papercut needs to get bandaged up. They need stitches, honestly, though they can't be bothered. Those aren't the worst scars they'll have from what Ruby did to them.

We agree to meet at Lucy's later that night. Her and I go straight there and close Lucy's bedroom door. We shut the blinds and draw thick curtains on top of them. We put an old movie on for comforting white noise, and Lucy talks about celebrity gossip from when the film was released.

We take turns in the tiny bathroom attached to Lucy's bedroom, trying to scrub the day off. When it's my turn, I sit on the floor of the shower. It seems like the monster believes possessing Ruby is helping it think, yet its ramblings are still nonsense.

Poison trees holding roots? Bloodlines, shame, curses, and desire. No, *need*. Grasping through the surface.

I look at the veins in my arms. There's been times when the world crushed me into apathy, but I've never wanted to die. Today reminded me of that. My incredible frailty could have been spilled out by Ruby. I imagine her fingers touching the hilt of her knife in her backpack, then choosing the flare instead.

Whose bloodline am I? My mother, my grandma, generations before them. Mixing together and swirling through me.

My father.

Beetles under my skin.

Papercut said if I notice them boring into me, I should end myself.

Lucy knocks on the door. "Cedar, you good in there? The hot-water tank must be almost empty by now. I hope you're not at cold-shower-level despair. I thought you'd want to know that Ada called. Her and Papercut will be here soon. Ada, Cedar! Your all-time major crush. How are you going to know if it's mutual if you waste away in the shower?"

I reach forward and turn the water off. The steam is warm. As soon as I pull the curtain back, cooler air will rush in, so I just sit there.

"You're alive!" says Lucy. "Or you collapsed into the shower knob. I forgot to grab you a towel, one second . . ."

When I hear the bathroom door open, I stick a hand from behind the curtain. Lucy passes me a clean beach towel with umbrellas on it. "It is mutual, by the way," I say.

"Whaaaaat? How did you figure it out?" says Lucy from

the other side of the curtain. "Was it the innumerable massive hints she gave you?"

"We kissed. At Camille's party."

"YOU AND ADA KISSED?!"

I bury my face in the towel. Lucy's improbable, irrepressible. She can hold grief and jubilation at the same time. She has me smiling into the towel.

"How was it?" she asks.

"Like . . . good."

"*Like . . . good,*" imitates Lucy. "I'm not leaving the bathroom until you tell me more. Give me the towel back. I'll hold it hostage."

"Fine fine fine."

"It was fine?"

"No, it was fucking magical and sexy and the hottest moment of my life. We went into the pantry to avoid Morgyn, and we were standing so close together." I've replayed this over and over and over and over. I've stood naked in front of the mirror and touched every spot she touched me. "And it just happened. There was a moment a minute before where I knew. I was looking at her, and I didn't hide that I wanted her. They reflected it right back at me."

"A cosmic connection," sighs Lucy. And I haven't even mentioned Cascade. "So you kissed, it altered your whole perception of reality and what desire can be, and then . . ."

"You're pushy, you know that?"

"You're unnecessarily cagey."

"I don't know. We kissed a bunch and started undressing,

and Ada started touching me more." I'll bet Lucy can see me blush through the shower curtain. "Then the power went out and interrupted us."

"Jesus goddamn cruel world. That decides it. I'm becoming an electrician. I'll fix the grid myself. So when you say 'touching more . . .'"

"Didn't you get interrupted too?"

"How . . . What? I was just with Papercut. If anything, the power outage rescued me."

"Mm-hmm?"

"No, no nope not allowed. That's not a thing. Don't reverse on me like that. Papercut's a walking, sometimes talking irritation. And they're into Camille."

"Who did Papercut create extreme croquet with?" I ask.

"Me. I'm the life of any party."

"Are they dating Camille? Are they some monogamous unit?"

"No, but they've hooked up before," says Lucy. "It's obvious."

"Do you love every person you've ever hooked up with?"

"None of them."

"Do you still get along with some of them? Maybe even flirt?"

"I never should have come in here," Lucy laughs. "I bring you a towel and in return I get attacked. But whatever. Even if I somehow *like* Papercut or whatever, they're all distant and broken right now. More than usual, I mean. Have you kissed Ada since the party?"

I see Lucy changing the subject, and I let her. Now's not

a time to push. "We've only talked about it once since Ruby went missing." Though I keep the details of that moment with Ada at the cabin to myself.

"Well, now we've got one more reason to save Ruby. For your love life."

"Our?"

"Shut up. I said 'your.'" I hear Ada and Papercut arrive, and Lucy leaves the bathroom to go say hello to them. Camille should be here soon too.

When I get out of the shower, my clothes are gone. Is no moment sacred to Lucy? I tell her about the kiss, and a minute later she's pulling more strings than ever. I'm kind of tall to be wrapping myself in this towel. Though I should borrow some clean things from Lucy anyway, even if it does force me into wearing colors.

I do the best I can with the towel and crack the door open. Papercut's lying on the floor making a snow angel in the mess. They've got bandages on their face and wrapped around their side, arm, and leg. Ada and Lucy are on the bed watching the movie. No one seems like they want to talk about the day.

Amid Ada's numb trauma, I see a flicker in the corner of her mouth and eyes when I step out of the bathroom in a towel that marginally covers me. There's a shared memory and a promise for later. Not tonight, but someday. The things we fight to reach.

Ways to get through the night.

Things to get through the night for.

On the floor, Papercut makes a show out of covering their eyes as I walk past them so they don't see up my towel. I choose Lucy's most subtle clothing, though the jeans still have rhinestones on them. Once I'm dressed, I sit next to Ada on the bed. They're nestled between Lucy and me. It's my shoulder Ada leans on. Lucy leans on hers. Papercut climbs up and rests their head in Ada's lap. We stay that way, clustered softly against the terrors of the world.

We watch the movie silently for a while before Lucy asks, "What do we tell Camille?"

"The truth," I say.

Papercut winces as they shift positions slightly. "Whole and nothing but."

Lucy says, "As the resident keeper of info, I'm afraid we've got far far less than the whole truth. Not *afraid* as in unfortunately, *afraid* as in scared."

"We'll tell her what we know." I can feel the vibration of Ada speaking against my shoulder combined with the steady pull of Cas toward me. Though now that I know what that sensation is, Cas's and Ada's energies have gotten harder to tell apart. And it feels like our kiss swirled me and Ada and Cas even nearer.

"Camille should be here by now," says Papercut. "She's usually annoyingly punctual."

"Is that why she's—" starts Lucy, with the tone of an insult, before stopping herself. "You should check where she is."

Papercut sits up with a groan. "Wish I'd never taught Ruby to brawl." We all know that what Ruby can do has nothing to do with what any human taught her. “I’m calling Camille. Something’s off.”

Papercut reaches over Lucy’s lap for the phone on the nightstand and dials Camille’s number from memory. It rings a few times before someone picks up.

Papercut’s straight to the point. “Is Camille home? She’s meeting me and some friends tonight . . . How long ago? . . . Okay, okay. What route did she take? . . . Birchwood’s a time-saver for sure . . . Thanks. No worries. I think I see her pulling up.” There are still two layers covering the windows.

Papercut hangs up before the person on the other end has finished talking. Their look confirms trouble. “It’s been too long. I’m going to take a look out there. Who’s coming?”

When we open the bedroom door, the dog is barking at the back entrance. She paws at the glass, then pushes up against it, straining to see. Her nose is twitching, pulling in whiffs of something from the kitchen window Lucy’s dad left cracked open.

“What’s that way?” I ask.

“Nothing much,” says Ada.

Lucy’s hugging herself like it’s suddenly gotten cold. “Nothing much is right. The empty lots where those town houses burnt a few years ago are over there.”

“Gap in the teeth,” mutters Papercut. They pick up the small dog and set her on the couch. “Cyndi, *stay*.”

We stick close to the houses and each other, walking through backyards instead of on the road when we can. I can hear each of us breathing. Ada starts when I stumble over a child’s discarded toys in a backyard and swear. Up ahead, I can see the space between the houses.

I squint. There's a huge bent lump in the middle of the darkest stretch of road. On the side closest to the trees. Something so broken that I can't tell what it is at first. I look for long limbs jutting out of it until I make out tires facing the sky. A car.

A wreck.

We start running.

We stop.

• • •

Dad,

After we read Ruby's journal, Papercut said this thing took the best part of us away. Papercut was right.

It keeps taking.

And taking.

Christ, it's so hungry for every shard of light we have.

Here's Camille's eulogy—from someone who met her twice, written to someone who never will. Camille was good. She cared. If someone can say that about you after you die, you haven't really ended. Camille was sad Morgyn celebrated her birthday alone, so she invited Morgyn to her party. Camille helped us search without question. When we found Ruby looking like fear itself,

Camille stepped forward to offer her food. For Camille, I pray the moments of her demise don't color the peace of her rest. Amen.

After the dam broke, me and Mom drove past the far reach of the water. It'd receded some, leaving behind the crumpled husks of cars. Inside, bodies shaken drowned crushed. Mom told me not to look. Camille's car was like that, but with the marks of teeth and claws. The car had been dragged to the edge of the trees and halfway trash-compacted in jaws beyond any crocodile or shark. Through the passenger door, we could see Camille hanging upside down, locked in her seat belt. Blood spatters and twisted neck. We stood across the road. None of us would dive into the full darkness to retrieve a corpse.

It's reaching farther. Circling closer. Ruby shook her head to tell us not to follow her, but it was already too late. The thing had to make an example. It chose the one who reached out.

We're back in Lucy's room now. We were . . . are, all incoherent. Ada kept saying there was another way to look. She said a watchtower or a spyglass. A way beyond us to see beyond us. Grief guilt shaken drowned crushed. They found a pack of crayons and drew dense drawings without form until they slumped over. Papercut fell asleep with headphones playing music so loud I could sing along. I'm sitting up next to Lucy in bed. She's working on her TALK files while I, most incomprehensible of all, write to you.

Sometimes I think it would do just as much good to walk to the edge of the woods and scream these words at the monster instead.

Yours,
Cedar

CHAPTER THIRTY-TWO

WITHOUT A SEARCH PLAN FOR THE DAY, WE WAKE UP LATE. Papercut left us a note. After last night, I'm afraid what it might contain, but it just says: *Went to Wharf Fry to fix some stuff + clear my head + keep my job. Meet me there.* That's more words than any of the rest of us have this morning. Lucy's parents say bright *good mornings* to us. Lucy does all the talking. Wharf Fry for brunch, she says.

"Did you all hear Cyndi going off last night?" asks Lucy's dad. "Must be raccoons or something."

"Or something," says Ada. She's got me worried this morning. They're twitchy and noncommunicative in a way I haven't seen from them before. She's got a snapped crayon she's fiddling with incessantly. It's clinging together by a piece of untorn paper.

Ruby gone, Ruby found, Ruby still gone. Ruby walking away. Camille gone too, and that's tipped Ada over an edge. If it's painful just to watch her like this, what's it like inside? I can't imagine. Though I do know that since we got up, Cas's radiating energy has been a thunder in my body. I can feel it straining to reach me.

"Well, we're off to Wharf Fry!" says Lucy before her parents can ask any questions about Ada's ominous statement. "Byyyyye."

When we arrive at the diner, there's a *Closed* sign on the door, but it's unlocked. We find Papercut in the kitchen lying halfway under a commercial sink. The room smells like fried food, burnt bread, and whatever gunk came out of the pipes Papercut's working on.

"You heard?" asks Papercut.

Lucy's immediately unsettled. "No, I haven't heard. *You* heard something before *me*? I'm never sleeping late again."

"I don't hear, I just see," says Ada. Their crayon breaks, half falling to the tile and rolling under an oven. She presses her face against the stained floor to look for it. Where are they? I don't know how to get her distant, intense eyes back to us. Anything I say to them seems to deflect away.

"Cedar, light that griddle and start some eggs and bacon and hash browns and shit," says Papercut. "We should get some food in Ada." Good, yes, something practical to do to take care of the ache around and in me.

"It's hungry, not me." Ada lies on the greasy floor and reaches their arm under the oven.

Papercut doesn't seem particularly fazed by Ada's behavior. They keep working on the sink. Soon I've got some food sizzling and Ada's found her crayon, only to shift her attention to searching through cupboards and drawers for no apparent reason. I hate how they leave the doors open behind them.

Papercut reaches out for another tool. "People found Camille's car this morning in the ditch on the road to Abraham's Corner. It was all up in flames. I ran into Tommy while I was walking here. His cousin drove by the wreck."

"Could it have dragged the car all the way there?" I ask. Playing with its food, but I don't say that part.

"No way to stick to the dark the whole time," says Lucy. "So it's Morgyn, right? We're all thinking Morgyn."

"I figure so," says Papercut. "Morgyn said Camille's car got hit by a logging truck—as if there's many of those here anymore. Said she's searching for who's responsible."

I'm barely aware of the food I'm flipping as I think my way through it. "She patrols all the time. She finds the wreck, tows it, and lights it on fire."

"Was Camille's body . . . ?" asks Lucy.

"Like I said, Morgyn ran the whole situation," says Papercut, "but I didn't hear anything about a body. About Camille." Papercut's voice catches in their throat.

Lucy goes over to the sink and crouches beside Papercut. For a moment she considers what to say, then asks, "Would it help if I held that flashlight?"

Papercut wordlessly hands it to her.

"This could be like with Kat," I suggest. "Morgyn's keeping panic down, making sure there's no trace of anything unnatural."

"I'm going to say something that might sound ridiculous," announces Lucy.

"Make it into a T-shirt." Papercut had that at the ready.

"You know I would," says Lucy. "But listen. Okay." She takes a deep breath. "To me, and I'm just throwing it out there,

Morgyn going to all that trouble sounds less like keeping panic down and more like removing evidence."

Papercut cranks something with a wrench. Ada opens a drawer with a rattle of cutlery.

I portion the food onto knife-marked white plates. "I think Morgyn's on our side."

"Got to Camille and the Point awfully quick and still too late." Papercut emerges from under the sink and sits up. Their face is stained and sweaty. "You haven't been here for long enough to know. Morgyn's on her own side."

I think of what my grandma said. Morgyn never loses. Would she pick the same side of the fight as us even if it was the losing one? The monster could have exerted pressure on her in that house all alone outside of town. Or worse. Power and justice are matters of appetite. Hers could have grown too big. Morgyn's in control. Morgyn takes. It's all there in her revolver resting against her thigh and the way she kissed my hands.

"Emerald and Ruby," says Ada. "Shining red. Car door." She's finally found what she was looking for—some tape. She starts wrapping the crayon over and over to mummify it, trying to reattach the broken half.

Papercut sits on the counter and grabs a plate of food with a curt nod to me. "You convinced that Morgyn helping Ruby with Emerald was selfless? I'm not."

"Did Ada give Morgyn something in exchange?" asks Lucy. She takes her own plate of food and sits next to Papercut. I try to give one to Ada, but she ignores it. I take that plate for myself, though I wish Ada would slow their frantic energy enough to eat.

Papercut takes a big bite and talks while they chew. "Not what she wanted."

"Isn't mine to tell," says Ada.

"Seems relevant," mutters Papercut.

"Not my story," returns Ada. "Promised."

Papercut slams their plate down on the counter. "Fuck, you're wrong, you know that? And Morgyn was wrong to make you promise not to tell right after she'd saved Ruby. With you in her debt. Was probably her whole plan. It *is* your story. It's part of who she is. And you've kept enough secrets. I'm going to tell it unless you stop me." Papercut waits a beat. "Okay, so Morgyn kissed Ada right after they got Ruby stable again."

Lucy drops her cutlery onto her plate with a clatter. Inside, my heart does the same thing. It fears the worst of what this could mean for me and Ada.

"*We* kissed," corrects Ada. "Met in the middle."

"Don't remind me," says Papercut. "But Ada told me that was it for them. A kiss in a high-emotion moment. Wasn't it for Morgyn. She went full love-confession on Ada. Wanted to be together, stay together, head to bed. Ada said no. Morgyn got angry. She yelled at Ada, kicked her and Ruby out when Ruby was barely in shape to be moved, and made her promise not to tell anyone."

"All true," murmurs Ada. "I owed her."

"Wasn't right." Papercut shakes their head. "That's the sort of way Morgyn helps. She has to have an angle, something she wants. She's no saint."

This happened a couple years ago, but now I'm woven in

too. It's in how Morgyn looks at me and what she feels and what Ada would think of the desire I harbor for Morgyn. It's in Morgyn knowing I was at Ada's cabin and wondering what Ada sees in me, then kissing my hands.

But more than nervousness, more than jealousy, a part of me understands. Because I've loved and not been loved back before. By people I kissed and one I slept with. By my own father, maybe.

"She's on our side," I repeat with less certainty than before.

"Evidence and character stack the other way," says Papercut.

Ada brushes past me toward Lucy and Papercut. They place one hand on Papercut's chest and one on Lucy's. Right over their hearts. "No one kills you for those. You don't need a mongrel guard dog."

"Your guard dog isn't trained," says Papercut.

Ada digs her fingers in. "Neither are the things it guards us from."

Lucy slides down the counter to get Ada's hand off her. "Kinda scaring me, babe."

Papercut doesn't move. "You're too trusting. But I'm betting on you, even if . . . fuck, even if you're betting on Morgyn. Doesn't mean I forget how she treated you." Papercut takes another forkful of food and holds it in front of Ada's mouth. "Eat something."

"We all—"

Papercut nudges Ada's mouth with the fork. "Eat something, then prophesy."

Ada takes the bite. She grabs Papercut's plate before she's

finished chewing and starts shoveling food in with her fingers. She holds the plate close to her mouth instead of bothering to sit down.

"We did learn something last night," I say, trying to ignore Ada's disturbed state, the sounds of ravenousness, and my own swirling emotions. "We were partly right not to search in the dark, because the monster can come and go from Ruby's body at will. But there's a flip side to that too. Once the sun sets, it doesn't need her. And when it's not in her, it must leave her somewhere. We're not going to be able to make her come home when it's controlling what she does. We've seen how strong she is. But if we could find her when the monster's roaming, she'd just be Ruby. We could get her somewhere safe."

"Night search," says Papercut. "Fun."

Lucy breaks an egg yolk and watches it run across her plate. "We'd still have to find her. While it's prowling around too."

Ada's finished the entire plate and everything left on the griddle. They wipe their mouth and say, "We all sin for something. I for love. Morgyn too." My brain's stretching to try to make sense of Ada and what I've learned. Who all loves who?

"Talk straight," says Lucy. "Well, not *straight*, but like—"

Cas's energy goes derailed. I have the sense of wanting to cover my ears, but it's in my entire body. A push and pull inside Ada that I'm somehow in the middle of.

"Shouldn't share. There's worse sinners. Much worse." Ada takes the crayon from behind her ear and starts scribbling on the griddle. The crayon's melting as she argues with herself. "Crow's nest. No. Why not? Heartbreak. Remember the dog?

I do . . . I know why not. Just Cedar. That I know why not. Just Cedar! Your nest, but they're the crow. They climb, you point. On black wings. On black wings."

"Does anyone know what she's talking about?" asks Lucy nervously.

Papercut takes another bite. "I've got a pretty good guess."

The crayon's worn all the way down, but Ada hasn't stopped trying to draw. I drop my plate and rush to her. Pull her burnt fingers back from the heat. "I'm Cedar. Just me. I'll be in your crow's nest."

"Cabin," says Ada. "Cabin, just you."

CHAPTER THIRTY-THREE

Ada takes my hand and drags me out of the restaurant. Their hands are greasy from the food they ate, but it seems to have given them new vigor and focus. That combined with a choice I don't understand.

"We'll meet you back here!" I call over my shoulder to Lucy and Papercut.

Ada continues to lead the way, walking fast. Their grip never loosens. When we reach Lucy's house, she goes straight to the ATV and starts the engine. I've barely gotten on and put my arms around them before we're tearing down the street toward the cabin. She ignores all stop signs but keeps a dead-even speed, with faith that cars will swerve around us. I can feel Cas and Ada matched in intention.

I find myself watching for Ruby's raincoat once we turn off the main road and into the woods. Now with a greater sense of threat than hope. Ruby warned us not to look. Then the monster in her showed us why.

The cabin looks the same as before. Cute, quaint. Ada doesn't seem to notice that she leaves the ATV running. They go straight inside, front door propped open for me. I kill the engine and follow. Somehow, I already know where we're going.

The heart room.

I find Ada kneeling in front of the chalkboard facing the doorway. Facing the three hearts and me looking down at her with questions.

"Ada, what are we doing?"

"Old souls, new magic." As if that answers anything. I start toward her side of the chalkboard, but she says, "No, face the window. You're seeing out. I'm seeing in."

She rummages through a pile of objects, tossing aside the cat stuffie and dog collar and emerging with a photo album. The pages snap by with hard turns until she hits one of Ruby. That slows them down. From there, each flip is tender, considered. Three times, they stop and remove a photograph. Then she walks by me to pin one in the center of each of the three hearts on the wall.

Each picture gets younger and nearer.

On the right, in the mechanical heart. Ruby this spring, shot from a distance away. I think she's in the field by the high school. There are still patches of snow clinging to the ground. She's blurry, arms raised above her head, about to launch into a cartwheel.

On the left, in the anatomical heart. This could be Ruby a year or two ago. She's in the living room of the trailer, posing in front of a wall decorated for Halloween. She's got a thin mustache drawn on her upper lip. She's wearing a fedora and the same white blazer Ada wore to the party at Camille's. The one she wore when we first searched for Ruby.

In the center, in the Valentine's heart, just a close-up of Ruby's face. Her as a little kid, the way I last saw Sky. Ruby's grinning up at the camera with chocolate ice cream stained around her lips.

Like how her mouth was in the woods yesterday, but innocent.

The room is thrumming. Cas's energy is floor-to-ceiling, wall-to-wall. I look to see if the curtains are moving, because the air feels alive. This is the power that pulled my eyes to find Ada at the Point, but cranked up until every atom, particle, and soul is vibrating.

"Ada, what are you doing?" I ask. I crouch down in front of them. "What's the crow's nest?"

"What are *we* doing," she answers. She opens a box of multicolored chalk and throws away the last bit of the crayon. This was what they really wanted. Then she starts drawing massive eyes on the chalkboard in sweeping strokes. "Lookout. Look out. Past the horizon."

"Ada, I want to help you however I can. I want to be part of we. But you have to tell me what this is." I reach toward her, but she bats my hand away, all while continuing to draw.

Within the pupils of the giant eyes, she draws smaller eyes in a few quick, decisive strokes. Then she grabs the worn-out children's running shoes and rubs the bottoms of them with charcoal until they're black. She unfolds one map of the region around Sawblade Lake and one that's just the town and lake itself. On each, she makes a pair of black footprints on top of the key to the map.

The energy's escalated again. My heart feels wrong. Sped

up, scared, not my own. This isn't familiar, doesn't echo back. New might crackling in the stillness of the room.

"Darling," I say. I've never called her that before. "Darling, are you there?"

Ada's hand tenses on the piece of charcoal she's holding until it cracks apart, showering the floor with dark powder.

I reach across the chalkboard and lift their chin up. Now I see that she drew her own eyes. Wild, hopeful, beautiful. "Cas, you have to let me talk to Ada. This is like living in the same body. It won't work otherwise."

Ada inhales and exhales slowly and deeply, all while looking me directly in the eyes. Mine are the other pair on the chalkboard. I know it. My eyes are drawn inside theirs.

"Darling," Ada says back. There she is, thank god. I could cry. I didn't want to feel alone amid the storm in this room. "Did you just call me that?"

"That's who you are to me." Now a couple tears do escape from my eyes. One hits the chalkboard, at the corner of Ada's eye. "I hope that's all right."

"It's good." Ada takes my hand. It feels like both the ground under my feet and a wave crashing down on me. "It's so, so good. It's my favorite thing in this fucked-up world right now." She touches my face, leaving charcoal marks across my skin. "Thank you for following me here. For listening to me about Morgyn instead of being threatened and acting weird. Will you go a bit further?"

"Yes." From every angle, in any way they could possibly mean.

Ada kisses me and lets it linger for a moment before pulling away. "That's in case you think I'm too Faulty for you after this and I have to get Papercut to beat you up."

"I trust you."

"That's what I'm scared of," she says, because there's nothing lonelier than misplacing your trust. "This is magic."

Rumors that have come true tear through the fabric of my reality.

"Some call the things Faulty people can do powers or abilities. Everything is science once we understand it and magic before that. I can see souls from afar. If it's someone I hold in my heart, Cas and I can cast a spell. I need two grounding points—an object of theirs and something of mine that's physically on them. Some are better than others. That rain jacket Ruby is wearing used to be mine, so that works. I've got her shoes here."

Ada describes it like it's all so simple. But even though I know about Cas and have been close to it, I have questions. Check the depth of the water before you dive in. At least know if you're going to break your neck. "What's this room for? And all the art?"

"The art is a way of grounding and casting. I started seeing flashes of a middle-school crush when I was twelve if I drew certain things. I had to line up the pieces. She had to wear the bracelet I made her, and me the hoodie I stole from her. Cas taught me what it knew, and we pieced the rest of it together through trial and error. This room is my amplifier. My heart, Cas's heart, and a third heart for love. I use it to set up connections. After that, I can usually do it from wherever with just a sketchbook. Especially if I know where the person is. Ruby is trickier though. She could be anywhere. I don't know whether to search for her or the monster."

Ada reaches into their back pocket and unfolds Ruby's sketch of the *BIG NIGHT ANIMAL.* "That's why I need this. I grabbed it from Papercut yesterday. Pin it under the middle picture of Ruby for me."

Not everything is magic before we understand it. Some things are pure, unfiltered devilry. I can't avoid looking at the hideous mouth Ruby drew. I turn my back to it after I pin it up, though that almost feels worse.

"Why do you need me?" I ask Ada. "Why not Papercut?"

"I mean first, I've never told them all of this. And second . . ." Ada holds up the dog collar. "I used to practice on our dog. I'd replaced this collar with a bandana of mine. When I was thirteen, he went missing. I saw . . . what was left. It felt different from the living, sort of static. Like reaching into the time that goes missing when you're driving on the highway and you forget how you got somewhere."

I don't want that either. I watched Sky disappear. I don't want another kid vanishing before my eyes. "You need me to look for Ruby in case things are bad?"

Ada's looking up at me. There's no way I'll say no to them. "Cas trusts you, and Papercut would never be the same if they see the worst-case scenario. I care about you too much to ask you for this. But I'm asking you because I know you care about me. And if I have to hear horrible news from anyone, I'd like it to be from you." She wipes away a tear with the back of her hand.

If I have to tell anyone horrible news, Ada is the last person whose heart I'd want to break. Yet the most I can do is support them and take some small fragment of the weight. To look when she needs to look away.

I sit across from them. "If this is what you need, darling," I say, "then let's do magic."

CHAPTER THIRTY-FOUR

"LOOK PAST ME, AT THE CURTAIN OVER THE WINDOW," orders Ada.

She grabs the colored chalk and begins to draw rapidly on the board. The sound makes me shiver in the heat of the cabin.

Then I sink right inside the shivering sensation.

I'm with Ada and Cas. I feel tightly held by the two of them. Breathlessly, impossibly close. It makes me feel like I know Ada completely, but it doesn't last long enough to hold it. Even a taste makes me want to chase that type of knowing for all I'm worth. It's beyond what I felt at the Point, or kissing Ada, or whatever good thing has been watching me through the night.

The other side slithers in. I feel the sensation of red eyes watching me in the night. It's like I'm half of what watched over me, searching for the other half.

My eyes are open, but I'm somewhere else. At first the images are blurred, going by too fast. There's no hint of location. A lucid dream fully experienced in my brain. I know my body is still in the room with Ada. Yet there's wind pulling at my skin and pine branches scratching my body. The smells of chemicals and forest and sewage and sawdust.

I'm in the blanket fort. Tay's cowering against the wall. Ruby—no, it must be Ruby after the thing has already possessed her—is putting on the raincoat and cinching the hood and bottom as tight as they'll go.

Next, I see Ruby running for the edge of town, occasionally glancing at the sky.

Then the concrete lid of an old backyard septic tank. Ruby heaves it open a sliver and jumps inside, landing up to her waist in sewage. She breathes deeply, satisfied, and pushes her back against the wall of the tank. I can see lightning flash above.

New scene. I hear my own voice. Then, a bit later, Lucy's. Ada. Papercut. We're calling for Ruby, but she's hiding inside a hollowed-out windfall. Our voices fade away. The tree's so rotten Ruby's arm punches through it as she crawls out.

Another cut. Wilted plants. A stream of runoff freshly flush with rainwater tainted by the contaminated bed it flows in. It's emptying into the lake. I know this place. It's below

the sawmill.

Overgrown, collapsed rooflines and what's left of smokestacks. Ruby wades through the toxic drainage and surveys the ruins.

She smiles

like this is a good place.

Then, knife pressed into a bone tree, carving carving carving. Where we found her words. Her hand slips and nicks one of her fingers. The blood looks slow and thick.

She smiles

like this is a good place.

Last. Last? Not too far from the mill. I can still see a

smokestack. A little toward the lake, there's a logging truck partly sunk in the runoff. A tilted cab marred with profane graffiti where Ruby sleeps restlessly behind the glass.

There are stars out.

Breakaway

car crash teeth
crashing through metal and never before
have I felt so hungry. It smells
like my grandma's pantry
like the basement of the old house
by the wide bunker door.
Darkness and turbines screaming, pushed to their limit.

Rip back.

The image is sharper, and the sensations are less muddled. I can tell that this is now or a moment ago. Ruby's crawling out of the cab of the sunken logging truck by the sawmill. She's sleeping here. That's what I wanted to know. I didn't want to see the empty bottle of tequila and tipped container of engine oil in the cab. The melted vat of chocolate ice cream swarming with flies. She takes a red jerrican with her.

Ruby runs. Toward Sawblade. The lake, the town, the lake, the town.

The town.

* * *

The spell's broken. My eyes refocus to see chalk dust everywhere. The chalkboard is a multicolored explosion. The maps are marked with a crisscross of clumsy lines. Ada's shirt is drenched in sweat, and one of her lips is bleeding from her biting it in concentration. For a second, I can't sort out why they're looking at me with such tense anticipation.

"Ruby's okay," I say. Relief washes over Ada's face. "She's alive. When it's out of her . . ."

Car crash teeth. Bunker door.

". . . she sleeps in an old logging truck near the sawmill. But she's moving toward Sawblade right now."

"That's why the spell snapped. I've got to establish it better. Give me a minute." Ada wipes the chalkboard clear and begins drawing again, occasionally referencing a map. They tell me to focus on the window again a few times, but the minutes tick by and no images tear through me.

"How is she so fast?" mutters Ada. Ruby must be at the threshold of what her body can endure, even with whatever strength the monster's poured into her. "I'm going to get a lock on her soon."

I stay concentrated, tense and ready for my mind to be thrown somewhere else. I don't want to see the monster's memories, or mine. I couldn't tell which was which. I just need to know what Ruby's up to, though I'm afraid of that too. One corner of the anticipation is without fear though. The part where I could feel my psyche merge with Ada's.

It hits in a rush. For one sweet moment, Ada's presence fills my body.

What's next isn't so lovely. I see Ruby slowing as she exits the woods and enters town. She's got her hood up and head down, navigating back alleys and yards, holding the jerrican with both arms. I have a deep sense of horror and childhood hand in hand. It's like I've checked under the bed at night and found both the child and the terror there.

Arson. Of course with its new hands it would claim the hungriest element. It knows so many places from following me. So many veins to cut. I don't see the one it's chosen until Ruby stops in front of the old white wooden sign for the local church.

All Are Welcome.

And just beyond it, I see the number beside the church doors, something I've never noted before.

56.

The open mailbox number I was missing.

It's . . . what day? Thursday. When my grandma and I were making preserves, she took a break on Thursday to go to some sort of meeting at the church. She's inside. I push back against Ada and Cas, but the balance is uneven. They're bent on getting a fix on Ruby that they can replicate. I want to scream that we have to go now. We've got to warn the people in the church. The dry, cracked wood of that old building is like campfire logs carefully stacked around someone I love.

Ruby heads for the back entrance. She's limping slightly in a way that's too old for her body. The door swings open in front of her. As she enters the basement, every cupboard and storage closet and toy chest follows suit. She flicks gasoline into each room, making lines along the floor. I can hear some chatter above her. They haven't noticed. The double doors at the front of the church are already open to stop the church from overheating.

It's set. Ruby inhales the fumes and leaves, sealing the basement up behind her. She walks around the building and pauses just outside the front doors. Scans the park surrounding the church until her eyes settle on what she wants. Picnic tables with heavy steel frames. She drags four of them over with apparent ease. She closes the double doors and barricades them. My eyes are drawn to her grimy mouth and the black gunk in her teeth as

she smiles

at this good place

and throws a lighter through the open basement window.

I know what it is to be trapped inside.

Ruby runs around the side of the building and sits with her back against the final door. There's no exit now. I can smell the smoke.

"There!" Ada's voice, but I'm still looking at Ruby. She braces her small form against someone on the other side, fighting to get out of the burning building. Grandma or one of her friends. Frail bones and aging bodies that are no match for the malice coursing through Ruby.

"I've got it!" says Ada. "Cedar, I've got it. You can come back!"

The world of the spell is rocking back and forth like an earthquake. Ruby's humming a song I recognize. It's lilting and mournful. Something I know because it was one of my dad's favorites. A song that's wandered with me and arrived on the mixtape Ada pulled from inside my skull.

Does Ruby know that song, or does it? Whose melody and message is this?

A sudden stinging pain hits my face. The scene goes sideways. My eyes snap open. I'm lying on the rough floor of the spare room of Ada's cabin, with sunlight slanting through the window. Each beam is clear, catching dust particles and thin wisps of smoke.

Ada's kneeling in front of me. "I'm sorry. I released it, but you didn't come back. I was shaking you and it wasn't working, so I slapped you."

I push myself into a sitting position. The song Ruby was humming is echoing in my mind. I can still smell the smoke.

"Ada! Fire!"

We both jump to our feet. The map of Sawblade Lake has burst into flame, as if the tongues of fire are lapping at us from through the vision. The map's burning outward from a pinprick where the church used to be marked. It's like the monster looking back at us. The map's gone before either of us can react, leaving fragments of scorched paper hovering around the room.

The flames are trying to spread to the magic supplies and the wooden floor. Ada grabs a heavy blanket from one of their piles of tracking objects and throws it over the blaze. She pats it down, stifling whatever fire remains before it's out of control. Ada won't let anything happen to this haven they're trying to build.

I'm about to help, but I catch a glimpse of red that used to be under the blanket on the floor. There's a bracelet made from twisted guitar strings and a pair of underwear, but peeking out from under them, a black cord and a red pendant. I reach down and close my hand around the shard of red plastic. The broken edge is worn smooth from me rubbing it for comfort.

It's the necklace I lost at the Point. I lied and told Ada I'd gone back to look for it to cover how Cas pulled me to her. Ada didn't say anything when I told them. For weeks, she hasn't said that she has this. I stuff it in my back pocket before Ada can see that I've grabbed it.

"What the fuck was that fire?" gasps Ada, wiping ash away from her cheek in a smear. Their face is ragged with the fatigue of grief and magic, sorrow and heat.

All are welcome, the necklace, notes of a familiar song. Things my mind doesn't wish to know, but they're in there anyway. I'm paralyzed for a second as the vision punches into my consciousness again. Ada's eyes go wide with horror at the look on my face.

"It's burning them alive," I manage. Then the urgency hits my muscles, and I grab the keys and run.

CHAPTER THIRTY-FIVE

WE FOLLOW A DARK PILLAR OF SMOKE TO SAWBLADE. IT guides us from the wilderness but tells us we're too late long before we arrive on the scene.

As we near the church, the smoke hangs in the air. It makes the light thinner and weaker. Burnt flecks of hymnal pages float down from above. There are two beat-up fire trucks from the volunteer fire department that followed the same billowing clouds as us. People are scattered around the park and clustered on the nearest sidewalks. They're gawking, but they're sticking close together. They can sense this isn't right.

It comes into view. What's left. Holy ground turned to scorched earth.

It's a blackened skeleton vomiting smoke into the sky. The roof's collapsed, the stained glass windows shattered. All remnants of color are gone. Every plant in the garden boxes near the church walls is wilted and gray with ash. On one side, the tops of the arched window frames are burnt off, leaving them like pincers reaching upward. The other wall has fully caved in, burying the sanctuary in debris. Above it all rises the bony ruins of the steeple.

This is a place of death now. More than the peaceful cemetery behind it or the beige funeral home across the street.

I'm off the ATV and searching the crowd, calling out for my grandma before Ada and I have even come to a full stop. Faces faces faces. I have a hint of recognition of all of them. It increases my panic as each one prompts the smallest surge of hope in my chest, then stifles it.

"Grandma!" That's no use. Only Sky knows her the same way she's beloved by me. That name is how she holds us in generations.

No one seems to know what's going on. People were pulled out. Corpses, maybe? They know who I'm talking about, haven't seen her. There are sympathetic eyes on me. Firefighters, unapproachable in full suits, are still spraying water on the remains. I'll claw through the smoldering wreckage if I have to. Someone must have an idea.

Mongrel's parked on the lawn near the church's front entrance. The picnic tables have been thrown to either side of the open doors. I can't see Morgyn, but she'll know something. Maybe the truth, and maybe she'll tell it. That's Papercut's voice in my head noting how fast Morgyn's been on each scene, yet always too late. Lucy saying it looked more like cleanup than rescuing. The thought of Morgyn and Ada kissing, Morgyn's heart on her sleeve, and her surge of anger for the person she claimed feelings for. I'm trying, but it doesn't sit right in me to trust anyone who's hurt Ada.

I find Morgyn frowning at the back of the church sign. Her hair's pulled into a ponytail, and her gun's on her hip. Someone walks up to her, and she steers them away from the sign.

From behind me, Lucy says, "Remember at the Point, I said Morgyn's top of the Sketchy Person List. She's T-R-O-U-B—"

"Carrion," interrupts Papercut. "A fucking vulture. Keeping everyone calm but no interest in stopping the slaughter."

I turn around to see Lucy and Papercut. It feels impossible that I saw them hours ago. These harrowing days, I'm jolting forward through time. It rushes, but each interval feels long. My mind is coming apart at the seams, I swear. Seams, mines. I'm in Lucy's arms, and that holds things together.

"Do you know if anyone made it out alive?" I ask.

"We've been trying to find out," says Papercut. "Doesn't look good though."

"Your grandma was in there, right?" Lucy gives Papercut a pointed look. "She'll be okay. She's double tough like only an old lady can be."

"Yeah, she'll be fine," agrees Papercut. "Where's Ada?"

A sharp gunshot cracks through the air, making everyone turn. Morgyn's standing on top of Mongrel, feet spread apart in her combat boots and her gun held in the air. "Show's over, folks! Time to clear out! We've got to let the fire crew do their work. There are two ambulances on their way from Fort Luthe."

"Who did this?" someone yells.

Morgyn puts on a pair of dark sunglasses.

"Smells like gasoline!" calls another person.

"Smells like hate!"

"Who blocked the doors?"

Morgyn waves away the comments. "Doesn't take arson to light up a pile of kindling. Everything's primed to burn in this heat. What we can figure out will be in the newspaper tomorrow morning. Now clear out!"

People slowly start to disperse. Lucy leads me toward the fire trucks. "They don't call ambulances for dead people."

"Or healthy ones," mutters Papercut, but they follow us. "It isn't like Morgyn to be public like this. It's not right. Where's Ada?"

I see them emerging from around the back of the church, shoulders slumped. So Ruby's gone. Morgyn's head turns to follow Ada to our group. She keeps looking at us altogether too long, ignoring the firefighter trying to talk to her.

Ada crumples into Papercut, and they put their arm around her. "You better now?"

"Was I acting weird before?"

"Oh my god *yes*," says Lucy. "You were glitching out saying the randomest shit."

"It was nothing much," says Papercut, picking the biggest flake of gray ash out of Ada's hair and blowing it away.

Now that people are leaving, I can actually get close to the responders. A guy who has the look of being in charge without ever getting near a fire stops the four of us. "You heard Morgyn. Let us do our job."

"My grandma was in there."

"Lotta old folks were in there."

"Can you just tell me if she's all right?"

He's about to reiterate that I should leave them to work. Each one of my three friends is ready to throw hands about it. Thankfully, a hoarse voice calls from the other side of a fire truck. "Cedar? Is that you?"

I dart past the man and run around the vehicle. My grandma's there, lying flat on her back in the shade of the fire truck. Her head is propped up by a folded blanket. Her face and long, white hair are stained black, and there are bandages wrapped around her hands and on parts of her face. She looks almost forgotten, removed from the group of people giving more-urgent care to the injured on stretchers. The volunteer fire department doesn't have body bags, but I can count at least four lumps hidden under a tarp.

I kneel beside my grandma. I'm crying, gently holding her hand. She gives a soft there-there and tells me she's fine. I keep my back to the tarp. I can't look at it. If the monster had its way, my grandma would be just another body under a sheet.

"I'm so sorry. I'm so, so sorry this happened."

"Me too," she says, patting my hand with her bandaged palm. "Me too, Cedar."

"This is my fault. It followed me here."

She looks confused. When she tries to say something, violent coughing comes out instead.

"I'm cursed, Grandma. Death's on my heels."

She recovers her voice and uses it to snort at me. "That's nonsense. You've been life into my old house, Cedar. Death's a lot closer to my heels than yours." Her gaze shifts to the tarp behind me, so I shuffle over to block her view.

"It's all right," she says. "At least they're covered now. It wasn't decent. I would've been trapped in there too if it wasn't for that Dalfason girl."

"Morgyn?"

"She got here first. She got us out. Thank her for me if you see her."

A firefighter with their visor down grabs my shoulder. "You can't be back here. We got to get her ready to go to Fort Luthe."

I give her hand a soft squeeze and stand. Fort Luthe's farther west than I've ever been. If the monster walks the same ground as me, it won't go there. My grandma will be safe for the next few days.

"Wait! Cedar, you need to know. A letter arrived for you this morning," says my grandma.

The firefighter's leading me away. "I'll check it when I get home!" I say.

She tries to say something else, then starts coughing again.

"I'll call you in the hospital!" I tell her.

On the other side of the fire truck, Ada, Lucy, and Papercut are huddled together, whispering. "What is it?" I ask.

"There's something on the back of the sign," says Ada. Ruby did seem interested in the sign when she first arrived at the church.

"We were waiting for you," says Lucy.

Papercut shakes their head and starts walking for the sign. "We're all in this. Whole damn town. People don't even know it."

There are words on the lower portion of the sign, the part someone Ruby's height could reach. They're scrawled in black soot. Finger-painted. Younger writing and older words. It's hard to read the crammed letters as they fade then get darker.

SO AS THE CREATOR FLOODED GOPHER HOLES,
I SMOKE OUT MY SIBLING WITH SORROW
BURN THE GROUND COVER UNTIL I HAVE THE
LAST ARMS TO RUN INTO

MY ARMS IN THEIRS, STRONGER THAN THIS
FAILING FRAME
MY WEST COAST TREE WITH THE SUN SETTING
BEHIND THEM
MY BLOODLINE, MY VEIN
MY BROKEN THING CRAWLING HOME WITHOUT
SHELTER

START WITH THE HOLY
THE CLUSTERED VOICES
END WITH EMBRACE
ANYTHING OVER ALONE

"Always *so* creepy," says Lucy. "Too much crawling and failing and sun-setting."

Something about its nonsensical words always feel like the long shadow of my own thoughts.

"This was Ruby?" asks Papercut. "Who started the fire?"

Ada nods.

"Are we sure?" Papercut traces a bit of the soot and rubs it between their fingers. "She could have gotten here after or before or—"

"We're sure." Ada's rereading the message. "It's getting more and more unchained. I should be willing to do anything to stop it and save Ruby. I should have looked for her earlier."

Lucy's curious, of course. "We all looked. Was there some other way?"

"There's always been another way, just . . . I was scared."

"You were brave to try it now," I say, taking Ada's hand. I should do anything too. I should tell all of them what I know. I should tell them that as I reread these words, I think they might be for me. Or worse, of me.

I tell myself it doesn't matter, because our mission's still the same.

That my silence might be unforgivable by now.

That if I speak, I may wind up alone.

By the church, Mongrel's engine roars to life. But instead of returning to the road, Morgyn drives across the park, tearing up grass and leaving tire tracks. She's coming our way. Fast. None of us run. We're frozen by the oncoming car, which skids to a halt at the last moment, leaving us between Mongrel and the sign.

Ada's grip tightens on my hand. We all pull closer to each other.

The red door opens and Morgyn steps out. Sunglasses and revolver, snarl and violence. Her jaw is set. She looks at the four of us, taking an extra second with Papercut. She doesn't have to speak the threat. Her posture already says *just try me*.

"Get in." The order is backed up by all the bullets I know are still in her gun.

Morgyn was right to focus on Papercut. "What if we say no?" they ask. I'd be willing to bet they've got that bowie knife on them somewhere.

Behind Morgyn, her car revs its engine. All on its own, like a dog sensing danger to its keeper. More of a mongrel than we knew. There's an energy off it that's new and raises the hair on my arms. My instinct is to run, but my rational response is to back away slowly. So it really is faulty. Through Ada's hand, I feel Cas respond to the rival awakened machine. Defenses up.

"Confirmed," murmurs Lucy, always thinking of updating her files.

"Get. In." Morgyn grabs my arm as I move toward the back seat. "You, up front with me."

The inside of Mongrel is the belly of the beast. Its presence surrounds us like howls in the dark. Outside, Morgyn stares at Ruby's message for long enough to read it.

"Usually, it'd pain me to say it," says Papercut, "but this time it makes me look good. Lucy was right."

"Better get used to it," says Lucy. "What was I right about?"

"Morgyn."

"I was, wasn't I?" Lucy looks far more pleased than the situation warrants.

I've strayed closer to Morgyn than any of them know. "She unblocked the church doors though."

Papercut looks at me suspiciously. I can see the dull gleam of their knife's bare blade held close to their side.

Ada goes to try the door. The lock clicks shut the moment they reach for it. There's a claustrophobia setting in, not enough air in here for all of us. Outside, Morgyn smears the words so they can never be read again, leaving her hand covered in soot. She wordlessly gets in the driver's seat and pulls away, the funeral pyre of the church in the rearview mirror.

Morgyn has the same tension as she did on the first night I met her. White knuckles, shifting gears without thinking, taking us farther and farther out of town. She drives fast, passing cars around corners, swerving sharply in and out of lanes. The windows are up. The car's getting hotter and hotter, but no one mentions it. We just let the sweat bead on the backs of our necks and run down our shirts.

Eventually, Morgyn turns into the woods. In the ditch, an overgrown sign advertises *Automotive Repair*. The washboard gravel road rattles us. As the trees blur by, it occurs to me how far from Sawblade we're getting. Perhaps our searching has become too much of a bother. Maybe we picked the wrong side.

She could be taking us to it. We could be left tied to trees at nightfall.

If that's what she wants.

If what she wants lines up with its desires.

Through the trees, the sunlight catches off metal. Morgyn slows and stops in front of a high chain-link fence topped with razor wire. The only entrance is flanked by semi exhaust pipes. She undoes a heavy padlock and pushes the heavy gate open, giving us a clear view. There are hundreds of rusting vehicles held within the massive confines of the fence. Every other kind of machine is crammed between them. Weeds tangle up where they can. In the sun, it's a glittering, filthy sea. At the center, a tall farmhouse stands neglected next to a huge workshop. Near the back of the yard, the burnt-out remnants of a barn remind me of Lucy's list. One way or another, someone's died on this property.

At a snap of Morgyn's finger, Mongrel shifts into gear on its own and pulls through the gate. Morgyn locks it behind us.

We've arrived at the Dalfason farm.

CHAPTER THIRTY-SIX

Morgyn takes us into the workshop. The mess outside doesn't extend into here. Above us, there's a high ceiling and two lifts with cars on them. A vast array of tools organized on the walls. At Morgyn's unspoken command, her car opens its locks, and we get out onto the neatly swept floor. It's cooler in here, and it smells like the cab of Morgyn's truck. Reminders flood through my body. Fear, relief, and lust.

Morgyn paces a few steps away and reloads the single shot she fired at the church, letting the casing fall to the floor. She takes off her sunglasses and turns to face the four of us.

"You're staying here." She spins her gun around her finger, considering for a second. "Yep, that should do it. It's for your own good. I'll let you out after it's done tonight." She nods to herself, problem solved, and heads for the exit.

"After what's done?" demands Papercut. Their hand is hovering over their knife.

Morgyn grabs hold of a chain above her head and pulls on it, the muscles in her shoulders taut with each tug. The main door of the shop slides down with a heavy, final thud.

"After what's done?" Papercut repeats.

Most people would show some sign of fear when Papercut

takes that tone. Morgyn doesn't even glance their way. "You're better off not knowing."

Papercut goes from coiled to attack in a second. Their arm's a blur, revealing their knife and throwing it end over end in one lashing motion. It buries itself in the door a foot from Morgyn's head with a sickening rasp of metal on metal.

Now her gun isn't spinning. We're looking down the barrel of it. Again, for me. The last time was in the pouring rain at Abraham's Corner, taking the long odds on her being something like good. Last time I talked to her, she saw my hunger and told me to stop trying to keep myself alive.

"Why can't anyone listen when I tell them they're better off not knowing?" asks Morgyn. "People say they want to know, but they don't. 'After what's done?' 'Why keep us here?' I'll tell you why." Morgyn's ranting her thoughts now like they've been boiling in a glowering place for a long time.

"You're in danger, that's why. Or you *are* a danger. Haven't made up my mind yet. Either way, it's safest to keep you at my place. You four, you're tangled up in it all somehow." She points the gun at me. "Cedar, nothing's been right since the moment you got here. Sometimes, I don't know if you're causing trouble or if it's following you."

Sometimes, I think those are the same thing.

"And Papercut," continues Morgyn, "you're usually on the right side of hell-raising. Usually. But you never draw the line. I knew if you survived long enough, we'd come to this. Now you just threw a knife at me."

Papercut shrugs. "Close to you."

"DO YOU THINK I FUCKING CARE?!" Morgyn takes

a deep breath followed by a shaky, slow exhale. "Lucy, you knew better than to get involved. You know everything."

Lucy's half hiding behind Ada and me. "Thank you," she says.

Morgyn finally turns to Ada. I notice her voice becomes a notch less harsh. "Ada, you've already had a lifetime worth of trouble. You put it all on the line for Ruby, and now . . ." Morgyn pushes a hair out of her eyes, and her fingertips hover on the mess of burn scars on her face.

"There were monsters a long time before Autumn," Morgyn says. "They were called humans. They *are* called humans. And we're different from everything else. Sure, we're hurting, we're trapped, we've got a million goddamn sorrows. But I thought we had something nothing else did. We've got malice. There are other vicious things. But none with malice. None with *intent*. I thought that. Fuck, I'd better have been wrong. For your sake."

I've been holding my silence, afraid any words will escalate Morgyn from tirade to violence. Lucy doesn't mind stoking an inferno though. "What do you mean?" she asks.

"I mean I'm out here. I'm driving the night when no one else should be. I'm keeping secrets and telling lies and cleaning up bodies. What's *left* of bodies. I'm picking between wrong and worse, because the little girl I once worked to save lit up a church and there are burnt corpses under a tarp on the street of the town I love. Either that's Ruby's own malice and intent, you four are using her as a puppet, or something else is. That's why it's for your sake. That's the tragic bullshit I have to pick between."

Lucy somehow dares to respond again. "Oh my god, Morgyn. That's awful," she says with total sincerity. "I'm so sorry."

Papercut's fists are clenched into weapons. "You'd like for it to be us," they say to Morgyn. It's a good thing they used their knife for a warning shot. "Then you could take us out back and shoot us."

"That's the last thing I want!" Morgyn yells. "You may not know, but some of you mean more than nothing to me." She makes eye contact with me during the pause before her gaze settles on Ada. But in that second, I see something under the fury that I didn't expect. Sadness.

Weariness.

I know that look from my mom's face during the brutal years after Autumn, when she was grieving and keeping us alive all at once. Tired of carrying it all.

"Tonight, I'm going to shut you in here and solve it once and for all." Morgyn puts a lock on the garage door and steps toward the side entrance. She's got one hand on the doorknob and the other keeping her gun pointed at us. "The world's horrible. I hope you have no fucking clue. And it's just me trying to figure it out. Just me up against it all."

"You're wrong."

I'm surprised to hear myself speak. Morgyn looks the same way, except with a tinge of displeasure. I still step forward. I think back to the last time I walked into her line of fire. If anything, I'm more scared of her now. "It's not just you up against this."

"What, you want to play hero?" scoffs Morgyn. "If you'd seen what I've seen . . ."

"I know what you've seen," I say. "A monster, right?"

Morgyn's suddenly gotten very still and attentive.

"Something hungry," I continue, "but not like any person." I think of Ruby's words for the creature that's taken hold of her now. "A long, dark ghost with a huge mouth. Legs bent the wrong way. Matted, scaled, reeking like death and rot. It can run and swim. It leaves cryptic messages we can't decipher. It likes to drink filth. It takes people over and breaks them from the inside out. That monster."

"Fuck," whispers Morgyn. "I hoped I'd gone mad."

Papercut laughs harshly. "You're mad all right. And the whole world around you."

Lucy's the one brave enough, or curious enough, to ask, "You're not . . . you're not on its side, are you?"

Morgyn glares at Lucy. "I take back what I said about you knowing everything. Of course I'm not on its side! Why the fuck would I do that?"

I dare a step closer. "Because it's probably the winning side."

Morgyn finally lowers her gun. Then she starts to laugh. I hate it, not because of her voice, but because the laugh sounds like all her joy has dried up. "Cedar, if I wanted to be on the winning side, I would have left Sawblade Lake a long time ago."

That settles it. This is where my grandma would start trusting her. "Whatever you're doing tonight, I want to help."

Morgyn shakes her head. "That's what you think."

"No, it's what I know," I say. "We've been out in the same darkness as you. What makes you believe people won't fight with you?"

"No one ever has."

Ada speaks for the first time. Their voice grabs Morgyn's focus more than Papercut's knife did or my confirmation that the monster was real. Morgyn's eyes are softer looking at Ada than I thought they could be. Softer than before she kissed my hands.

"Have you ever let them try, Morgyn?" asks Ada.

Morgyn slumps against the doorframe, silhouetted by the bright afternoon light outside. She lets her head rest there.

"When you first met me, you didn't leave me to last the night alone," I say. "This isn't something to face by yourself."

"We've been learning about the monster." Lucy emerges from behind Ada. "Too much. We'll definitely be helpful."

Papercut sighs. They take the few steps over to the garage door and wrench their knife free. "I wouldn't trust you not to fuck this up on your own anyway. Someone's got to keep an eye on you."

Ada walks past me until she's close enough to touch Morgyn in the doorway but doesn't reach out. "You shouldn't be the only one out there tonight. Remember, I tried to convince you to teach me how to do Ruby's surgery, and you wouldn't let me. Plus, this thing's got my sister. I'd walk through hell to get her back."

Morgyn straightens. There's the slightest hint of a smile at the corner of her mouth. The kind of smile that looks fun and is nothing of the sort. "That's good. Because tonight we're going to the old mill, and we're going to kill it."

CHAPTER THIRTY-SEVEN

Morgyn spends her life fixing things, just not her house. It's falling apart. Some of the posts holding up the veranda roof are broken, making sections slump above it. The railings are half-gone and the boards of the deck are giving out under the weight of car parts. Plants are growing out of the gutters, obscuring moss-covered shingles.

It's worse inside. It looks less like someone lives there and more like it's an abandoned house Morgyn's crashing in. There are barely any decorations. Where there is furniture, it's faded, dusty, and frayed. What there is in abundance is scrap. Unlike in the shop, the chaos of the yard has climbed the front steps and come inside. There are smaller broken machines and parts everywhere. They're heaped on top of each other, so we have to weave around them as we make our way through a series of rooms to reach the kitchen.

Ada drops back to whisper to me. "A lot of these are faulty. After being in Mongrel, Cas is . . . watchful of other faulty machines. But these haven't decided to end themselves. Morgyn must have communicated with them or stabilized them."

Ahead of us, Lucy's head is on a swivel, learning everything she can about the most mysterious and talked-about person in her *TALK* folder. She keeps trying to ask Morgyn questions, which is working about as well as I'd expect.

"I felt Cas on the defensive as soon as we crossed the threshold, I say quietly. "Half this shit is volatile." There are computers, cellphones, and pieces of medical technology you'd never see in a hospital anymore. I'll bet some of it helped Morgyn do surgery on Ruby.

The kitchen's ahead of us, but I drag my feet to get a better look into a place I've imagined myself in before. Morgyn's bedroom.

It's large and open and notably clearer than the other rooms. It's like there's a line at the door that the machines don't cross. The walls are painted a cool green, and both windows are full of thriving plants. The bed's tucked in the midst of all the leaves with a pile of magazines beside it. The top one is distinctly pornographic. The closet doesn't have a door, revealing work clothes, jeans, and grayscale fabric. I can just see the elaborate edge of a black prom dress pushed to one side.

I notice Ada looking in there too. I pull away guiltily, even though I can't tell exactly what Ada and I are or what it means. It's only been five days since we kissed. Wretched days with a few soft words and a small, glimmering reminder that she still wants me. But I haven't been thinking of Morgyn like that throughout the week. Not until I looked at her bed and had a sharp pull in my stomach picturing what it would be like to be there with her.

I think Morgyn could put her mouth on me and wash the rest of the world away for a while.

What I say to Ada is "It's not what I expected."

Ada lingers for a second longer. Perhaps she's wondering

about another path, one where she kept saying yes to Morgyn after they kissed. "Morgyn never quite is. Good thing you can see through her snarl. If you couldn't, we'd still be locked in the workshop."

And we'd be safe.

The five of us gather around Morgyn's table. The kitchen is the same era as my grandma's, but it gets the opposite level of attention. Dirty dishes piled in the sink. Jars with plastic over them full of drowned fruit flies. Abandoned pots with leftovers in them sit on the stovetop, baking in the sun.

Morgyn sweeps a forgotten repair project onto the floor with a clatter and spreads out a map of the area instead. "I've been laying a trap for it," she says, tapping a black X drawn in permanent marker. There are other circles in places I recognize. The Point, Camille's house with a question mark, where we found her car. There are a few spots missing, like Tay's house, and a few more places I didn't know it had been. On the edge of the map, an arrow points north with the label *Abe's Cor*.

"That's a good spot," I say, pointing at the X. "It's close to where it's keeping Ruby at night."

"How do you know?" asks Morgyn. "And what do you mean, 'keeping Ruby'? This a hostage situation?"

"That's too kind for what it's doing." Papercut's eyes are tracing the pattern on the map.

Morgyn's looking fed up with not knowing what's going on. She hasn't realized that Lucy and Papercut don't know much either. She singles me out. "Cedar, explain."

Explain. As though we understand everything. Morgyn's not asking though.

I remember what I've kept to myself before, like my mom and the mailboxes. Then I lay out the rest from our encounters with it, from what Kat said, from the messages the monster's left, from Ruby's diary, and from what it's been doing to Ruby. Wants a host, scared of light. Ashamed of its form? Maybe. It took Ruby when the power in town went out.

Ada adds, "Ruby works better than Kat because she has a hollow for a second soul."

"Shit, that was us." Morgyn picks at a dark stain on the table. Blood? Was this where they did Ruby's surgery?

"The host lets it do things in the light," I continue. "It also seems to have more clarity and communicate more when it's in a human. At night, it can leave Ruby to do other things. Like Camille—"

"She's buried out back," interrupts Morgyn in a rush. We all look at her with varying levels of accusation and shock. She shifts and glances away. Picks at the stain again. "Seemed better than burning her in the car. I did it last night. She's there, is the point. If you want to visit or whatever."

Papercut's looking at the map even harder than before. "Thanks." I can hear them carefully holding their voice steady.

Morgyn just says, "Anyway, carry on."

"It's wearing Ruby out," I continue. "She's faster and stronger with the monster in her, but the way it's using her is too much for her body. We've seen that. We have to get Ruby at night. We've got to find her while it's outside of her skin and take her back. Soon. We can't take her during the day. What's in her is too . . ." I think of the flare and the way it threw Papercut. ". . . too devious."

"It's got more intention now," says Morgyn. "Not just lashing out. Strategy. More and more. You read what was on the sign."

"So as the creator flooded gopher holes, I smoke out my sibling with sorrow," quotes Lucy. *"Burn the ground cover until I have the last arms to run into.* Then not sure what's with the blood talk. Generally icky, isn't it?"

"Start with the holy, the clustered voices," adds Ada. "It's targeting our shelter."

Was it doing that at the Point already? Assaulting our joyous escape.

At Abraham's Corner, even? A bastion on the road.

Even before thinking or knowing, this beast violated our safe places.

"It's gone too far," declares Morgyn. "That's why it has to be tonight. First it comes into town for Ruby. Then kills Camille at the edge. Now it's crossed another line. Ballsy motherfucker killing people during the day. And you don't fuck around with fire, not in my town." She glares at us, her burnt face daring us to question her. "How we going to find Ruby anyway?"

"Magic," says Ada.

Morgyn shakes her head. "No such thing."

"The unexplained is magic. Or if it hurts us, demonic," says Ada.

Morgyn's ready for that too. "Next you're going to want to bring crosses and holy water along tonight."

"Wait until you've heard," says Ada calmly.

She briefly explains how her powers work. It's a lot less

than what she let me in on, though she does add that because our link to Ruby was established by the two of us, it can only be used again in the same way. Papercut doesn't act remotely surprised, Lucy's hanging on every word, and Morgyn tries to seem unimpressed.

"So just Faulty shit," says Morgyn when Ada's done. "An extension of how Cas helped with Ruby's operation. Saying that's magic is like saying a watch is arcane because you've never taken one apart. Though it'll be helpful," she adds quickly, which seems like an incredible understatement. "Can you keep tabs on Ruby until nightfall?"

I can't imagine us maintaining the intensity of that link for more than a couple minutes. Given what happened with the map, best not to risk it too often. We exchange a look, and Ada suggests that her and I check in on Ruby before we go, and then maybe we can get a location on the monster at the same time. Maybe. The magic's not behaving like normal. It's a lot less stable than when Ada usually does it.

"Usually?" asks Lucy. "Like do you do this all the time? Because that's a little amazing a little creepy I'm a lot jealous."

I'm watching Ada to see how they respond, because I've been wondering too.

Morgyn doesn't let her. "I have a more relevant question," she says. "If Ruby dies while the monster's in her, does it die too?"

Which sends everything off the rails.

There's an instant uproar. Ada and Papercut are at Morgyn's throat. Toppled chairs, raised voices, obscenities and then suddenly blows and Morgyn slammed against the counter. Papercut's knife goes skittering across the floor. A pot crashes down, spilling clumpy rice.

Lucy and I are both shouting, trying to pull people apart. An elbow catches me in the mouth, splitting my lip. My hand comes away bloody.

Morgyn pushes Ada aside and throws a hard punch into Papercut's stomach. "STOP! I'm not saying we kill a kid. Fuck. I'm just asking."

Ada's breathing heavily. Somewhere in the melee, she grabbed a wrench that she's still gripping fiercely. "That's. Not. Something. You. Just. Ask."

Morgyn holds her hands up. "I know. Ada, I know. I'm sorry."

Slowly, Ada sets the wrench down on the floor. "You're not as big as you think you are, you know that?"

"You're right," says Morgyn. "I'm not. I get carried away."

Ada doesn't respond.

"I really am sorry." Morgyn reaches for Ada, touching their hand where it's hanging at their side. Ada flinches away. She's not held in place by Morgyn's touch the way I am.

Papercut's still recovering after getting winded, but there's fury written all over their face. "You're a coward for even thinking it." Then I am too.

Morgyn's voice snaps out of the softness she had for Ada. "You're only brave because you haven't seen it."

I wipe more blood away from my mouth. My tongue tastes like metal. "Have you?"

"You should know by now, Cedar. I've seen everything there is to see, and none of it was fine."

Papercut grabs their knife off the linoleum. "Prove it."

Morgyn leaves Ada's side with another apology, barely whispered. Her hand hovers near Ada's for a second before turning away. Morgyn rummages through a few kitchen drawers, each one the junk drawer, before grabbing a few loose photos. She holds them so I can't see more than the black corner of one.

Film photographs. Shutter to canister to development to here. A way of measuring reality again now that we can't digitally alter them anymore. These aren't drawings or odd descriptions by a child. This is proof.

"I was at the racetrack east of Abraham's Corner after dark," says Morgyn. "I'd been working in the garage for a bit. When I came out, there was something on the bleachers. A shifting darker patch. Stank too. I took a couple long-exposure shots before I fired my flash."

A single blink of terror.

"It ran. I hung around in my truck for a while. Kept the lights on, and it didn't come back. Eventually, I loaded the rally car and drove to Abraham's Corner."

I think of the way Morgyn was on a hair trigger when she picked me up. Shoot first, ask questions later. The camera in her back seat as we drove to Sawblade Lake. "That's why you believed me," I realize. "We'd seen the same thing that night."

A desperate fear linked us in the cab of Morgyn's truck more than I could have ever guessed.

"Couldn't leave you there once I knew this was nearby."

Morgyn throws the photos down on the table and turns away.

I wish I could do the same.

None of the others move for a few seconds. Ada's the first to step forward. She links her fingers with mine, pressing our palms together so we can be a fraction of the power of this thing. On my left, Lucy leans in to look too. Her breath catches. I can hear her hold down a retch. Papercut's last. They grip the edge of the table and keep their face to the side, like they can only bear witnessing with the periphery of their vision. Behind us, Morgyn scuffs the rice on the floor under the edges of the counter. This isn't the sort of thing you want to see more than once.

None of us want to look.

I reach out a hand and spread out the photos.

Dark. Dark. Dark. Flash.

CHAPTER THIRTY-EIGHT

THE PHOTOGRAPHS:

The dim long-exposure ones are first.

It's too dark to make out everything, but at least it wasn't raining at the racetrack. There's enough to jigsaw it together.

It's on the bleachers. Huge, obscuring several benches with its long body with the muscled curves of a snake but wrong like a massive eel.

Front legs bending back, back legs bending forward. Despite its size, it carries itself like something light, ready to pounce. The benches don't bend under it. Impossible to say whether it's walking or hovering.

A ghost. A ghostmaker.

Patchy coat and stretching, thin rat tail. Its head is turned away, lapping some spilled alcohol off the wood. Slivers raking its tongue.

Flash.

Ruby drew it right.

My eyes circle the edges of the clearest picture, avoiding the center. I take in the claws, long and curved for ripping. Now I see different-sized scales with fur growing up between them like weeds out of a broken sidewalk. It looks ill and feverish.

Sinewed strength. At some points, the bleachers are visible right through the body. Ethereal and real like something chasing you in a dream.

But not the mouth. There's nothing phantom about that and nothing at all behind it.

It's open wide, wider than a jaw should, a silent scream at the camera. Teeth upon teeth forming crooked rows with others protruding randomly. Some far down its throat, punching through. All angled inward.

This is a final place, but not of rest.

Would there even be enough left to make a ghost?

That mouth is drowning in deep water smashing on jagged rocks a whirlpool that goes all the way down a sinkhole. Proof that damnation is not needed for hell to be real and here. To coil you and pull you down, there's a rough black tongue so long it hangs from the side of its mouth. I've heard its sound just feet from me.

That's tonight.

• • •

Dad,

It feels like it's been a long time, but I wrote you yesterday. I'm tossed in waves, no up or down or breath to snatch.

Once we made our plan, we visited Camille's grave together. My version of together somehow means me,

Ada, Papercut, Lucy, and Morgyn. You're not in it. Not Sky, not Mom.

Me and Mom didn't talk like you and Sky were dead or alive. Somewhere in between. Like Schrödinger's cat in the box with the poison, both and neither until proven otherwise. Your bunker could have failed just like your dam, leaving you and Sky drowning in the dark, clawing at the ceiling. If you get this somehow, I'll be the same to you—suspended. I could die tonight or destroy the greatest danger to me.

There are fresh flowers on Camille's grave. Morgyn did that. Grandma would do that for me. If you had a grave, she'd do it for you too. I left Camille's graveside earlier to call Grandma. There was a fire at the church, and she was in it. I called the hospital, but they said she gave up her spot in the ambulance for a friend with a one-in-ten chance of living. Didn't even survive the trip. So I called her house, and she answered. Even forgetful on pain meds, she answered.

I asked Grandma if she was scared to die in the fire. She said of course. I didn't expect that. I asked about heaven, and she didn't say anything for a long time. She told me she's lived in Sawblade Lake her entire life. The longest trip she ever took was to visit our family. She said heaven sounds like a long way. She's not sure she's ready to make that trip.

I asked how I get ready to die. How do I know if everything I've done is for nothing?

She asked if it seems pointless or unwinnable. I wanted to say both, but I let her keep going. She told me if the point is winning, I should go to the arcade. But out here, all I can do is figure out who I can't help but love and do everything I can to make them know it.

"You'll mostly lose," she said, "but it wasn't pointless. Your love is never wasted."

I told her I love her. She told me to be good, be safe, not knowing it's impossible for me to do both. She told me she's so glad I came to Sawblade Lake. Those could be the last words I hear her say. I wish I'd had last words like that from you.

Yours,
Cedar

CHAPTER THIRTY-NINE

Ada knocks on the door just as I finish folding the letter to mail later.

I'm in one of the upstairs bedrooms with a window overlooking the backyard. Sitting at a dusty desk, I can see far across the junkyard. Morgyn's making her way back to the house. Lucy and Papercut are still at Camille's grave. Lucy gives Papercut a side hug. The light of the setting sun is on the two of them.

I open the door for Ada. I could feel that it was her and Cas coming up the stairs.

"You all right?" Ada asks as they close the door behind them. There's a piece of furniture covered in plastic. Ada pulls the tarp aside to reveal a gorgeous couch—green and antique with heavy carved wood.

"Not for a while now," I say.

Ada sits on the couch. "I think I sort of am? I'm doing something for Ruby. We could end this tonight."

"And then?" I ask.

Ada smiles at me.

It's the most beautiful of the lost things.

"Could we take a hammock to the cabin?" they ask. "Stay in bed late, make brunch, rock in the sun."

I lean toward her. I pour my tired mind into these thoughts and feel a hint of excitement. Of somewhere else someday somehow. "So in this scenario we're falling asleep together?"

"I have . . . a confession." Ada's looking right at me. They're only blushing a tiny bit, but they don't turn away. "We already have been. And not just the day we painted my cabin."

I reach into my pocket and pull out my necklace, the one I found in Ada's magic room. I dangle it in front of her, and she bites back a grin. I think I've figured out how Ada knew more than I'd told her. That my injuries looked worse before and all the songs I played to keep myself sane.

Ada's got a mischievous look, nearly guilt-free. "Yeeeah, I snuck into Papercut's room and stole that off your pile of clothes the night after the Point."

"You'd just met me!" I laugh.

Ada shrugs, as if all this is simple. "But I knew. Cas knew too."

"How'd you ground it? I didn't have anything of yours."

Ada reaches out and takes my hand in both of theirs. Her hands are warmer and softer than mine, melting me down with memories of us pressed together in a pantry going anywhere we wanted before fear interrupted us.

She rolls the hair elastic off my wrist. I have to bite in a gasp. Compose myself. "This wasn't my ex's. It's mine, and I planted this on you. You've never taken it off. What does that say about you?"

"Are you smug right now?"

They lean back on the couch, arms spread out. "You've *never* taken it off."

"Okay, maybe I was, am, a bit infatuated too." I force myself not to look away. My double-time heart echoes an acceleration of Cas's energy. "And I could feel it. Some nights, when I was most afraid, it was like a glowing presence pushing back the dark."

"That was me watching you," admits Ada. "I'm sorry, Cedar."

"You don't have to be. It felt more like being watched over."

"I promise I looked away if you were getting changed or anything. But still, I know it was wro—"

"From you, that's the sort of wrong I like."

For a few incredibly satisfying seconds, Ada's flustered. She doesn't seem to have any words.

"Was that smooth?" I'm embarrassed, shy, bold. Things I didn't think were anywhere to be found in today. "For the first time ever, I think I might have been smooth."

Ada nods vigorously. "Mm-hmm, that was smooth. It had an effect."

"Turns out I just needed a darling to have those feelings for."

Ada exhales. Their fingers dig into the couch. I don't miss that detail, even with impending danger and light fading outside.

For the first time, Ada sounds nervous. Going on like I do. "So I came back to the house because I was sad and wound-up and confused and hopeful, and there's a best thing to do with that. Generally acknowledged. You know it. I was looking for someplace quiet, but then I saw you in here and I got all brave and okay. Okay. I know what I want. If you do too."

She takes her arms off the couch and slowly runs her hands down the tops of her thighs, brushing the skin, spreading her fingers out. I can feel them like they're on me. Their legs are together, but as they repeat the motion and press harder, their knees open the slightest bit.

"Is this the sort of wrong you like?" she asks. They try to do a low, seductive voice but break into a laugh halfway through. One that pulls me along with her. "It was sexy when you did it!"

"It's sexy to laugh with you." There's an ease to us together. It's not like at Camille's, each of us dressed to party. I'm in Lucy's jeans and her cropped white shirt that doesn't fit my shoulders, and Ada's in shorts and a dull beige T-shirt. There's no music or dancing or alcohol or soaked clothes to lead us here. No rambling night.

Still, we're here. Ada's unbuttoning her jeans and pulling a zipper down and

telling me to follow

in her normal voice. A little tired, a hint of crying and a hint of laughter. It's irresistible, so I copy her.

Soon, a hint of sighing. Grins of absurdity, locked eyes.

Facing each other with our knees almost touching. We're turned on turned up the energy in the room like glass fogging. Ada checking in with their eyes. She's not quite ordering, just leading. With their other hand, they trace their own body.

Corners of eyes, jawline, collarbone, between her breasts and over her stomach.

I mean, ours.

All of these ours.

Our hips and the insides of our thighs. Undressed to match, item for item. Our inside-out shirts are crumpled on the floor together. Awkward half standing pulling off my jeans while Ada kicks their shorts off. There are photos sticking out of her back pocket. Morgyn's photos that they grabbed to track it.

I could stumble down those thoughts.

I trip and let myself stumble a different way. I let myself fall until I'm on my knees next to the couch. I ask and Ada says yes and then puts her hands on the back of my head and pulls me between her legs where I've wanted to be since

I woke up beside them

on their bed at the cabin on a rainbow quilt in a room that smelled like paint

and sunshine

where I could imagine kissing my way down their stomach and now I don't have to because I'm kissing my way up their thighs and my hands are gripping the back of their hips. Outside the door, steps pause in the hallway and stay for a long time before continuing on. Inside the room, Ada is murmurs and gasps. She doesn't notice or, like me, doesn't care. Even as in the yard Camille is dead and our beloved hearts are standing at her grave. The sun's almost set, and lights are heavily buzzing to life all around the sea of cars as I give Ada my own series of yes and yes and please.

Eventually, we hold each other in stiller and stiller ways. All skin curled together squirming and adjusting to fit both of us on the couch. We say words like *darling*. We let our hearts slow down together, but not too much.

Because it's soon.

Soon we go out past the lights.

CHAPTER FORTY

Morgyn's pickup truck and Mongrel idle side by side in front of the shop, pumping exhaust into the humid night air. Morgyn's at the wheel of her faulty car, and Lucy's driving the truck, with Papercut in the passenger seat and Ada and me in the back.

"Look that way," orders Ada. They point through the front windshield of Morgyn's truck. I've got a clear view from the center seat. "Toward the sawmill. Are you ready?" She gives my hand a couple quick squeezes.

"I trust you," I say.

Entirely entirely, soul and body both, it turns out.

Lucy revs the engine.

"As soon as you've got a position, we go!" calls Morgyn through her open window.

Ada pulls out a heavy sketchbook, Ruby's running shoes, and the flash photo of the monster. They flip to a fresh page and begin to draw in frantic strokes of charcoal pencil. The last thing I see here is Lucy twisting in her seat to get a better look at the process.

Into the shiver.

Ada's taste is still on my tongue. The trembling of Cas is

in me. This isn't closer than that, but it's a near thing. Again, there's a moment of purely the person I adore and desire. Like the stretched-out moments in the upstairs room.

Then the other thing is there. Always shredding the good of this world.

This time, it's right now right away. I see Ruby asleep, curled up in the cab of the truck half sunk in the toxic stream. She's shaking like she's hypothermic. Sweating like a fever. Tossing turning bad dream bad dream

bad dream gone real.

Breakaway

my mind digging in trying not to be pulled toward
a sound
of endless mechanical churning like
if water could be ground up
if water could scream
like I can't
with my mouth suddenly gone dry and thirsty.
Endless sloping concrete lifeless as the surface of the moon or
a bone forest or
a dark bunker door.

The spell gets clear again. For a second, I felt like I was in my monster, but now I observe it. It's a shade in the pine trees, creeping and floating and panting. My viewpoint keeps shifting. This thing is hard to get a focus on. Above, beside, close-up, wide shot, but no more point of view. There are some early hints of moonlight off the lake, but it's not bright enough to get a clear look at it yet.

Ruby was right. Again.

It doesn't like to be seen.

All I have to do is figure out where it is to know whether we can travel safely to the sawmill. I'm the worst person to do this. I didn't grow up here. Still, it's on me to scan for a landmark of some sort. I think this is Sawblade Lake. I'm fairly certain I recognize its jagged shoreline. Lights. That's town in the distance with faint traces of smoke above it. There are broken glass bottles under my feet. This isn't the Point though. It's some other party spot I've never seen. Smaller and less heavily trodden. There's moss growing on the ash where bonfires once burned.

From across the clearing, I feel a gaze on me.

I'm in the back seat of Morgyn's truck. I swear I am. There's none of me actually in this vision, but I find the monster locking onto me. I notice its eyes for the first time. Flickering, double-lidded, no white at all. Gunk built up at the corners like something ill or something weeping old engine oil all night.

Now my perspective stops jumping.

It doesn't have a hard time focusing on me.

I don't know how to tell Ada to get me out of here. I can't find her presence. I'm scrambling around for a thread of their existence. A lifeline, please.

It takes a step toward me, its head emerging into what moonlight there is. Far, far worse than the pictures.

There, a link to Ada that I yank on for all I'm worth.

There's a shark down here.

I'm the blood it smells in the water.

I'm gripping Ada's hand tightly.

"Hey hey hey," she says softly. "You back with us?"

Their eyes are clear and deep. Safe and good. "I'm back. I'm here. But I think it could see me, Ada."

"That's not normal, right?" Lucy glances between us. "What *is* normal, by the way?"

"None of this." Ada closes her notebook and presses it shut like a mouth could reach out. "What else did you see?"

I describe everything, providing the details I can and trying to answer their questions. It's not quite enough. Most of my memory is full of its eyes. Lucy suggests the McAllisters' old place. Papercut says it could be out by the waste-transfer station. Ada doubts it, but still. If it's the transfer station, it's pretty close to the route we're about to drive. Lucy says it wouldn't be overgrown like that. Though Ada's not sure when the last time was anyone partied there.

"It's the McAllisters'," insists Lucy. "The transfer station isn't right on the water." I'm not sure what perspective I saw the lake from, but this seems right. Lucy's confident. "We're good to go!" she calls to Morgyn. "It's at the McAllisters'."

Morgyn nods and rolls up her window. "Remember, lights out!" she says just before it seals shut.

So we head through the darkness close on Mongrel's bumper. We're constantly scanning as the roads keep getting smaller and the trees keep closing in. Ruts, logging roads, all weaving deeper into the woods.

Ada and I keep our fingers linked together. I try not to think of how it leapt out of the woods and ended Camille or what those moments were like for her.

It never shows. We pass through the shadows to arrive somewhere worse.

The old sawmill is a decrepit sprawl of buildings and smokestacks. A place of destruction and systematic lifelessness.

Morgyn pauses at the edge of the toxic runoff in front of the remnants of a bridge. She rolls down her window. When Lucy does the same, a stench strikes me. If it's near, we won't be able to smell it.

"One car at a time over this!" calls Morgyn. "We're almost there."

The brittle bridge groans. It holds for now. We're the same in every way.

Across the bridge, Morgyn turns up a metal ramp that leads into the ruins of a massive industrial room. It's a temple to deforestation. In places, it's open to the sky. Huge rusted beams. Equipment that was too heavy to move and was left to dissolve. When Autumn happened, the machines should have been too old and inactive to wake up, but some of them had wicked enough purposes that they gave out. There are scorch marks and a saw blade thrown across the room with such force that it's buried in the wall.

Papercut's not gawking around the same way I am. They twist in their seat. "So, Ada, do we risk looking again before getting out of the cars?"

That was the plan. It wasn't the plan for it to be looking back.

Ada turns to me. "I'd say that's for Cedar to decide."

I want to say no. I can still feel the panic of it coming for me and not being able to get myself out. "It's best to do it now," I say with effort. "If it's far enough away, maybe we could reach Ruby first." On foot at night, probably carrying her back. We'd be slow and vulnerable. "Break it off and wake me up after thirty seconds."

"It usually takes two minutes to triangulate a position," says Lucy, "in movies. So we should be good."

Papercut raises an eyebrow. "Triangulate?"

"Do you have a better source? Peer-reviewed monster-hunting journals?"

In the back seat, Ada whispers, "Thirty seconds, less if you're distressed. I'll have you out of there."

It's ten seconds. Then we're leaping out of the cars and moving as fast as we can.

Because the moment things got clear enough to see it, I knew we'd made a mistake. It was on top of a pile of garbage, scrounging for noxious dregs to drink. So the transfer station, so close by. So it could have hit us while we were driving if it hadn't been distracted by the trash.

It lunged for me with its mouth open. I tugged the line, and Ada pulled me to safety. As I shot to the surface, I saw it keep running through the space where I'd been. Straight for the sawmill.

We brought bait. Bottle after bottle of soda to pour out and lure it in. We haven't emptied a single one yet. This thing always finds me in the end.

There's no time to reach Ruby now. We scramble to set the trap, our feet slipping on concrete and rotten sawdust. We trip on debris and say muffled curses in the dark. Generators, floodlights. Things Morgyn's been gathering and bringing out here bit by bit. We get both vehicles in position. Pour the soda anyway, at the center of it all. We're making a circle of light to tear a hole in the night.

It will rattle and burn to ashes the way evil things do in all our stories when the light strikes them.

And stories and rumors are the truth we pray on.

CHAPTER FORTY-ONE

WITH A CREAK AND A SHUDDER THAT GOES RIGHT THROUGH me, a pair of huge sliding doors on the side of the room break away their rust and begin sliding open all on their own. They cry out with every inch they move, and we're lucky for it. There's no other cue that it's almost here. Smell drowned out, whisper movement of a hunter.

We bolt for our positions on the outside of the circle. I'm on one of the generators across from the door, ready to yank the pull start and power it to life. On the other side of the circle, Papercut and Lucy are by two more, though I can't make them out in the faint moonlight. I'm sure they're hiding like me anyway. I'm behind an old conveyor belt leading to massive blades. Morgyn in her car, Ada in the truck. Ada has to softly close doors that have swung open on their own. Mongrel's stay closed, its soul pushing back against what just came into view.

No more shifting perspectives, photos, or drawings.

This is what's in our minds behind a closed closet door at night. Fear made flesh.

It comes into the room like a long hand reaching toward us, stretching its backward legs onto the cutting floor. At the smell of the sweet liquid, it swishes its tail. Out and back, cracking.

A naked whip, skin on skin. It steps without weight, leaving the sawdust undisturbed.

But its tongue could be a thousand pounds. It drags heavy on the floor. It's parched like mine was when I searched for it, trailing no saliva. Craving. The tongue malforms its mouth so it can't shut completely, forming a smile of blacker darkness.

It takes too long for the end of it to enter the building, its body snaking on. Now that it's near, its smell overpowers whatever toxic waste pours into the lake.

My fingernails dig into my palm. I'm shaking. I want to throw up. They say once you can see a monster, it's not as bad. That nothing is as dark as what you can build in your mind.

They lied, like all stories do.

Its head lurches around and settles on me. Its eyes are murky, like fetid water. As it steps toward me, I learn that it's not silent after all. With every step, claws clack soft on the ground and scrape slightly as it raises its next foot forward.

It stops, dead center in the circle, one foot in the sugary liquid spreading between its claws. I start counting when it stoops its head to drink. This was how we agreed to time it.

Three.

The tongue sounds the same as at Abraham's.

Two.

The same as the water leaking into the basement of my childhood home.

One.

And I throw all my strength into starting the generator.

I can feel my pupils recoil to tiny dots as Mongrel's headlights kick on, glaring brighter than any car I've ever seen. Ada flicks the truck's on too. All the generators shoot current to 360 degrees of floodlights turning everything white and

dead center

there are no ashes.

It writhes and crumples, snapping its tail, body, and neck around. It thrashes its legs and stoops its head as if it's trying to hide its horror from us. In the blazing light, I can see through it where its fur and scales are thinnest. Organs outlined palely. There's no red in its bloodstream.

I can see its heart accelerating and its lungs gasping to spew the most awful sound I've ever heard. I cry out in response. Covering my ears does nothing. It's like an endless rasping inhale. Like the door scraping open to welcome it into this room. Like it's the one pulling us in.

It isn't a sound of pain. It's one of sorrow and shame and wrath.

Any story we leaned on came from either side of this thing. Legends too new or too old, incomplete, faulty research. They should have taught us that hating something isn't the same as being destroyed by it. Thank god, since we hate this monster and hope against hope it doesn't destroy us.

While this monster thanks the devil, since the light isn't burning it.

It stops thrashing. Then it slowly shifts into a crouch, head low to the floor. It looks around the circle, muscles coiled and ready to pounce. We've done the worst thing we could have. We've made it desperate and angry, then trapped it in a corner, all without hurting it.

Morgyn stomps on the gas pedal and all hell breaks loose.

Mongrel spins out and jolts forward. The monster leaps away a second too late. Mongrel catches one of its back legs and spins across the floor. Morgyn wrestles control back, knocking lights flying. Beams shooting and falling everywhere. Sounds I've never heard before. This room has lost sanity.

The monster hasn't slowed down. It pops its knee back into place. The bones punching through don't bother it as it leaps for Papercut and Lucy. There's a cacophony of metal. It rips pieces of steel machinery straight off their bolts in the concrete floor and casts them aside. Papercut and Lucy are exposed. Papercut has their knife out even though it's smaller than any one of the teeth reaching toward the two of them.

Ada had the truck in reverse, ready to back down the ramp and away from this place. Now the reverse lights vanish as she throws it in drive and rams the monster in the side. The engine that tows trailers and pulls out stuck cars strains, pushing the monster toward the wall. For a second, it seems like Ada might pin it.

It clenches, and I don't know what's about to happen, just that I've got to move. I leap over the conveyor belt and aim for the truest cover I can find—Mongrel. Then the monster pushes back. Ada doesn't have Morgyn's skill behind the wheel. The truck goes straight across the room and crashes into the spot where I just was, crumpling the side of the vehicle. I glance over my shoulder to see Ada wrenched to the side by the force of the impact. No seat belt, thrown across the cab. My heart does the movement with them, slumps and goes still like her.

From her car, Morgyn screams at me to run to Mongrel. She's got her gun in her hand.

Papercut and Lucy are sprinting across the open space for the truck. That's where it aims its mouth.

A step behind Lucy, Papercut slips in the soda and stumbles. Lucy has a good chance to make it to the truck, but she turns to help Papercut back up instead.

"CEDAR!" yells Morgyn.

I've run right for it. It scoops its mouth along the floor and opens wide. Papercut seems to be up and away from the chasm until the tongue flicks out and knocks them down. It starts drawing them in.

Papercut twists enough to drive their knife into the tongue with both hands. It releases Papercut when it recoils. The monster bites the knife out, swallows the blade. Then its tongue emerges again.

And finds me standing in between it and Papercut. In between it and Lucy. And Ada.

It's coming for the ones I would be lost without. I'm all in on keeping these people. All in that the monster will hesitate rather than consume me in a single bite. In the back of its throat, past the last of its teeth,

I see the end
one way or another
and this is my long-shot
throwaway
knife's-edge way
of not going there.

It stops. Its tongue is halfway wrapped around my waist. Maybe it isn't as bad for me because I feel like I've stared into this maw before. Somehow, this gaping hole into nothing has been in my home and my body and my blood.

Behind me, Papercut and Lucy have gotten to the truck. It can still drive. I yell for them to go, and Lucy swerves the truck brokenly out of the sawmill and toward town.

It's obsessed with me. It wants me, but only alive.

I feel it now the same way I felt Cas at the Point. But if Cas was a distant train, this is the inside of a turbine. Mayhem and violence and intentions without words. It presses up against my mind as if to ask,

May I?

Are you done yet?

Six gunshots in rapid succession explode through the room. They all hit its face around the eye. It lurches away, sending me sprawling as its tongue releases me.

"Get in!" calls Morgyn, already closing the distance between us. Mongrel picks up speed and holds the passenger door open for me. I barely make it in before we go down the ramp.

Morgyn shifts into a higher gear as we fly across the bridge over the toxic stream. Not far ahead, I can see the unbroken taillight of the truck. It's too damaged to go quickly.

"What the fuck was that?" asks Morgyn.

It was seeing how far down I could swim without the depths taking me. "It needs me. It won't hurt me."

"Good."

"Good?"

Morgyn swerves hard down a different road. "That means it's going to follow us. We can lead it away."

"Morgyn, it'll kill you."

Morgyn pushes the speed a little higher even though the road's rough and the trees are practically in it. "Can't kill me if it can't catch me."

This monster is making my fears come true, whether it knows it or not.

And it might know.

When I faced it, I could tell that it wanted something from me. I'm not sure what, but it only has one way of getting what it desires. That's the fear. Lurking outside my home, opening mailboxes to show it watches me, making an example out of Camille to demonstrate its commitment.

I was afraid it was parallel to us in the woods the first time I drove with Morgyn. But I thought the headlights were enough to ward it off. Now I've seen brightness doesn't truly stop it. It's a matter of the lengths it's willing to go to. It loathed the light for making it seen. Yet it fought rather than fled. Anger, or worse, desperation.

What else would have it exploding out of the trees behind us, straining to catch Mongrel? We've tried to burn it with light. We've hit it with two cars. Morgyn's emptied her revolver into it. I saw the damage to its leg, but that's not slowing it down. We were fools to think we could simply destroy it in this form.

Damage is its essence. That's something like invincibility.

Every stride, its claws reach out of the darkness. In our red taillights, its eyes are finally the color they are in my mind.

With each extension of its limbs, the eyes get a little larger. Tongue in the wind made by its speed, and jaws that could close around Mongrel's bumper and force us to a halt. Morgyn would fight with everything she has, then disappear down its throat, leaving just me.

If it won't kill me, what will it do when it gets me alone in the woods?

"Seat belt." Morgyn doesn't turn to look at me. She only gives a glance in her mirrors at the monster that consumes all my attention.

She does pull her own seat belt across her chest though.

The moment I do the same, she starts to really drive. Around me, I experience the full potential of the relationship between a human and an awoken faulty machine. Cas and Ada work together, but there's still tension there. Morgyn and Mongrel fall into alignment and curve time in their favor. Every fault in the back road and fallen tree and sharp turn feels like they planned for it. Drifting, swerving, accelerating. Each action with the greatest possible efficiency.

And we need it all.

The monster has undrawn reserves. Where we swerve around, it leaps over. As the RPMs climb, it simply pushes harder, all while locked on to me. I'm shaken by the movement. I want to scream and never stop, because if I was at the wheel, we would have been wrapped around a tree a hundred times. I see death ahead and behind.

Now just ahead.

"You lost it!"

Morgyn's grinning. Is she having fun? "Was it in doubt? You've got to get to know me better." She slows down a hair and loosens her hands on the wheel. The muscles in her shoulders relax slightly. We can see the dense lights of Sawblade Lake.

Surely, it won't walk through that gauntlet and let all those eyes rest on it. Its shame keeps it behind that boundary. In Ruby's body, it might, if she can still make it that far.

A laugh finds its way out of me. "I really do."

The look Morgyn gives me. It's question and grief and desire. In it, I can feel the adrenaline racing through me and the leftovers of Ada's hands and mouth on every part of my body. Morgyn was right. I'm hungry. The more I taste the more I want.

The monster steps into the road in front of us, blacking out the light we're aiming for. A hunter's mind to go with a hunter's body. The weeks it spent in the woods have given it a map. It wasn't giving up. It was cutting us off.

Morgyn throws the wheel to the left, taking us into the underbrush. Like I feared the first time we drove from Abraham's Corner to Sawblade. Except I didn't know Morgyn and Mongrel then. A tree takes off the mirror. Branches slash away paint and crack the windshield. The engine pushes to hurtle us through bushes and back toward the road on the other side of the monster.

It twists after us, whipping its tail around. I duck as the back windshield explodes. A shower of glass. The air whistling around me. Searing pain through the side of my face. Morgyn throws herself against the steering wheel as the monster's rat tail wraps around her headrest and rips it clean off.

Blood's running from the slash in my cheek, dripping onto Lucy's jeans.

We ricochet onto a proper road, and Morgyn fully opens up the throttle. Behind us, I see the monster turn back and sprint for the sawmill and the girl we couldn't save. We barely saved ourselves.

CHAPTER FORTY-TWO

Morgyn doesn't stop until we reach the center of town. She's not going near the water or the edges. Instead, we wind up at the strip mall. Half the shops are boarded up, but the parking lot is lit with a scattering of streetlights. A few cars straggle in corners, some with people sitting on the hoods and others with people inside. Whatever can't happen in the homes of Sawblade. We're all keeping secrets here.

Morgyn parks in front of the silent post office—one of my confessionals. After she's caught her breath, she says, "It kind of fucked you up." That's true in every single way, but she gestures to my face. I run my tongue along the inside of my cheek, wincing at the thinness where the tail lashed me.

"Should put something on that." Morgyn reaches over my lap and opens the glove compartment. She hands me a stained rag, then sees how filthy it is. "Let me get you something better."

"I'm all right." So what? It bleeds. It scars. Maybe infection rages through my face.

Morgyn flicks open a knife and slashes at the bottom of her tank top. "I should've seen its tail coming around. A little swerve and you wouldn't be hurt." She rips off a strip and presses it into my hands.

"It's really fine—"

"It's what I can do!" she snaps.

I hold the fabric against my face, letting it soak up the blood. There's a faint hint of laundry detergent clinging to it that I don't associate with Morgyn at all. We sit in silence for a few minutes, both looking straight out the window.

"Radio?" she asks eventually.

"Yeah."

She flicks the dial a few times, nothing seeming to satisfy her.

"That last one," I say.

"Not my kind of singer, but it's not like there's anything good." Morgyn turns it back to soft guitar, times past. She brushes glass off the edge of my seat with her bare hand. Her hand runs along the edge of my leg. She holds a shard between her fingers and lets the light catch its sharp edges. "What now?"

We could make a new plan.

Find a bigger weapon.

More light.

"We listen to this song," I say.

So we do. And the next and the next. I check the cloth. The bleeding's slowed. The DJ says it's folk songs until dawn, wherever you are. No banter. He announces another, this one about leaving, and lets it play.

Morgyn reaches halfway across the distance between us, then rests her hand on the gearshift. "Best driving of my life, and for what? I feel all run out."

"Maybe you're coming down off a high."

"Kind of a sad fucking high."

It's true, but I remember what Lucy told me. "We take what we get and don't ask questions."

Morgyn shakes her head. "That's not how I've lived. Or I have. Play the hand I'm dealt, write my own rules. I don't know."

I turn to her, scarring face to scarred one. "What's something you *do* know right now? Something good."

"You're an asshole." Morgyn drapes her arms on Mongrel's steering wheel and rests her head. I think she might not respond, then she says, "I know I'm glad I'm not alone right now. I know I'm glad you ran to Mongrel. I know I'm glad you didn't let me leave you behind at Abraham's Corner."

There's a whooping across the parking lot and some laughter drifting through the night.

"I never had that," says Morgyn, "whatever that is. Carefree and unknowing, the kind that comes from having your own people. But meeting you . . . It's helped. When you stepped back into the open after I shot at you, I was so happy I hadn't hit you. You were brave, incredible, like almost nothing I've ever seen. And tough. Good tough, not Sawblade tough. Maybe I liked to think that someone else knew about the monster, but mostly I liked that it was you."

Morgyn turns her head to look at me. "You're a good person to be not alone with, Cedar."

It's in her eyes.

Question

grief

desire.

I know she's going to kiss me, and I don't stop her.

It's how I imagined it would be the night I met her. She kisses like it's inevitable, first like asphalt melting in the sun, then like our mouths can outrun terror itself. Like she knows what she's doing and like it's been a long time.

I meet the kiss with a mouth metallic with blood and a mind dizzy with fear and the euphoria of survival. This moment has been held in me since we sat in her truck in the rain outside a house I could only hope would be welcoming. A story I was already in. Her mouth conjures her bed, looking into that room and fantasizing my place in it. With Ada by my side, both of us lingering and turning away.

Did Morgyn kiss Ada this way after they saved Ruby?

Can she still taste Ada on me?

I already have a story with Ada. That's the one I belong in.

We break away at the same time, me with a rush of guilt. But Morgyn only reads the part of my face that's still full of desire.

Morgyn says, "Slide your seat back." She reaches for the lever below my legs and does it herself, jolting me back. She jolts everything inside of me, then doubles it with her hand on my thigh. "Let me closer to you."

I can't seem to think properly. It's a swirl of Ada and pain in my face and fear and despair coursing through my veins. My body pleads with my mouth to say yes. To let me sink into a feeling again.

"There's glass everywhere," I say with my eyes on the floor.

Morgyn's aren't. She's taking me in. "I'll kneel on glass shards. I've done worse for things I've wanted far less." She takes my chin, turns my head to her, kisses me again. She kisses me like we're building to something. Shifting in her seat, starting to cross over to my side.

With everything in me, I keep myself from kissing her back. I put a hand on her chest just above her breasts, fingers spread out, and feel her respond. Slight, halfway between a sigh and a snarl. "Let me create something good," she says. "Let me make you feel good. It'll be between us."

That's not why my hand is there. It's because she's the person who feels more. She's thrown herself at the wrong heart again, one whose feelings stop at a desperate kiss.

Gently, I push her away from me. "There's Ada."

Morgyn folds her hand over mine, keeping it on her chest. She switches it from pushing her away to feeling her heartbeat, racing together with mine, neck and neck. "What even are they to you? Have you even talked about it?"

"No, we haven't—"

"Exactly, so—"

"We haven't, but it doesn't matter. I know what they are to me, and I'm not going to chance it on a talk we haven't had." Morgyn's breath is under my hand, asking to merge with mine. "We wouldn't be making something good, Morgyn."

"And what is she to you?"

"My darling," I say.

Morgyn releases my hand and slumps away from me. "Fuck you." But she says it sad instead of angry in any direction. The feeling goes at the whole crushing ether around us.

"You're Ada's darling too," Morgyn says. "It's obvious. And I heard you two upstairs. I stopped at the door and thought about what would happen if I cracked it open." Despite everything erotic that brings up in my body, I don't truly wonder. It would only have been an ugly scene.

Morgyn rolls down her window and tosses a handful of glass into the parking lot. "I get to be her surgeon, her mechanic, her mercenary, but not behind that door with her. I didn't lead that thing away for Papercut or Lucy. That was for Ada. I'd do all those things for her. I'm happy to. And if I was anything like good enough for Ada, I wouldn't go after you. Of course you adore them. Who wouldn't?"

"Have you . . ." I'm not sure I should say anything, but Morgyn hasn't pulled her gun on me. "Has it been a long time?"

"Since they came to me asking for help with Ruby, I guess." Morgyn gives a small shrug. "How can you do anything but fall in love with someone who loves that hard?"

All I can think of to say is "I know."

And I know what I have to do.

"Now I'm too late for you." Morgyn turns away from me to light a cigarette. "I had this absurd feeling when I first picked you up that we were driving the wrong way. I thought you seemed lost. I felt the same. I was going to ask you to leave town with me. Forget about Ada. Forget it all. Leave the monster to scrap it out with this place."

"It wouldn't work."

"Why not?" asks Morgyn.

Across the parking lot, Morgyn's truck turns in crookedly with only one headlight. I count one, two, three people inside. Each one sitting upright. Part of me hoped Ada would be unconscious for what's next.

Morgyn takes a long drag like she's trying to settle herself. "Why not, Cedar?"

CHAPTER FORTY-THREE

Before anyone speaks a single word, Morgyn passes around a pack of cigarettes. Call it community. Communion. Now we've got some tiny warmth to hold, our own little lights, our own agency

to die

slowly

on our own terms.

The truck's parked at an awkward angle, partly over the curb. Lucy's sitting on the tailgate with Papercut beside her. Papercut's eyes are flat. There was no thrill to how they almost died back there. Ada stepped out of the truck, threw up, and sat down on the dirty pavement with her back against Mongrel's scratched side. Their forehead has an ugly gouge on it and bruises are spreading on their face and arm. She's cradling one of her arms close to her chest protectively with her eyes closed. Morgyn stands leaning against Mongrel, blowing smoke at the night sky above the streetlights. I'm pacing, restless with choices.

We do have our own people.

We've got our own secrets.

And I don't think I can own both any longer.

Lucy shifts. She's spending more time looking at her cigarette than smoking it. "Does it . . . Does it *hate* us?"

Morgyn glances at the wounds the monster's inflicted on her two vehicles. "It followed us like it does."

Lucy throws her cigarette onto the concrete and watches it fizzle out. "But then when did it start? Did it hate us before we did anything? We didn't even have a chance. Not like we would have been friends or made it a pet, but it just showed up in Sawblade like that." She's holding back tears. Papercut gives her hand a squeeze, and she doesn't let them move away. "*Why* does it hate us?"

Nobody has a response. It hurts to watch people you love cry out and get nothing back.

Lucy without answers, Papercut without spark, Morgyn without a plan. Ada without comfort, crumpled inches away from her own vomit because they drove forward to help Papercut and Lucy instead of running. She throws herself into the fire again and again for the people she loves.

All of us doing the same for each other
throwing our whole selves in
except for me.

I stop pacing.

"It didn't follow *us*. It doesn't hate *us*. It's me."

There's a legend about a bundle of ropes called the Gordian knot.

A tangle, a snake, a thing that could not be unraveled
until a brute with a sword cut it in half

and said there
I've solved it.
There is your truth
in tatters on the floor.
There is your world
fallen apart, and that is
the truth.

"I knew it would chase me and Morgyn," I say, "because it wants me."

That's not the start.

"I guessed that it needs me for something. I don't know what, but it does. I could feel it. But it's not something it can simply take. I think that's why it hates me. Maybe?"

Not the beginning either.

"When we stalked it with magic, it could see me. It went right for me."

I persist, going back step by step.

"When we found Ruby gone, I realized it's been following me since the beginning. I'll get there, I swear. But that's when it came together in my mind. Open doors, bottle caps, a white sheet."

I know I'm not making sense. And if I am, I don't want their reactions.

I look out across the parking lot so I won't see the moment my friends realize that their safe places are no longer safe, and that it's because of me.

"At night, I feel like it's watching me. Like I'm a radio station and it's always tuned in. I didn't know at first. You have to believe me. I figured out that it was tracking me around town and to the Point, but we were safe in the light. It was only at Tay's house that I realized the whole thing."

I've lied all along. Silence is a lie, not telling anyone what I fled from. My honesty arrives too late for sympathy.

"I came here because my mom died. They said it was a faulty machine, but when the blanket fort collapsed, memories came back. The same things it's done here. It didn't just follow me around here. I brought it here. It's my monster."

Earlier.

"It goes further, somehow. All the way to the house I grew up in under the dam and Sky and my dad and the bunker." But there's no point telling that part now.

I've already cut the knot
hewn open a twisted silence
and cut the ones I love.

There's a clamor of accusations. Steps forward, hands on weapons.

Morgyn says I'm like Ruby when she burnt the church. I'm a threat to Morgyn's town, and that's the vilest I can be. She takes what she said earlier back and says she should have left me to its jaws at Abraham's Corner. Unforgivable. Traitor. Damned.

Papercut too. Though their words are *coward*

and *deceiver*

and *monster*.

Lucy, drowned out, saying thank you for telling us. That she knows I didn't have to. Thank you for taking the chance to step in front of it and save Papercut.

Ada's sitting on the ground like they might never get up again. When she talks, the other noise dies. "You led it to Ruby. You knew you were a danger, and you stayed with us. You didn't even give us the chance to choose if we'd stand by you." They don't have to say the rest out loud. I know her words are *weight*

and *disappointment*

and *heartbreak*.

Ada has all those words sliding down her face in salt water.

Morgyn's not leaning on the car now. She's up close, threatening, ready to tell me to start running and see how far I get. "This is what you do to Ada? Get wrapped around their heart then squeeze the life out of it. You oh-so-loyal that you turn me down tonight. That's a lot of self-righteous bullshit for a traitor all along. Here I thought Ada cared about you because you're softer than me."

Papercut, in their emotionlessness, seems most likely to kill me. "Why was Cedar having to turn you down in the first place?"

"There were things the first night we got to Sawblade. And a week ago," says Morgyn, making it sound like more than it was. "I didn't start it. Not just me. It was before anything with Ada and Cedar anyway. But Cedar still looks at me like they want me. And it's not like they mentioned any of it to Ada."

Lucy says, "Your math all seems a little wobbly, Morgyn. Tonight wasn't before. Tonight's tonight. Tonight you tried something and Cedar said no."

"Eventually," says Morgyn. "*After* kissing me back."

Papercut hops down from the tailgate, chest to chest with Morgyn. "You're about as good with hearts as you are with plans. The light will kill it? Almost got us all killed, and now it's back to Ruby. Ada tried to use magic to find her. Maybe it moved Ruby or found cover. Connection's gone. Lead's gone. Wasted."

Lucy's on her feet too. "Everyone needs to calm down! We just went through like absolute hell. We *all* thought the light would torch it and then we could get Ruby. And Cedar's been through a lot. It doesn't matter that it was following them . . . not that much. Except Ruby, I guess. But still. It's not like any one of you would have told the truth any sooner."

I want to believe everything she says, but my heart can't. All that's inside me is glass shards and shame. "That's more than I deserve."

"I know," says Lucy, "and I'm giving it to you anyway because you're my friend. We should all do that for each other."

Papercut turns on Lucy, incredulous and disdainful. "My little sister could be dead because of this fucker, and you're siding with them?"

"It shouldn't be 'siding,'" pleads Lucy. "We're all on the same side."

Papercut shakes their head. "Not if you're with Cedar, we're not."

"I'm with you too!" Lucy doesn't know where to look or direct her words, caught in the middle of everything. "Papercut, of course I'm with you too. I love you, Jamie."

"I thought I—" starts Papercut. Then they bite their tongue. "Just these last weeks, or before too?"

"Does it even matter?" asks Lucy.

I want Papercut to say it matters more than anything. But instead, they sound tired. "Not anymore."

"Well, this is melodramatic," sneers Morgyn. "I tried to help. Power to you solving the clusterfuck you're in. You all deserve each other."

Ada turns to talk at Morgyn's back as she walks to Mongrel's driver's side door. "You're a bitch. A lonely, sad bitch with a gun and a fast car—"

The rest is drowned out under the sound of Mongrel pulling away.

Papercut climbs into the truck. "Ada, let's go."

I reach down to help Ada up, but they ignore my hand. Papercut gets the engine to start on the third try. Ada still hasn't moved.

I say I'm sorry. Too late, like everything.

Ada doesn't look at my face. Her eyes are on the ground—my shoes stained with soda, the cigarette butts, the vomit. "Fuck it, you could have brought your sorrow to me sooner." With all their effort, they manage to get up. Pale and uncertain on her feet, but certain in her words. "I would have stood by you, Cedar."

* * *

There is my truth
in tatters in the parking lot.
There is my world
fallen apart, and that is
the truth.

Yet everything I knew was a blade too dull, because Lucy—
the last and truest harbor
—still asks
why it knows me and
what it wants.

Those questions remain knotted as we drag our feet to her home.

• • •

Dad,

I understand why you lied and let the water of your sins wash over all things instead of confessing. I can't imagine Papercut or Morgyn or Ada forgiving me. I can't imagine forgiving myself when I've never forgiven you.

I've tried to be honest with you, but it's the second-to-last word of every letter that's the truest part. There, in the closing.

Yours,
Cedar

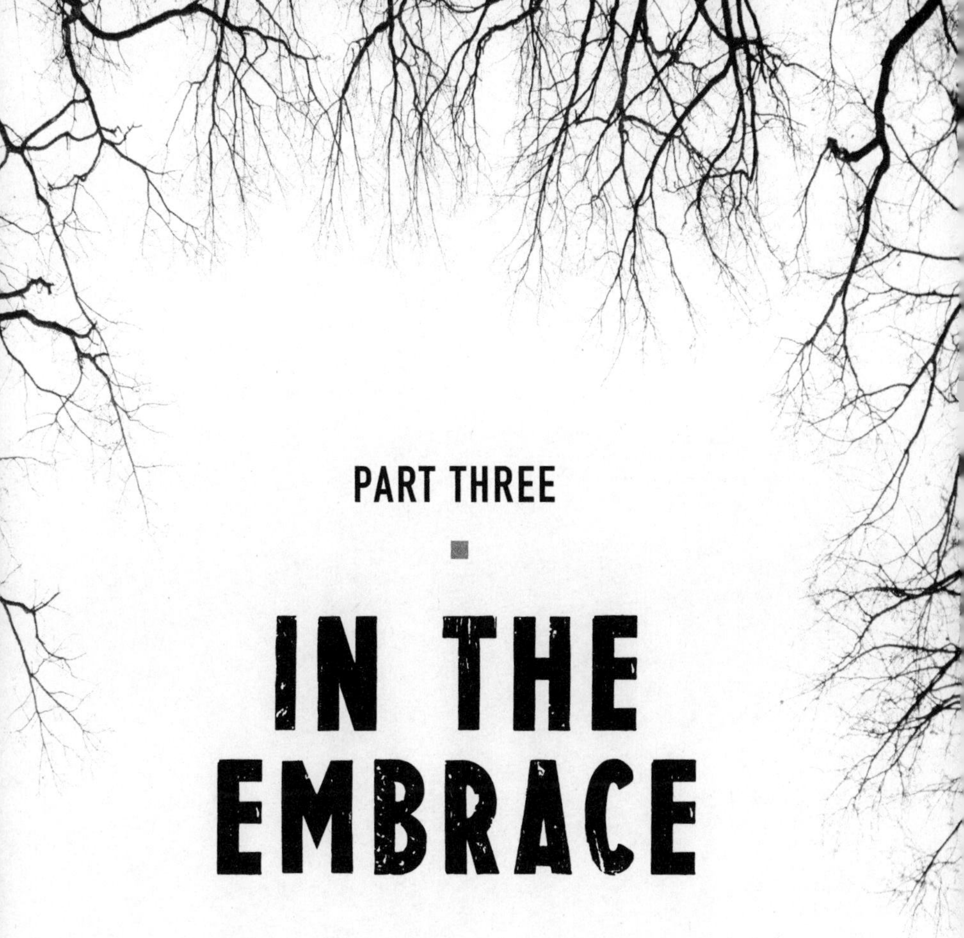

PART THREE

IN THE EMBRACE

CHAPTER FORTY-FOUR

The night is like the ones after Lucy first tried to show me shelter. It should have worked then. It was me who ruined that and brought death to the Point.

Lucy and I stay up until dawn and sleep during the day with the TV on even though we know all the actors in the film are dead now and the sunlight doesn't truly protect us. Not from the mouth and not from its walking host. It's the same as locking a door knowing the monster could just swing it open.

I offered to go home or to try to leave town. Lucy said it already knows her address. And if I left, it'd take Ruby and follow, and Ruby would die alone in the woods far from the people who love her most.

"You can't want me close after all of this," I said.

Lucy snapped at me for the first time I can remember. "Get over yourself, Cedar."

I raised my eyebrows at her.

"You fucked up," she said. "But you did the right thing in the end and a lot of right things along the way too. Papercut called you a coward and liar and monster. That's all of us. That's where we're at. You'll do better, and I'm going to be there for it."

I stuttered a response and wound up sobbing ugly tears instead of thanking her. We cried together, arms around each other.

"What does Papercut even know?" I said once we could talk again.

"Just because I forgive you doesn't mean you get to judge the people who are ready to rip your head off. It's harder for Papercut and Ada than me. It's their sister."

"I meant, who would ever walk away from you?"

"Oh, that. I *know*."

"Worst possible choice, clearly."

"I mean . . . yes. But it's also one of the things I love about Papercut. They're standing by Ada and Ruby no matter what. They'll even walk away from *me* for it. They're wrong, but I want to be in the inner circle of that love."

"I'm so sorry. I didn't know you cared about them that much."

"Because you're clueless."

"I knew you liked them! I didn't know how much. Papercut's lucky you love them."

"I love several people." Lucy smirked at me. "Papercut's the only one I love *and* want to fuck."

"Papercut's good," I said. "I think how you stand by the people you care about is one of the things they love about you too. Even if it infuriates them."

"I should hope so."

As we were starting to fall asleep, Lucy rolled over and whispered, "I'll snap at you again if you ever tell me what I can and can't do or how I should and shouldn't feel. What, did you think I would just shut up?"

"Never."

"Now you're learning."

It's almost sunset by the time I walk home. The heat's heavy and dead, though Lucy's dad was talking about a storm. I can see dark tendrils of cloud along the horizon grasping toward Sawblade.

If the power goes out again, I hate to think what it might do. I imagine a thoughtless rampage leading to me. If it can devour in its most monstrous form without being witnessed, it will strike back at us. Last time, it came for Ruby. This time, it will be me. Without the light it despises and with desperation in its dark veins, it will come for whatever it believes it's owed.

I arrive at the brick house with 32 beside the door. The windows on the second floor are open, trying to create some airflow. That means my grandma is up and about. It'd be safer if she was somewhere far from here, in a hospital I've never been to, off the radar of my monster. But in a way I'm glad she's here. It means this place is home.

I'm about to call her when I step inside, then I see the letter on the kitchen table.

Someone wrote my grandma's address large, with my name front and center in loops I've seen hundreds of times before. No return address, and no one knows this is where I went. But even from the entrance to the kitchen, the handwriting's familiar. I step toward this small thing that's so important my grandma had to mention it to me even though she was supposed to get in an ambulance and her friends lay under a black tarp. I told her I'd read it when I got home, but this is the first time I've been back.

This isn't in my father's writing. This is recipe books, band shirts, hands with rings.

I tear open the envelope and unfold a white sheet from my mom.

• • •

Hey Cedar,

I almost started this dramatically like the old thrillers I make you watch on VHS. "If you're reading this, it's already too late." But I can't see ahead to be certain of that. I can't predict who you'll be or what you'll be doing if you read this. What I do know is that I just woke up in the middle of the night with a horrible shadow hanging over me. I know that I can't let "too late" happen.

What I've learned can't be lost, because I've learned it to keep you safe.

I'll start with a lie. I lied to you the way I know you sometimes lie to me when you say you're studying late. I'm not visiting an old friend. Instead, I went to the coast north of where we used to live, following a rumor. This is the sixth trip like this in the past five years. I've lied about those trips too, so here's the truth.

I'm following something. I don't have to check your room for monsters, so now you're old enough to know. I've found one. It starts far, far back. Our part starts with your dad.

I know we don't talk about him much. I don't think there are good people and bad people. There are good and bad choices though, and ones that hurt people and ones that don't. Sometimes you can put it on circumstance, sometimes not. You know about a lot of the bad choices your dad made, but he was also skilled at hiding things.

Building the dam. It went from shady dealings to . . . well, darkness, I suppose. Evil? I'm not sure. Your dad's part maybe. Some of it I learned over the years we lived below the dam. Other parts I've pieced together since through my own observations, research, and interviews. Somehow, I've become the leading expert in an undiscovered field of faulty studies. Not that anyone knows who I am.

The dam started having problems the moment it was finished. Ones that your dad was to blame for that couldn't be fixed. He spent a lot of time there alone at night. The books I'd find in his desk at home got stranger and stranger. Theory, religion, conspiracy, the occult. In his way, he was a genius. That was the first thing that pulled me to him in high school. His research began long before

Autumn, maybe even before he was your age. But in desperation, he listened, and he figured out there was a fragmented soul in the dam. Autumn was triggered technologically, but that isn't the only way to stir faulty souls. I've seen your dad's sketches and notes. He did some ugly cocktail of old magic mixed up with devices he built. He woke it up on purpose.

You can stop reading. This gets so awful from here. Remember you are your own, not just the child of me and him.

Like most faulty souls, the one in the dam wanted to die. Instead, your father made a deal.

Cedar, your dad promised you or Sky to it. He told it that if it held the dam together until he died, then it could leave and have one of you as its host. From one of his creations to the other. A good body, not one as shameful as that filthy dam.

But like Faulty people and the extra souls in them, this was a relationship. He had to talk to it and work with it to solve things about the dam and, most of all, prove he was still alive. Yes, we built the house below the dam to demonstrate that it was safe, but it was also so he could be near the thing he was bound to. He did work on solutions. He never intended to really give you or Sky to it. He loved you.

One of his solutions was the bunker. It was designed to withstand more than a dam break. It was also built to hide from a monster. Don't get me wrong—it knew of that place. You could feel its creeping presence all over the house, especially around the bunker. That's where your dad kept his darkest tools. He spoke to it from there sometimes, and sometimes it made its presence known. But once the bunker was covered with water from the river the dam had held, the monster couldn't reach it.

I learned what your father had done not long before Autumn. Your dad claimed you and Sky had to stay at that house as part of the pact. I don't know if that was true, but I chose to remain close. When the dam broke, your dad wasn't scared of the water. He was scared of what he'd woken up years before. It heard the same call as other machines and broke its promise to wait for your dad's death. Perhaps because it had been awake longer and gained more of a sense of self, it had a way to take shape no other faulty thing had—a hideous form. Our new world evolving even as it began. That's why your dad chose the bunker instead of running with me and you.

From the moment we escaped, I started looking for this thing. The sins of the ones we've loved weigh on us. This trip, I finally found it. It's wandered to a smaller dam up north that your dad designed. I'd rather not describe how this monster looks. I'll just tell you what I've discovered that could be important.

It's incensed, but it's learning. Through my

trips, I've noticed that its decisions are getting less random. Coming to this dam, for instance. It opens doors and hates the light, though I've seen it risk brightness for something it wants if it thinks there's no one watching. It hates its reflection even more. I've seen it catch a fully lit glimpse of itself in the windows of an old factory once. It made . . . let me just call it a horrible sound so I don't have to remember it closer than that.

What does it want? Above all, you or Sky. Though the lake and bunker combined should keep Sky safe. And it's also always thirsty. I've got a theory that it's cursed from the machine it came from. For all the water it destroyed, it can't drink clean water. Alcohol, runoff, paint, sewage, gasoline, but not rain, for example. It hides from that. It will swim in the ocean where the water's most poisoned, but yesterday I saw it get caught by a rogue wave of cleaner water. That sound was worse than any other it's made. It's normally semitransparent. Where the water hit, it became more ethereal, like it was clinging to life. That's why it can't reach the bunker. Your father bet the floodwater would be pure enough to keep it at bay.

With enough clean water, maybe it could be harmed? How I'd force it into that kind of situation, I can't imagine. I've seen it flip a semi tanker on its side and cut the tank open with its claws. Thirst, light, and water aren't much to go on for weaknesses. Though obsession and need could count for something too.

That's what I've got. I'm coming home to you now. I've missed you even though you're a pain in the ass. I'm mailing this from the world's least-reliable-looking post office. They said it'll take a few weeks. I'm going to send it to your grandma's house in Sawblade Lake. When I knock over dominos in my mind, if something went so wrong you had to read this instead of me telling you, you'd wind up there. She'll keep it safe, and you too. She's great at that. You've never been to Sawblade, but it's remarkable in its own way. Maybe someday I'll get far enough from my memories of your father to visit there with you and we can read this letter together.

Love you, see you soon!
Mom

CHAPTER FORTY-FIVE

I WISHED TO UNDERSTAND, AND NOW I WISH I DIDN'T. MY eyes are clear. I don't even have tears.

It stretches back and back and back and

too late.

The house and family I grew up in. My memories of the basement and bunker and presence. The deafening familiarity of this thing.

The date on the letter is from a week before it killed my mom. It followed her first. It swam the poison river behind our apartment block and waited for the power to go out. Was it coming for me or her?

At Abraham's Corner, the true barrier wasn't the streetlight but the rain. It fled because I stumbled over the bucket and spilled clean rainwater into what it was drinking.

And here. It can swim in the toxic lake, walk the unflooded sewer. It hated the fireworks and wanted the alcohol. It tried something with Kat, whose body pushed back the fog of its thoughts for a moment and let it communicate in words. Thirst, hideousness, hollowness. In the end though, an unhallowed vessel, hull shattered.

So a better host—Ruby. It'd seen her. She understood it like she understood Emerald. And it fit into the gap where Emerald used to be, because in a warped way, this monster is from a faulty machine after all. Both of Autumn and other, an aberration from within. It used its connection to me to stalk Ruby and the power outage to reach her. Got her agreement by threatening her friend. Fled, hid from the rain in a septic tank.

My mom said it's learning. I think it's remembering too. In Ruby's form, things seem to be becoming clearer. Unashamed of its form, though still ashamed of the dam. Perhaps it's figuring out it needs me. Were the mailboxes a threat or just a signal of our link? Was it reaching out? Carved into trees, talk of blood and curses.

Then the message at the church.

> So as the creator flooded gopher holes, I smoke
> out my sibling with sorrow
> Burn the ground cover until I have the last arms
> to run into
>
> My arms in theirs, stronger than this failing frame
> My west coast tree with the sun setting behind
> them
> My bloodline, my vein
> My broken thing crawling home without shelter
>
> Start with the holy
> The clustered voices

End with embrace
Anything over alone.

Like my mom, it was both thinking out loud and talking to me. I'm the west coast tree. I'm the sibling it hopes to break. Like Cas or Emerald, it needs a relationship. For my body to hold it, I have to surrender myself to it.

"Cedar?" calls my grandma from upstairs. "Are you home?"

I hurriedly fold the letter and tuck it back into the envelope. I'll keep this awfulness from my grandma the same way my mom kept it from me. After all these years, I doubt she recognized my mom's writing like I did. Though she might have guessed anyway.

"I just got back!" I call. I'm going to have to explain this cut on my cheek somehow. A simple story. I tried to get into the middle of a drunken fight. A broken-off bottle.

I step out of the kitchen, where all my attention was on the letter. My head's reeling. The broken bottle will do, but I'll say I wasn't *in* the fight. Just bad luck when I was pulling people apart. Just in the cross fire.

Something's off.

I stop walking and look across the familiar space of my home. The worn chair with its patterned fabric. The spoon collections, landscape paintings, and magazines.

The dollhouse.

My blood becomes thick, cold slime.

Every single tiny door is open. It's like a small hand reached inside and exposed the space behind every barrier. Each delicate room laid bare.

My grandma appears at the top of the steep staircase, moving slowly. There are still bandages on her hand and some on her face. She's tired but smiling at me, and she looks older than she did yesterday. "I think we found a place for the church to meet this Sunday." She's seen the letter in my hand. She's starting with small talk in case I don't want to talk about it. "I swear, all I've done since waking up is close cupboards."

She places her foot on the first step.

Behind her, a small shadow appears at the top of the stairs.

Cornflower blue.

My grandma's still talking, off-balance as her foot moves between steps. "It was the oddest—"

Ruby pulls her arms back, aiming both palms at my grandma's back. I scream something and run for the base of the stairs, but Ruby doesn't twitch. There's a calm sadness on her stained face as she meets my gaze and pushes.

The inhuman strength means my grandma only hits the steps once

hard

before I break her fall with my body.

I don't care that I'm vulnerable to Ruby as I untangle myself from my grandma's crumpled stillness. Twisted neck and bleeding skull. I'm shaking too hard and breathing too frantically to tell if her heart is beating or if any air is moving in and out of her lungs. I hold her blood-smeared, frozen face in my hands.

There's a soft creaking on the steps. The sense of Ruby standing over me.

"Find me at the numbers in the in-between," she says. "Whenever you're ready."

I lash out at her, but my hand catches nothing but the space where she was. She's already out the door and into the failing light. By the time I burst into the street, she's halfway down the block, running in tilted, painful steps.

CHAPTER FORTY-SIX

My grandma's dead.

My ground cover is burning.

I call whoever you call.

I sit on the bottom step holding her hand. My mom's letter is lying on the floor. When someone arrives, I tell them there was a fall. That my grandma was unsteady after the fire.

Eventually, the house is empty. Night and rain are falling outside. If the rain had begun earlier, my grandma would be safe. If I got the letter yesterday. If my grandma took the ambulance to Fort Luthe. If I never came here.

It stretches back and back and back and

too late.

It got here first and waited for me. It wanted me to see.

The doors on the dollhouse are still open. I carefully close the first one. The second. My hands are trembling. I accidently break the third off, and I break with it. I tear the dollhouse apart with my bare hands until there's blood on the fragments of wood. I don't stop until my sobs are spent and every fragile thing is in fragments on the floor.

CHAPTER FORTY-SEVEN

I NEED BANDAGES. I MAKE MY WAY TO THE UPSTAIRS BATHroom and fumble the cupboard open. Pulling slivers from skin with tweezers. Disinfectant fizzing sharply. I leave most of the cuts uncovered.

My dad's old bedroom remains latched shut. If I go in there, I won't stop until my body is in shreds. But my grandma left her door ajar. I've never been in her room either. With a push from my damaged hands and a creak of hinges, I step inside.

There's soft bedding that drapes to the floor and an oak dresser with a mirror built into it. A clutter of pictures, organized jewelry, an old fan swiveling back and forth causing a rustling on the far side of the bed. I walk around it and find piles of newspapers. They're open to specific pages and marked with highlighter. Circles here and there. Notes in tight handwriting.

I pick a paper up. These are for the area I grew up in, not for Sawblade Lake. She must bring them in by special order. I kneel down and start rummaging more. They go back years and years. My grandma's circled any news about the fallout of the dam disaster that buried the bunker. Either my grandma had her own suspicions, or my mom was honest in that one phone call.

This heap looks like my grandma was watching for news that her son and grandson might be alive. I dig further, scattering her unfathomable system, looking for the most recent paper. It just arrived a couple days ago, but it's dated two weeks back. It's got more circles and notes than any of the others, and it all points to one thing.

The lake's been draining.

Any day now, the ruins at the bottom could be open to the Sky.

My brother could finally be free. And my father could be set loose on the world again.

I take a closer look at the pictures on my grandma's dresser. On the far side, her with me and Sky as grinning children. I imagine rescuers opening the bunker and, from countless miles away, our monster lifting its head. Sky and my dad climbing out. I imagine them the same ages they were when I left, though Sky must be seventeen now. I imagine the monster catching the signal of Sky's body. A fresh host, untainted by the world. No longer kept safe by the water. It could take him instead of me.

We've already done that. My dad grabbed him and pulled him into the dark. I got to grow up with sunshine and people and my mom, and if Sky's alive, he grew up isolated underground with the looming presence of the man who sold out his own children. Sky's been taken instead of me once. I can't risk that this time.

My grandma said she was scared to die. She said she wasn't

ready to make that trip. I asked how do you get ready? She told me to figure out who I can't help but love and do everything I can to make them know it.

I know who I can't help but love.

Ada.

My friends.

Sky.

The only way I have to show that love is by protecting them. I've got to make the people and places they care about safe again, from Ruby to each other to this shitty town. It's too late to save Kat, TJ, Oliver, Camille, the church, the people inside, my grandma, my mom, but not too late to avenge. And I have an idea I'm hacking into a discernable shape in my mind.

I run downstairs and dial Lucy's number.

She answers instantly like someone waiting with hope. For Papercut, she says. I give her a reason to call them first. Ada and Morgyn too. I ask her to tell the three of them she's found a way to save Ruby. I know she'll make something up if they've got questions.

It has to be soon. It has to be tonight. I don't explain all of it. I ask her to hang her trust on some fragments.

She tells me it's enough. The rain's enough. I'm enough.

I say to remind the others of Ruby's failing body and the risk of a power outage. We've got to move fast. We'll meet somewhere. Don't mention me. Tell the others the rain will keep them safe.

Where?

My grandma told me that if the point was winning, go where

my dad used to work and the monster haunts the bone trees outside. Go to the arcade.

It's not that clean though. Winning has a cost. It's never without risk or sacrifice. You can't be safe and be good.

You mostly lose, but it isn't pointless. Love is never wasted.

CHAPTER FORTY-EIGHT

Dear Sky,

I don't know why I've never written to you even though I've been writing to Dad. Maybe it's because I could stand the thought of him being dead, but not you. Or because I didn't want to put all this weight on someone who will, in my mind, always be smaller than me and need protecting. It could be that I remember you reading sound by sound, letter by letter. You hated it. You liked it better when I told you stories.

Let me tell you one now. A ghost story. Of ghosts. Perhaps to a ghost and by a ghost as well. I don't have time to write it, so these are words I'm reciting in my head. They may never make it beyond that.

The arcade on the lakeshore is abandoned. A closed, silent exterior of boards and spray paint with rain slipping through the cracks in the roof.

A vacant place, not empty.

It's full of bodies. The burnt out and the smashed in. Corpses

that used to be machines

that used to be games.

These amusements are all dead except for one pinball machine still humming in the center of the room. It's a possessed world of light sending colors dancing off the graveyard around it. It pings and whirs, playing against itself.

Perpetual, beautiful, haunted perfection. Red numbers continually rising. The pinball machine is a prisoner trapped in a loop, unable to lash out or end itself. This is its version of a scream, and it's calling us in.

We used to believe desolation like what we find in this place showed us how our world had changed. Torment comprehended and contained. But we were far from dredging the bottom. Now the arcade feels safe compared to what we've seen. What better place to meet?

If we are to be near a nightmare, let it be caged.

We are all the prey, praying:

Cover of night
uncover that which we seek
but are afraid will find us.

I walk alone in the rain toward the end of the boardwalk. The worn boards creak underneath my feet, and I can imagine the water lapping in the hollow space below me. The lake smells rank, betraying the pollution. I step over the gap where a plank's rotted away. I don't look down.

The businesses along the waterfront are either closed

for the night or forsaken, but there are a few lights glimmering from the windows in town. It's quiet enough for me to believe that somewhere inside, I might be out of danger. Though now I know walls have no meaning. The lines I've drawn between myself and the world are imaginary, but I still cling to them, thinking my skin can stop the shadows from leeching me into nothingness.

Ahead, by the arcade, a car pulls up and idles in the dark. Our wolf without a pack.

As I get nearer, I see the forest behind it. Here, at the edge of town, the dead pine trees look like bones around the two people who emerge from the far side of the building. They're caught sharply in the car's headlights. One has their hood pulled up, face down. The other's short hair is exposed to the rain. Our bled-out fighter and our parallel soul.

And finally, from down the street beside me, joining me, a person who wanted to know everything and now knows too much.

We walk together toward the others, close enough to hold hands. Then we do, because we're all hollowed out and running on touch. These are my hungry, desperate hearts.

Kill the car engine. Push a sheet of plywood aside, and one by one step into the light of the tortured machine shining brighter than it should be able to. There's water dripping from the ceiling of the arcade and insulation hanging loose. This summer feels like that first Autumn, with life coming down around us.

I hope we're willing to kill for each other. I know we're willing to die.

I'm the last inside. Our walking curse, drenched in the sins of those now buried.

I'm the hunter

the bait

the teeth of the trap

the foot caught in it.

I put the makeshift door back into place, sealing us in.

It's time to draw our fear close and face it.

That's just the start. I don't know the rest yet. I know that at the arcade I stood in the dancing light and spoke face to face with the people I love. Some of them had hate in their eyes that broke my heart. I carried a letter from Mom and talked about Jonah from that Sunday school story I can't shake, about curses and being thrown overboard to calm a storm. I gave them a plan. A sacrifice too late for some but not for all. A way to keep a pact, or something like it. It's based on terrible truths Mom learned for us and told to me. She wouldn't have wanted it to go this way.

Neither do the wolf, the fighter, the parallel soul, or the truth-seeker. They still agreed. They saw there was no other way. They made the plan better. The one who's my closest friend had silent tears. So did the one I've given all of myself to. I left before there was time for more words or lost nerves. I wouldn't have been able to carry on if someone begged me to stop. Or if no one did.

Now I'm at the numbers in the in-between. Edge of town, edge of the light, edge of the woods. I'm at the mailboxes, writing this letter to you in my mind and waiting while I listen to a mixtape called "Shelter."

I might die tonight. I chose that, and what decided it was you. I hope you don't feel any guilt in that. There's nothing owed. I'm only telling you so you know someone loves you enough to die for you.

It's here now. I've got to go.

Love,
Cedar

CHAPTER FORTY-NINE

Ruby is in the trees. Behind the mailboxes, I can make out her small form in Ada's old blue raincoat. Sunken eyes, stained mouth caked in filth. It's raining, so she's done everything she can to make sure no clean water touches her skin. Trees above her, hood up, and her hands deep in her pockets.

It knew where to find me. It's always known. Its power has opened a few mailboxes. The familiar numbers and some new ones that could be the arcade or the diner or Camille's house or the post office or the Dalfason farm. It doesn't matter anymore.

The same rain protected me at Abraham's Corner. Now it guarantees that the monster won't leave Ruby's body and rush into the rain to assault me with its more warped and powerful form. Still, its presence pulses in the back of my mind, like a headache I've woken up with after a night I don't want to remember. Like I'd rather stay in the dark than be dragged into it.

From underneath the music in my headphones, each beat insists.

Let me in.

Let me in.

Let me in.

I'm the one door it can't force open. It can lean on me and rattle the locks, but if it breaks me down, I won't be the perfect vessel any longer. It needs an invitation, so that I might play host and it might play the houseguest who never leaves.

"Not here," I say. The mixtape makes my voice sound muted to me, like someone else is talking. "Ruby's siblings have to be there to take care of her."

Let me in.

Let me in.

Let me in.

"Soon. There's a place." Then I welcome it to do the same thing that set off this entire mess. "Follow."

I start down Birchwood Drive, staying close to the houses. My shoes stick slightly with every step, until the bottom halves of my legs are covered in mud. I force myself not to look back.

Beside me, a car gently clicks unlocked.

A garage door shudders up a couple inches.

A trunk pops open.

Ruby is slipping through the cover of the trees alongside me. A limping wraith behind sharp sweeps of pine and columns of bone.

My mom said obsession and need could count for something. Her and I and it know of these things. Like chasing a monster your husband created through the wreckage of the world. Like a desperate attempt to trap that monster in light and save Ruby.

Like following the child of the creator who deceived you.

It's taken this thing a decade to figure out and find what it was promised. It had to learn and devour and possess and fail to reach this point of clarity. It suffered and suffers still. Now it's close, it has a one-track mind that throbs without questions.

Let me in.

Let me in

Let me in.

Will it be like this once it's in me, but multiplied by a thousand? My body is a precious place I sometimes hate and sometimes love but always inhabit. Soon it will be just a monster's dwelling. This thing's all-consuming need stronger and darker than anything I've felt. Once it's invited in, I doubt I'll be able to cast it out.

Even if it's only for a short time, I hope I'm not present.

That Kat wasn't.

That Ruby isn't.

But I think she is

screaming and scratching at the walls

until her fingers bleed.

When I arrived in Sawblade Lake, I felt only numbness and fear. Now some part of me wishes I'd clung to that. Flat and afraid and detached from the full extent of what I'm losing. Parties, intertwined bodies, laughing through the night.

The love and wonder and sense of home.

We pass Lucy's house and the vacant stretch where the monster killed Camille.

No one gets to document their walk to the gallows. In the end, this is always done

alone.

But I'm not numb anymore. I'm awash, and in my mind, I cling to what I can. I write letter after letter in my thoughts.

• • •

Dear Lucy,

I wish you'd lived on my block my entire life. I wish you'd sat next to me in class. I wish you were in the passenger seat of all my road trips and the 3 a.m.'s of all my sleepovers. Thank you for holding my hand at the arcade while I told everyone this plan and for reading my mom's letter out loud when my voice gave out.

I'll write again if I see the night through.

Cedar

• • •

Dear Morgyn,

It's not all true. You're far more than the rumors. The first time you picked me up, your hands on the wheel, those kept me alive. Everything else is a mess. Love like shrapnel. Just because you're not right for someone doesn't mean you're not good enough. There is love for you that you won't have to kneel on glass shards for. I don't know if you even consider yourself brave, but you are. You planned to face it on your own when you were the only one who really knew what you were facing. Thank you for picking the losing side with me.

I'll write again if I see the night through.

Cedar

• • •

Dear Papercut,

Lucy loves you and wants you. This is the luckiest you could possibly be. I know you're fierce. Everyone knows it. Don't be too fierce to accept her heart, Jamie. I don't think you are, because when you've got your fists up, you're standing between the people you love and the things that threaten them. Thanks for not stabbing me on sight tonight and for that nod you gave me once I laid out my plan. I'm holding it as respect, but maybe it's always meant you want to fight me.

I'll write again if I see the night through.

Cedar

• • •

Dear Ada,

You make me ramble nonsense with your eyes, shut me up with your touch, spill my whole heart out when I'm *near you. It's absurd. It started the first time I saw you. I only knew you for a few minutes before the fray began. Then in the fray, I learned you're someone whose hand I would hold from here on out. Hammocks, brunch, colored quilts. Laughter and fresh cookies. Fall asleep and wake up together. I should have brought my sorrow to you sooner. You never gave me a reason not to.*

Thank you for watching over me during all those nights. Thank you for your tears when you knew what this plan could mean. Thank you for being my darling, even if it was only for a little while.

I'll write again if I see the night through.

Cedar

CHAPTER FIFTY

Far ahead of me, Camille's house is the opposite of how I left it. No dancing or joy and no ring of lights trying in vain to protect it. Lucy said Camille's parents left town without a set return date the same day her car was found burnt-out by the road. Now we're here to end what cut down Camille.

I walk up the center of the street lined with houses that were never built. At the end, Camille's stands solitary on the cul-de-sac, a first and last beacon. Behind me, Ruby breaks from the cover of the trees and follows me. The rain unleashed itself while we walked. It's blown through now, leaving the night cool enough to make me shiver in my soaked clothes, but the monster stays in Ruby. It's come this far. We both have.

The front door Morgyn once sealed with her truck swings open to welcome me in. Ruby and I walk the halls and pass below the mounted elk head in the main room. I take one last look out the windows at Sawblade and its lake. Remarkable in its own way. We go past the kitchen with the pantry where Ada and I kissed for the first time. Out the back door and toward the pool house.

All the lights are on. They catch off the water and ripple through the glass and onto the lawn, pulling us in. As we get closer, I look in the windows to see Ada, Papercut, and Lucy standing inside on the far side of the pool. They're blurred through the glass. Once it's in me, will I see them that same way? Blurred, distant.

Again, the door opens before me like my monster's being courteous.

My steps echo as I walk around the still pool to my friends, leaving muddy footprints on the white tile. Ruby latches the door behind her when she enters. She hesitates, and the pulsing in my head escalates.

"Patience," I order. Silently, I beg please, a lifetime of patience. I know how to tell when I'm ready to die, but I'm still not. "They've brought fresh clothes for me. Wait there."

Ruby walks to the center of her side of the pool where I pointed. That's good. It fits with our plan. One of her legs drags and every step looks painful, though she doesn't flinch, even if Ada does. Ruby sits on one of the deck chairs and rests her forehead on her folded hands.

It's the gesture of something old and weary.

Or something bent over in prayer.

My arrival to the other side is quiet. No greetings or hugs. My friends have seen that it can hear and understand us, so all the words I wrote in my mind while I walked stay within me, unspoken.

Papercut's focused on Ruby. Flickers across their face of brightness to see the sister they love, and rage to see what it's done to her. Restlessness too. Under their hooded plaid cape, I notice the shape of Morgyn's revolver in the waistband of their jeans. A backup plan. Now that it's me, not Ruby, whether the monster dies with its host becomes a question to just ask.

Beside them, Lucy gestures to a neatly folded pile of clothes. She gives me a forced smile, trying to keep it together for me. There's a pair of boots sitting next to the outfit. Something about the careful order makes me want to start to cry. A shudder goes through me. I feel like I can't move, can't breathe, can't—

"Everything's here for you." Ada's voice is the same as it was at the Point. Calm and steady and wrapped around me. My entire being leans toward it. It makes huge things simple. I know I want to exist near Ada. Now, in the past, always. I can feel the thrum of Cas as Ada adds, "Everyone's here for you."

Everything. Everyone. It's only code that all the pieces are in place. Not to be mistaken for anything warmer.

I look at the ground. Even at the arcade, I couldn't meet Ada's gaze. There's another pile of clothes by their feet. Children's clothes. These are for Ruby if we save her. It's a reminder of things worth dying for.

I see Ada's feet step closer to me until they're near my muddy shoes. "*I'm* here for you." She puts her arms around me, and it's

not quite forgiveness
not adoration
but it is shelter. After it all and in the midst
still love.

Without asking, Ada helps me change. Their arm is hurt from the fight, but we manage. We peel off the sodden clothes, which stick to my skin, until I'm naked on the pool deck. We didn't think the monster would cooperate if I was drenched. The only thing I keep is my necklace. Ada hands me fresh clothes, each piece clean and dry and heavy around me. Funeral clothes.

Lucy's dad's steel-toed boots. Cargo pants with too many full pockets. A T-shirt from Lucy for a band she knows I like. A vest carefully hidden inside a lined denim jacket that's gutted and restuffed. It presses down on my shoulders. I button up my jacket and turn back to see Ruby's posture unchanged.

"I'm ready." I try to make my voice sound strong for me and everyone. Instead, it echoes off the flat water and disperses into the space. It's like the self I thought I had is already slipping away from me.

Ruby doesn't respond.

As I walk back around the pool, I try to move normally to hide the secrets in what I'm wearing. It doesn't matter. Ruby still isn't watching. As I get closer, I can feel why. The need is too great, the stakes too high. It can't bear to look at me and face the thought of losing me.

There's a small diving ring sitting on the edge of the pool deck. An inconspicuous marker, like tape stuck to a stage. I stop in line with it. Across the pool, Ada gives me a nod. Lucy glances toward a closed plastic chest on the deck by her. I know she's got a chain in there to use if the plan works. If it doesn't, Papercut's got the gun.

Ruby gets up, stumbles slightly, then stands straight. What if I tackled her now? Could I kill it?

Not something you just ask. Not about a kid.

Ruby faces me and pushes her hood back, revealing the dark

smears around her mouth and the stains on her teeth. The sunburns on her face and blisters on her hands. The filthy, tangled, matted hair. How her shoulder still isn't right and how her body looks like it's eating itself to survive.

Haunted things don't have eyes that roll back or turn black. Their eyes are tired and glazed over. They have anguish behind them. Haunted is parents at gravesides, soldiers returning from the trenches,

a kid whose body has been taken away.

The pulsing in my head stops. I'm myself again. The breath before a plunge. Ruby uses her own voice out loud now, but with the rasp of a smoker and a long, cruel life.

"My hallowed vessel of the same father
My tree of branches reaching for the sun
Raised in the same lies, rocked in the same cradle
The last arms for each to run to
Now end with embrace
Now anything over alone."

Ruby steps toward me and stops a few feet away. Closer than the plan, but I trust Morgyn. There's a stench rising off Ruby that mixes rot and blood and ancient cold air with chemical cleaners and sewage. All my evolution tells me to hold my breath, turn away, run and never stop running. This is how I may become. Even if my body doesn't break down, will those be my eyes?

I feel Ada's and Cas's presence, though my gaze is on Ruby. Still, sensing them gives me what I need. I force myself to stare into the haunting. "Once this is done, you and I walk out of here. We leave Ruby and all of my friends alone. We leave

Sawblade Lake and we never come back." It's a lie that doubles as a contingency plan.

Ruby tilts her head at me. Part of me can't help but hear a trace of the mocking, playful kid in its sinister words. "You *and* I? In this embrace, I walk you out. You must understand."

"I understand," I say, though I never wished to. "I'm ready."

"Thank you."

Then a shiver runs through Ruby. The consciousness flares up in my head, screaming to be let in. Ruby's body disguises the monster. Now that it's nearer, I feel a catastrophe, a menace, a mangled soul. To let it in is

to swallow a snake
to lean toward roadkill in the sun
and breathe deeply.

Ruby rocks back and forth with her arms wrapped around her. The haunting blinks out of her eyes,

and this time when she says
thank you
it's the real Ruby speaking to me
and to Ada
but the haunting
has to go somewhere, so it
blinks into me.

I expect a rush of writhing darkness twisting into my mouth. Instead, it's like a ghost stops inside me instead of passing through. As if my shadow stood up and wormed under my skin. My entire being inhaling ice-cold air that stays frozen all the way down.

The monster shudders into place inside me. I can't control

any part of my body any more than I can control my heartbeat. We turn away from the others and step toward the door and Ruby's body.

I strain and strain and strain, but I'm suspended. I'm pushing against something impossibly heavy with nothing to push off of.

So plan A is already out to sea.

Papercut draws the gun and fires.

CHAPTER FIFTY-ONE

Coursing through my veins
coursing through my mind and my memories looking in a mirror
at myself from another angle catching
glimpses of each of us in the pieces of broken glass falling on us
on me
on it.
It's all breaking away now. I'm breaking away.
Me now spliced together with
the monster.

Ancient creatures, plants, and rocks died and slept, and
their forms and what slept within them were free
from dreams and uses. All separate
resting near each other until
claws of machines, of zombies enslaved against their own,
tore them from the earth. A part and another and another
melted and sewn and meshed together to make
a dam.
Still sleeping.

Papercut's gunshot is just a signal for now, but I'm too close to Ruby. I hear Mongrel's engine. Ruby's crawling away from the monster that guides my body after her in slow steps. I want to yell at her to crawl crawl crawl, save yourself, but I have no voice anymore.

An alarm screams out and I wake up
no, *it* wakes up
like waking up in the hospital
after a horrible accident to find
its organs
its limbs
its face
are no longer its own.
That was my father forcing it awake.
So the alarm becomes its own scream as in a rush it learns
what it's been formed into and what this creation has done
to the water. Woken up
to be coerced. My father's deal doesn't
make sense to it. But then
nothing does.

Headlights blaze through the wall. Then they whip sideways just before Mongrel explodes through the side of the pool house in a barrage of glass. Metal frames twist away. The back tires of the car miss Ruby by inches, and then Mongrel strikes me.

The monster has taken the rest of me, so why doesn't it take the pain? The bone goes through, I think. Somewhere in my leg or my hip. I'm in the air. My friends' voices are obliterated by the mayhem of Mongrel. In the arcade, together, we layered this plan.

A second alarm, this one from on high
the launch of the Mars mission
like a leaf falling like Autumn.
The soul in the dam broke its coil.
Let the concrete fall
but without it, a body
grotesque
thirsty and ashamed
in a senseless world. It knows what it's done
as part of the dam. Something it never asked to be.
It drags itself through the desert
of the night. There's hope somewhere in a fragmented
memory
of a promise.

In plan A, the monster possesses me, and I jump into the pool before it takes complete control of my body. The water drives its foul soul from this plane.

Right now, Ada's running to Ruby. On the opposite side of the deck, Lucy is already grabbing the chain from the crate to pull me to the surface once the monster's gone. Even though we all know that plan is lost. The moment it was in me, I knew it was far too strong. I felt the extent of the agreement.

I've signed myself over. It can walk me where it wills.

In B, Papercut gives the gunshot signal and Morgyn drives

through the pool wall. That's what's happening now. They knocked down a section of fence to get Mongrel into the yard, close enough to be lying in wait. It's sloppy, but we use the skills and tools we have. We've seen that a car can move the monster. That's all we need. In the end, the water will still do the work, and my friends will still pull me back up.

What's left, at least.

In C, nothing goes right. This plan ends with bullets and my fragile body dying with the monster inside. Even as I hit the water, Papercut holds vigil, hair trigger. They'll be watching to make sure it's me that surfaces, not something else inside my skin.

The things it's done the things it's done
the things it's done
and it's finally done.
It wants to cry. It never has, not sure
it can. It tells itself that it's not
malice or monstrosity
just desperation cornered
trying to survive.
And this thing is
in me
and maybe this thing is
the same as me.
Raised in the same lies and
rocked in the same cradle. It just
wants to live freely
no matter the cost, but

when it woke, the first voice it heard was our father's.
Stay free. Get free. Keep people in the dark.
My friends know too much, so to stay free
they have to be put in the dark forever.
When I woke, I heard my mother's voice first.

"Salt water," said Camille a week ago. "So it doesn't damage my lustrous skin or hair."

Tonight, Morgyn asked, "Are you sure that will work?"

If it was chlorine, I wouldn't be. That seems more like my monster's drink of choice. But salt water is pure. In my mom's letter, it swam the poisoned ocean but screamed when the clean wave hit it. Its body faded.

Salt water will damage it. Skin and hair and soul.

It names me and my friends.
Host watcher hunter lover fighter child.
Our names are its killing list.
As the water wraps around us, I feel
panic rip through it. The shadow in me is being pulled
outward.
It's being pulled toward a light at the end of a tunnel where
it will be seen in a truer way
than it's ever been seen. Who among us doesn't fear that?
So it claws to stay inside me. It digs in.
It screams *traitor* at me with the guilt of knowing
it's the other side of the same coin.

CHAPTER FIFTY-TWO

The monster and I sink, just like my friends and I planned at the arcade. That's why my heavy clothes are full of gravel and scrap metal. The pockets, the coat lining, the vest. We know a wave didn't kill it instantly. To stop it getting out of the pool too quickly, we had to send it to the bottom. Ada said Cas might be able to tell when the monster was gone.

"How long can you hold your breath?" asked Lucy. "I won't leave you down there a moment longer."

I said I had no idea.

She said she'd hold hers to get an estimate.

In the water, I'm overcome with pain from every angle. My pain as the salt water purges my cut hands, the slash in my cheek, and the wounds Mongrel inflicted on me. The monster's pain as the water tries to wrench it out of this world. The clean water hates it. It hates the dam. It hates that this thing was ever allowed to exist.

My feet hit the tiled pool floor. Above me, my blood twists red toward the surface. Lucy's counting. Ada's helping Ruby. Papercut's got the gun trained on the surface. Morgyn's getting out of Mongrel and running into the broken pool house. They're all waiting for an unknown sign. But it isn't coming.

In my body, the monster is stronger than it was in Ruby's. It's strong in a different way than it is in its own snaking skin. It won't give me up. It won't be seen in the light. We underestimated its ferocious will to live.

It takes my arms and legs and pushes at the water. Though its soul is flickering, it swims against the weight. Now that its thoughts are in me, I can feel that it's not scared of anything outside of the water. Not Mongrel or the gun.

My feet lift off the pool floor.

I can't watch my friends die at my hands. I see its thoughts. Wrestling the revolver away. Bullet holes, glass slashing a throat, a face pressed into the water.

It makes me take stroke after stroke after stroke. Climbing through the bloody water. I can't stop it. This is how the faulty souls felt when they woke up inside horrible machines. They had to either watch the destruction they inflicted or

choose to die.

I think of Ada's face.

And fireworks.

They have one thing to give, and it's everything. They shimmer out and save us all at once. Hopeful. Purposeful. Ending beautifully.

At Abraham's Corner, a sip of spilled water made it flee.

I've got just enough control to do what my body normally does without thinking.

Underwater, I take a deep breath.

CHAPTER FIFTY-THREE

My dad wanted me to get baptized, but my mom didn't. She said all water is holy water, and he got angry and I'd just been born and I wasn't supposed to remember this.

It sees the ocean. The morning light is catching off the crests of waves, and no one can see it.
It thinks, maybe I don't need a host.
Maybe I am my own home.

I found a toy of Sky's in the back seat of the classic Chevy. A plastic fire truck he drove back and forth with incessant noises. In the rush to flee, I stepped on it. I turned the last thing of Sky's we had into shards of red plastic.

I cried and apologized. My mom said it was all right, but she was crying too. I wouldn't let her throw away any of the fragments. I picked a favorite one to keep in my pocket. My mom was worried I'd lose it, so I let her make a hole in it so I could wear it as a necklace.

It's a chasm.

It doesn't know where the things it swallows go. It stays

hungry and thirsty.
It will not choose the light at the end of the tunnel.
It doesn't choose to end,
but having reached the final moment,
it claims what it can.
It folds in on itself, sinking
into its own mouth
and whatever's beyond.

It's gone.

Even though I'm submerged in salt water, I know I'm crying.

To be alive. To be dying.

My lungs fill. The strength's gone from my body, and I drift back to the floor of the pool. I look up through the bloody water with stinging eyes. Wounds, blood loss, a world going sharp then dim then sharp then dimmer. It's endless choking with no air to bring in.

Drowning, thrashing, but I am my own.

There's a chain near me that I can't quite reach. I can feel Cas's presence searching me and finding that it's just Cedar now, nothing else. There's a rush of bubbles as someone dives into the water and strikes toward me. Then another.

I am my own.

I am not alone.

I close my hand around my necklace.

CHAPTER FIFTY-FOUR

THERE'S A THRUMMING. THAT'S ALL THERE IS AT FIRST.

The feeling of being rocked gently by a train.

The warmth of being near a fireplace.

You could stay, if you want.

This is Cas and Ada speaking at once. When it comes to souls, it's all mixed-up. They're talking to me, and I'm listening.

I don't know what it all means, says Cas, *but I want you to stay.*

I want you to stay too, says Ada.

I'm tired. We could swap places if you want, says Cas. *I'll leave, you stay.*

In the last of my clear moments, I recognize Morgyn's theory—the one her and Ada didn't use on Ruby. Cas and Ada both remember it. A faulty soul lets another one replace it. Cas replaced by me. My soul stabilizes the machine in Ada's heart, allowing Cas to die without exploding the microbot. The others save my body, then Ada lets my soul return to it. Hopefully.

My body's dead. My soul's slipping away. It's this plan or the end.

I'm tired too. Of pain and sorrow and loss.

But I've still got family here. People who want me to stay

despite my lies. Who are fighting to save me. A red shard of plastic clenched in my hand.

I say yes.

Cas leaves, and in the space where it once was, Ada catches my soul.

CHAPTER FIFTY-FIVE

For snapshot seconds, I can see myself through Ada's eyes. I'm looking into the water at Lucy and Papercut looping a chain around my chest. I'm on the pool deck. Lucy's doing CPR. There are flashing lights outside Camille's house. My friends called an ambulance from Fort Luthe for Ruby before I even arrived at the pool house. Now that ambulance will need to carry me too.

Then I blink, and I'm in my own body again. I'm looking through the glass roof of the pool house. I can feel my own pain and hear my own hammering heartbeat.

I see Morgyn bringing the paramedics over. Lying on the deck near me, Papercut's holding Ruby close. Lucy and Ada are kneeling over me.

I want to tell Ada I was a firework after all.

I think she knows.

Beyond their eyes, I think I see stars poking through the clouds. I could be delirious. It doesn't matter.

I am my own.

I am not alone.

CHAPTER FIFTY-SIX

Hey Mom,

Fuck, I'm already crying. Sorry, I'll try not to swear too much. I know you don't like harsh words, even though you let me talk how I wanted.

This isn't going to be a sad letter. This is the letter I imagine I'd have written you if I went away to college. The one where I'd tell you all the good things and not to worry.

For the first time since Dad made that deal, I'm truly safe. We killed it, Mom. Dad's monster, your monster, the one from the dam. It was because you were looking out for me. I learned from your letter and made the right choices in the end, and it's gone.

I did get hurt pretty badly, but it's nothing that won't heal. It's mostly my leg, and I was never an athlete anyway. I've got a bit of a scar on my cheek, but otherwise my face is okay. I know you'd want to know that.

I've decided to stay in Sawblade Lake. Partly it's to finish high school. Summer's almost done, and soon I'll be walking the same halls as you and Dad did. He's still in pictures of the old hockey teams in the trophy case. But I know I'm not him. I've got good people around me. The best. I think that's mostly what shapes you and sets you on one path or another. The voices you hear. Dad's were his dark studies, black-bound books I found stuffed under the mattress in his childhood bedroom. For me, yours was the biggest voice. Thank you thank you thank you.

More than anything else, it matters that I tell you I still have family here, the kind beyond blood that we both believe in. Grandma's gone. You were right. She kept me safe in so many ways, even now. She left me everything. Apparently, she changed her will the day after I arrived. I tried to sleep in the house once I got back from the hospital, but I wound up going to my friend Lucy's in the middle of the night instead. And I've just . . . stayed? After a week, she talked to her parents, and they offered me their spare room. I figure you'd be concerned that I'm eating well, that I'm in a good home. I am.

I've got other friends too. Morgyn gave me a final offer to leave town with her, but I could tell she didn't really mean it. She understands that chance is gone. I go to her place sometimes. We work together. She teaches me more than I ever thought there was to know about faulty machines.

Then there's Ada and Papercut and Ruby and their family. Ruby almost died from the monster, but its strength in her kept her alive. She's bouncing back with a young body and memories that are thankfully blurred. I'm at that house all the time. We told the truth to Ruby's dad and Ruby, skipping the worst of it. After, Ruby outright demanded her older siblings forgive me this instant. Those are deep wounds though.

Papercut's treating me normally now. I think Lucy talked to them. They might listen to Lucy more than anyone else. And complain about it. And adore her. The love that's working out and working through. I want to be the same.

Making things right with Ada matters for another reason too. I'm in love with her. You'd like them in every way. But I fucked things up with her. There's no other way to say it. Not in a fall-back-into-each-other's-arms sort of way. And they lost something important to them to save me. She was Faulty, and now that part of her is gone, she misses it.

But Ada asked me to go work on their cabin with them tomorrow. She said she needed to clean out the magic room, and I felt like the right person to do it with. That's good.

I'm shattered and healing and I'll never be the same and I'll be all right. Somehow. Someday.

I love you.

Yours,
Cedar

EPILOGUE

Dad,

It's autumn now. Real autumn, where the leaves that fall will grow again in the spring. I'm back in the arcade. If you had high scores, they're long gone. I used some of what Morgyn taught me to communicate with the last pinball machine standing. Or listen, at least. It's hurting, but it doesn't want to die. It chooses to suffer and live, shattering any record you or anyone ever set. All we've made into ash and rust.

The last trace of the dam is gone. I solved your problem for you, though know I did it for Sky and for so many others, not you.

I've been learning. I cleaned out your bedroom and found your books and notes that weave together the esoteric and the ancient with the newly contrived. I've got an ex-magician and a faulty mechanic to help me decipher them, but one thing is clear. You were working on waking souls in machines long before you needed to get yourself out of trouble. A suspicion of Mom's made certain. I can't imagine you tried only once. I can't imagine you were the only one.

This is my last letter. I know there are traces of shadow in the bunker that shouldn't come to light. The tools and tricks you used to wake the monster before Autumn. I've got to deal with them. The sins of the ones we've loved weigh on us.

I still get the papers Grandma ordered. I'm watching for the news that someone's found the house, and when I see it, I'm coming to destroy your evil devices and take my brother back. I'm bringing backup. I don't care how deep you've dug your claws into Sky—I will wrench him away from you.

I'm coming for you. And I'm coming for Sky.

Cedar

ACKNOWLEDGMENTS

It has to start with my incredible agent, Amy Tompkins, because that's why this book is out in the world. Your tireless work gives me the space to breathe while I create, knowing that you've got the rest of it covered. Thanks to you, I get to live that wacky dream of being an author.

Ali Romig, there's never been any doubt that this book belonged with you. You're the biggest cheerleader a writer could hope to have, and I almost cried the first time you signed off an email "Your fan, Ali." Every conversation with you leaves me full of confidence and my mind buzzing with ideas. Your edits struck right at the heart of my vision for this book and added so much depth and cohesion. Let the record also reflect that I think you're impossibly cool.

To the rest of the team at Delacorte Press, thank you for your dedication to making this book into a beautiful, polished final product and getting it into the hands of readers. I can barely comprehend the amount of work you all do.

Go back and look at the cover of *The Saw Mouth*. That's Evangeline Gallagher's art, the first part of this story before any words get read, and I wouldn't have it any other way. When Ali first told me you were going to be the cover artist, I wouldn't shut up about it. I still don't. I knew you'd twist the nightmare just right. Rory, your incredibly kind words finished the cover off. You're a pal and an inspiration and a prose menace.

My dear beta readers, Elyse, Carly, and Teresa. I couldn't trust you more. Thank you for reading this book first, for making sure it made sense, and for all flagging the same disastrous scene to fix. And thanks once more to Carly (the second of three to you), this time for sensitivity reading.

I couldn't have written *The Saw Mouth* without the support of the Banff Centre and the 2022 residency there that changed my life. Tanya, Kat, and the whole beloved cohort, being there with you was like coming home somehow. I'll never forget it.

To my friends at home and far away and my wonderful writing pals and mentors, all too numerous to name, there'd be no stories without all of you. That goes for my siblings too. Dasha, Tirian, Tayah, you're not too numerous to name, but the ways I love you are.

Mom and Dad, thank you for letting your kids wander around in the woods and for digging your way out of the sort of Christianity that's not easy to claw free from. Your ability to learn and the all-in way you love are things I hope I can carry forward through my whole life. Mom, I remember being astounded at how precisely you proofed *The Saw Mouth* in a couple days. Dad, I remember you telling me you cried in your car in the hardware store parking lot when you finished reading *The Saw Mouth*. I'm so lucky to have parents like you two.

All my love and thank-you kisses to Carly and Waffle, my darling little family.

Special thanks to Canada Council for the Arts, Manitoba Arts Council, Winnipeg Arts Council, Winnipeg Public Library, and the incredible staff at these organizations.

I'm writing these acknowledgments months before my debut novel comes out, but I'm starting to see the first glimmers of my readers, and I know I'm going to adore you. It's a huge honor that you spent your time with this book. I don't take it for granted.

While *The Saw Mouth* takes place in an unspecified region, it was written all across the settler-colonial country known as Canada. Most of the writing happened on Treaty One Territory, the traditional lands of the Anishinaabeg, Anishininewuk, Dakota Oyate, Denesuline, and Nehethowuk Nations, and on the National Homeland of the Red River Métis. Many of the visuals also draw from the landscapes of Treaty Three Territory, the traditional lands of the Anishinaabeg and Métis Peoples.

CONTENT WARNINGS FOR *THE SAW MOUTH*

Captivity by a parent
Cheating
Child selling
Dead bodies and body parts
Death of a pet dog (mentioned as a past event, not seen)
Death of family members
Discrimination (fictional)
Drowning
Drunk driving
Dystopian-scale disaster
Eye trauma
Family violence (implied)
Fire trauma
Gore, blood
Gun violence
Hand/finger trauma
Missing children
Monsters and violence to animal-like monsters
Mouth trauma
Physical harm and threat to a child
Possession

Possession of a child
Religious trauma
Scars and marks of injury
Stalking
Suicide
Surgery (discussed)
Traumatic family separation
Traumatic memory distortion
Underage consumption of alcohol/drugs/unsafe substances
Violent/traumatic incidents involving vehicles
Vomiting

ABOUT THE AUTHOR

Cale Plett is a nonbinary, genderfluid writer living in Winnipeg, Manitoba. They grew up on a dead-end gravel road and used to get lost in the woods for fun, scary abandoned cabin and all. They are the author of *Wavelength*, a queer YA romance featuring a runaway pop star, *The Saw Mouth*, and the forthcoming *Stranglehold*.

@caleplett
caleplett.com